DO NOT KISS 'TIL CHRISTMAS

She hadn't put her keys in the door. And Bret became aware that his pulse had started racing.

It was a classic scenario, and he suspected Chloe realized it, too. He didn't feel like an editor and an employee. He felt like a boy walking a girl home after a first date. Her door didn't face the street. No one would see. Except that he was her boss again and he needed to start remembering that.

No matter how tempting it was to pretend he wasn't, just for a few more minutes.

Professional ethics, he reminded himself, and took half a step back. Just half a step. "Thanks for coming," he said. "Today would have been just an obligation for me. You made it a lot better."

Chloe's face softened into a smile, and God help him, it was one of *those* smiles, its glow soft and genuine. "Thank *you*," she said. "I had a wonderful time."

She hesitated a fraction of a second. Then she stepped toward the door, and Bret turned to go. Mission accomplished. He'd gotten through the day without crossing the boundaries, professional ethics intact. And doing the right thing had never felt so stupid.

A voice in his head said, *Screw professional ethics.*

The moment was almost gone and it would never be here again, so before it was over, before he could stop himself, before Chloe could get her keys in the door, he wheeled around, pulled her into his arms, and kissed her. . . .

Books by Sierra Donovan

NO CHRISTMAS LIKE THE PRESENT

DO YOU BELIEVE IN SANTA?

WE NEED A LITTLE CHRISTMAS

DO NOT OPEN 'TIL CHRISTMAS

Published by Kensington Publishing Corporation

Do Not Open 'Til Christmas

SIERRA DONOVAN

ZEBRA BOOKS
KENSINGTON PUBLISHING CORP.
http://www.kensingtonbooks.com

ZEBRA BOOKS are published by

Kensington Publishing Corp.
119 West 40th Street
New York, NY 10018

All Kensington titles, imprints, and distributed lines are available at special quantity discounts for bulk purchases for sales promotion, premiums, fund-raising, educational, or institutional use.

Special book excerpts or customized printings can also be created to fit specific needs. For details, write or phone the office of the Kensington Sales Manager: Attn.: Sales Department. Kensington Publishing Corp., 119 West 40th Street, New York, NY 10018. Phone: 1-800-221-2647.

Zebra and the Z logo Reg. U.S. Pat. & TM Off.

First Printing: October 2017
ISBN-13: 978-1-4201-4152-8
ISBN-10: 1-4201-4152-X

eISBN-13: 978-1-4201-4153-5
eISBN-10: 1-4201-4153-8

10 9 8 7 6 5 4 3 2 1

Printed in the United States of America

*For Charlie, for your love and all your patience
over the years. I couldn't have written a love story
without you, and there's a little bit of you
in every hero I've ever written.*

I love you.

ACKNOWLEDGMENTS

Special thanks . . .

To Sharon Wild, who started this journey off when she gave me my first Nora Roberts book. Love you!

To Stephanie Newton and Roberta Smith. You're on opposite coasts and you've never met, but you're the two most steadfast critique partners a girl could ask for. You encourage me, keep me grounded, and let me know when I'm on the right track.

To Tania Ramos, for providing valuable medical advice to help me with a plot point. Any errors in translation are mine.

To the baristas at the Starbucks at Bear Valley Road off the I-15. You've seen a lot of me over the past few years. Special thanks to Adam, Carleton, Marina, and Chelsea, for smiling when you see me, remembering my name, and never complaining about the table space I take up. And a very special thanks to Sergio, for keeping the place running.

To my readers. A book isn't worth the paper (or e-ink) it's written on unless the story reaches someone. Thanks for picking me up off the shelf or tucking me into your e-reader, and giving my characters a few of your precious hours. May you all live happily ever after!

Chapter 1

"Just once, couldn't somebody kill someone?"

Bret Radner bit out the words as soon as he hit the period at the end of his latest story for the *Tall Pine Gazette*. The headline read: EVERGREEN LANE SHOPS PREDICT SUCCESSFUL CHRISTMAS SEASON.

Shocker.

"I'll get right on it." Bret's fellow reporter, Chuck Nolan, didn't even glance up from his own computer screen. "Who've you got in mind for the lucky victim?"

Bret released a long, slow sigh. Chuck had heard it all before. And there wasn't really anyone in Tall Pine he was *that* annoyed with.

"Okay," Bret said. "A tourist."

Chuck battered out a few words on his keyboard with his oddly efficient hunt-and-peck method. He was in his early forties, and somehow Chuck had never learned to type. "And how about the murderer? I'm not doing your dirty work for you."

"Another tourist. How's that? Two really *rude* tourists."

Bret returned his attention to the story on his screen, running the cursor down the text to proofread it once more before he sent it to his editor's in-box. Holding back another sigh, Bret reached for the writing pad that contained the notes from his interview with the head of the local water district.

"Radner." His editor, Frank McCrea, stood in the doorway of his glass-walled office, twenty feet from Bret's desk. "I need to see you for a minute."

A summons to the editor's office at four o'clock was pretty unusual. Too quick to have anything to do with the story Bret had just sent over. And if it was a reaction to his mini-rant, that would be a first.

Only one way to find out. Bret followed McCrea into the editor's inner sanctum, aware of Chuck's curious stare behind him. He sat in one of the straight-backed chairs facing McCrea's massive oak desk. Massive, but scarred with age, like just about everything in the *Gazette*'s offices. At thirty, Bret sometimes suspected he was the youngest thing in the newsroom. Including the coffee machine.

"What's up?" Bret asked.

McCrea—middle-aged, graying, and broadening around the middle—took his seat in the larger, cushioned chair across from Bret. "I've got a curve ball for you."

Bret's brows lifted. Ordinarily, he loved curve balls.

McCrea continued, "I had a call last week from our corporate office in St. Louis. The editor at their paper in Chicago stepped down about six months ago, and the associate editor they promoted is making a hash of things. They asked me to step in and do some damage control until they find somebody permanent."

Bret blinked, trying not to show signs of whiplash. After all, it was logical enough. McCrea had headed up the Chicago paper before he moved his family to Tall Pine a decade or so ago. If he'd been looking for peace and quiet, he'd certainly gotten what he was after. What Bret had never understood was how McCrea had ever found Tall Pine. Tucked away in the mountains some two hours from Los Angeles, it was barely on the map.

But any good newspaper story led with the most pertinent point of the article, and Bret had the feeling his commander-in-chief had buried his lead.

McCrea moved quickly to correct that: "I'm putting you in charge."

That, too, was logical. McCrea had hired Bret when he came home from college, and Bret had spent the last seven years living and breathing the job, such as it was. When McCrea took vacation time, it was Bret who filled in. Although he couldn't recall McCrea taking as much as a full week off at any one time.

"Okay." Bret couldn't hold back a half smile. "Sure you don't want to trade and send me to Chicago?"

"Were you listening? I'm going there to clean up the mess from another guy with years of experience in a major metropolitan area." Bret flinched at that. McCrea pretended not to notice. "You'll have your hands full here, I guarantee. The Christmas season is coming up next month, so you'll have to work smart, with the holidays to schedule around. I know you're not big on Christmas—"

"It's not my favorite thing, no," Bret responded automatically. McCrea knew that better than most. And he'd remember why, better than most.

"—but on the up side, as I said, this will keep you busy. It's no secret you'd like more of a challenge."

Bret inclined his head. "You think?"

"Trust me. There's more to running this place on an ongoing basis than you realize. We get by okay on two full-time reporters plus me. But you're going to need to delegate. I know your work ethic, and if you don't watch out, you could end up trying to write the whole paper by yourself. By the time you figured out you were in over your head, you wouldn't have time to look for someone else. So I hired one of our freelancers to fill in while I'm gone."

"A freelancer?" Bret kept his features still.

Generally, freelance reporters were amateurs. They worked from home, usually as a sideline to another job. Their skills left a lot to be desired, and they didn't tend to last long. More trouble than they were worth, in Bret's opinion.

"I know what you're thinking. But this one's consistent. She's been working with us for nearly two years. Chloe Davenport."

The byline rang a bell, but barely. Freelancers were entrusted with less timely articles, the kind that even Bret tended to skip over. Church bake sales, prize-winning pickles, interviews with this year's valedictorian. McCrea added, "She was in the office yesterday."

Bret remembered glimpsing the back of a blond female head through McCrea's glass walls. "I thought it was one of your daughters coming in for lunch money."

McCrea shook his head. "Chloe graduated college a couple of years ago. You've probably met her. She's a waitress at the Pine 'n' Dine."

Bret frowned. He didn't know of any blond waitresses at the local diner. Unless . . . A faint image surfaced in his mind.

"She works nights most of the time," McCrea added.

The picture snapped into focus. Bret didn't usually go to the Pine 'n' Dine in the evening. But a couple of months ago, he'd stopped in to write up his notes on a town council meeting before he came back to the paper to file the story. A petite, blue-eyed blonde had waited on him. She looked like a china doll, for heaven's sake.

He dredged his memory further. She'd made some sort of joke. . . .

Whatever it was, it wasn't important right now. But he wondered if McCrea was suffering from a touch of middle-aged crazy. His editor was a family man, ethical to the core, and Bret didn't think he'd ever dream of cheating on his wife. But that didn't mean a pretty face couldn't cloud his head.

"Are you sure about this?" Bret picked his words with care. "She's awfully young."

"Older than you were."

Hard to get around that one. Bret flicked a brief smile. "Yeah, but I was a prodigy."

"Then you should have no trouble getting a newbie up to speed." McCrea leaned back in his chair. "Unless you're not up to it. I could always put Chuck in charge."

It was a transparent bluff, and both of them knew it. Chuck was a great guy and a good worker, but organization wasn't his strong suit.

"Hey, they say print journalism is a dying field," Bret deadpanned. "No point in rushing the process."

"It's a yes, then?"

"I didn't know it was a question. But sure. I'm your guy."

"Glad that's settled. I'm leaving this weekend. You take over Monday."

Monday? "You're telling me this on two days' notice?"

"Didn't want to listen to your griping any longer than that." McCrea sat forward again, resting his arms comfortably on his desk. "Now get out."

Most of their talks in McCrea's office ended that way.

"Fine." Bret stood. "But you're going to freeze your butt off in Chicago."

He walked back out, his head spinning. A lot had changed in ten minutes, but he'd be lying if he said he wasn't salivating just a little bit. He loved a challenge, and he was overdue for one. Now McCrea had given him the keys to the kingdom.

And a freelancer to babysit.

Chloe Davenport pushed through the door from the reception area to the newsroom Monday morning, brand new briefcase in hand, trying not to feel like a kid on the first day of school.

It was only her third time inside the *Tall Pine Gazette* offices. All of her other contact had been by phone or e-mail. Just like school, it was a roomful of desks. Instead of thirty small ones, a half-dozen big ones stood lined up in two rows. And at the far end of the room, the mystical, glass-walled editor's office.

The editor's office was empty, and only one of the desks was occupied. Behind it sat a brown-haired man, probably about forty, rifling through disorderly stacks of paper on top of his desk.

"Good morning," she said.

He looked up, startled, although Chloe hadn't exactly tiptoed in. "Hi." The man gave her a puzzled, but not unfriendly, smile. She was a few minutes early, but he didn't look as if he'd been expecting her.

She smiled back and put out her hand. "I'm Chloe Davenport." As he rose to shake her hand, his puzzled expression didn't clear, so she added, "I'm looking for Bret Radner?"

The man looked distractedly over his shoulder. "He's around here somewhere." He turned back to her. "Sorry. I'm Chuck Nolan. I'm on my way to an interview at the school district office." He sifted through his papers again until he fished out what he'd apparently been searching for: a blank notepad. "You must be the freelancer?"

Good. They did know she was coming. "Right. Well, not a freelancer anymore. I'm here full-time, at least until Mr. McCrea gets back. He said to come in at nine. I guess I'm a little—"

A door opened at the far side of the room, and a trim, dark-haired man burst through it, wearing glasses with thin black wire frames, a cell phone in one hand, a cordless phone handset pressed to his ear. As he spoke into the phone, his calm tone of voice belied his rapid stride. "There's been a delay. We'll have your photographer out there shortly." He hit a button to disconnect the call, then punched a few keys on the handset. "Jen?" His tone was more brisk. "We still haven't heard from Ned? Okay, thanks."

He lowered the phone to his side, eyes closed as if in thought. Or as if willing someone to spontaneously combust. "Who dedicates a plaque at eight-thirty on a Monday morning?" he said to no one in particular.

She recognized him.

She could only hope and pray he wouldn't recognize her. Chloe glanced at the pleasant, laid-back Chuck. *Why couldn't it have been the other one?*

Bret Radner had been one of her customers at the Pine 'n' Dine a few months ago. She'd noticed him because he was one of those men who looked good in glasses, which she liked. And he'd been typing away at a laptop, which intrigued her. Especially since the Pine 'n' Dine didn't have Wi-Fi, so he was probably writing something.

But he hadn't looked up from his laptop since he ordered. Not once.

Curiosity warring with frustration, she approached his table when his cup reached the half-full mark. "Would you like more coffee?"

"Please." Not taking his eyes from his screen, he unerringly maneuvered his cup under the spout of her coffeepot.

A little demon prodded her. "Excuse me."

She had to wait several seconds before he seemed to realize she wasn't going to go away. Finally he raised his head and met her eyes with a dark-eyed stare behind the black wire rims.

Now that his gaze was fixed on her, unblinking and waiting, she started to regret her gumption. But the little demon spurred her on.

"Thanks." She tried not to stammer. "We're required to see all of our customers' faces at least once. That way, in case you turn out to be the Unabomber or something, I can give a good description."

His stare sharpened, and she knew she'd had it. *No tip for you, baby. You'll be lucky if he doesn't complain to the owner.*

"They caught the Unabomber in 1996," he said. "You're way behind on your current events."

Then his lips twitched in a faint smile. "Thanks for the coffee," he said, and returned to his laptop.

It all made sense now. The laptop, the writing, and especially the crack about current events. No wonder he'd known the Unabomber's capture date off the top of his head.

Great. He probably thought she really believed the fugitive was still at large, over twenty years later.

Maybe he wouldn't place her. Maybe she looked different enough without her uniform. She'd pulled her blond hair into a bun this morning, in an effort both to keep it simple and to look professional. Unfortunately, she realized, that was pretty similar to the way she had to wear it when she waited tables.

Right now, Chloe wasn't sure if he'd noticed she was standing here or not. He was speaking to Chuck. "Ned's missing in action. I'm going to have to steal the photographer for your nine o'clock. Can you shoot it on your phone?"

Chuck shrugged. "Sure." He nodded toward Chloe. "Uh, Bret? Miss Davenport is here."

Sharp dark eyes fell on her from behind his glasses, and Chloe's stomach did a twist. Maybe he remembered and maybe he didn't, but he looked as if he'd just found an overdue bill underneath his refrigerator.

Resolutely, she put on her best smile and put out her hand. "I'm Chloe Davenport."

He accepted her hand, his smile tight. "The freelancer."

She held his stare and kept her smile. "Not anymore."

"Right." He released her hand. "You're early."

Early was generally a good thing. Clearly, not today. "A little."

"I'm putting out a few fires this morning. I'll need about an hour to get my feet under me. Hold on."

He thumbed out a number on his cell phone.

"Winston? Bret." His voice returned to the brisk-but-polite tone he'd used with the receptionist. "I need to move our ten o'clock. Can we bump it up to eleven?" He nodded. "Great. See you then."

She only knew of one Winston in Tall Pine—Winston Frazier, the oldest member of the town council—but she couldn't imagine anyone speaking to him in that brusque tone. He was a regular at the Pine 'n' Dine, and every waitress called him "sir."

Bret lowered the phone and zeroed in on Chloe again. "You're my new ten o'clock."

"Okay. Where do I—" She hefted her briefcase awkwardly.

Bret glanced over the two rows of desks. He nodded toward the one behind Chuck's. "That one." It was littered with a hodgepodge of newspaper sections, a phone directory, a vintage-looking computer monitor, and a telephone Chloe hoped was actually plugged in. "How about if you get yourself situated, have a cup of—" His eyes darted to a coffee maker on a small cabinet against a wall, with about an inch and a half of coffee at the bottom of the pot. It looked lonely and cold.

Chuck sidled to the exit, sending what might have been an apologetic nod in her direction.

Bret took no notice. "Could you make a pot of coffee?" he asked her. "I'll get with you at ten. Sharp."

As if that were settled, he turned away and headed for a side door at the other end of the office at high speed, dialing the cordless phone as he walked. Leaving her alone in the newsroom. With the coffee maker.

If her new boss had paused long enough for her to draw a breath, Chloe would have been tempted to object. Probably just as well. His quick departure gave her time to remember her mother's advice whenever her dad or her brothers were being sexist: *Pick your battles.*

So, Chloe laid her briefcase down on top of the desk Bret had indicated and got to work.

Her first day as a full-time reporter, and her first assignment was to make a pot of coffee.

For the next hour, Chloe watched Bret Radner with a mixture of apprehension and fascination.

She'd only met McCrea in person twice, and she missed him already. The editor had definitely been a no-nonsense type, brief and to the point; she'd learned to keep her e-mails to him short, because sometimes he'd miss a question if she surrounded it with too much extraneous detail.

Compared to this guy, McCrea was a model of patience and leisure.

Bret made his way in and out of the newsroom with the speed of a tornado, but no tornado was ever so purposeful. The air around him practically crackled as

11

he wore a path between the editor's office and the desk across from Chuck's, making and taking phone calls in quick, clipped tones. Physically, he wasn't as imposing as either of her two brothers, but even from across the room, he intimidated the heck out of her.

He got over to the coffee maker moments after the pot had finished perking and poured a cup with a brief glance in her direction before he vanished through another door, this one at the back of the room. The *Gazette* didn't look that big from the outside, but obviously the building branched off in all directions.

Midway through the hour, Bret got the call he'd apparently been waiting for. "Ned? Where the heck are you?"

He'd come to a momentary stop in front of the desk across from Chuck's. Standing with one arm propped on the desktop, he said, "I don't get it. Your wife's in labor, not you."

Chloe studied his face for any sign that he was joking. She saw no change in his expression.

Then, as the person on the other end responded, he grinned—an expression she'd never seen on him before. "Same to you." The grin faded as he eyed the desk blotter calendar in front of him. "This is early, isn't it?" Another pause. "Okay. Keep us posted. Give Debbie my best."

He switched from the cell phone to the telephone on his desk. Chloe wasn't sure what had happened to the cordless handset. "Jen? Could you get me McCrea's list of freelance photographers? Ned's going to be out for a while. Debbie's in labor. Yeah, two weeks early . . . Do you know if we have an account with the florist?" He nodded. "But hold off until we hear how it goes."

As he hung up, Chloe volunteered, "Two weeks isn't that bad."

He looked at her as if surprised to see her still there. "So he told me."

And he sped off to the reception area.

Chloe sipped her coffee and returned to the task of straightening—or finding—her desk. The newspapers covering the top ranged in age from two weeks to two years old; she set them aside for recycling. The phone did, in fact, have a dial tone, and the computer hummed to life when she turned it on. The drawers were filled with curious archeological artifacts: stray teabags, broken pencils, absolutely no working pens, and half-filled memo pads with scribbled notes dated three years ago. Had it been that long since they had another reporter?

She thought Bret might forget her, but he returned to stand in front of her desk promptly at ten. "Okay. Let's back up and start from the beginning." He extended his hand to her again. "I'm Bret."

"Chloe." She leaned across the desk to shake his hand again and got the same brief, firm squeeze as before.

Did he remember her from the Pine 'n' Dine? He gave no indication. Good.

Bret leaned back to sit against the top of Chuck's desk, arms folded in front of him. Chloe wondered if he realized what a closed-off posture that was. She wondered if it was intentional.

"So," he said. "This is your first full-time news gig?"

"Yes."

"Okay." He closed his eyes briefly, as if he'd just witnessed a ten-car pileup. "Basics."

Then his eyes opened, and the onslaught of instructions began.

"Work day starts at eight. Deadline is two-thirty, but we've never taken that literally. It was designed for the best of all possible worlds, and this isn't it. But unless you have an appointment, which you'll let me know about, you need to be back at your desk by then. We're short-staffed here, as you can see, so I need boots on the ground pretty quick. By the end of two weeks, I'll expect you to be filing ten stories a week. . . ."

Without taking her eyes from Bret, Chloe felt around on her desk for the pad of paper she'd left there. Thank God she'd brought her own pens.

Bret nodded. "Yes, put that at the top of your list: always have a notepad ready."

If he saw any irony in that statement, Chloe couldn't tell, because as soon as her pen was poised, the torrent of information resumed.

"When you're doing a phone interview, use a headset and take notes on your keyboard, not by hand. It's faster and it's way more accurate. And when you quote someone, make darn sure it's what they said. No paraphrasing."

That was almost insulting. "I would never—"

"Good. No profanity of any kind, even in a quote. We're owned by Liberty Communications, which owns over four hundred newspapers across the country. They're very conservative, and believe me, we want to keep them happy."

By the time Bret came to a stop, she'd filled five pages with scribbled notes. She just had to trust that she'd be able to read them later.

He pushed up from Chuck's desk. "Generally I'll be meeting with you on Mondays to go over story proposals for the week. We've already lost too much time today, so have at least five ideas ready for me tomorrow morning. Meanwhile, I'll get you some press releases to write up into news briefs. That should keep you busy."

As Bret retreated to the office formerly occupied by McCrea, Chloe sat back, took a deep breath, and exhaled it. She had a feeling it would be her last chance to breathe easily for quite a while.

She could do this.

Writing for a newspaper hadn't been her first choice for a job, but then, her career plan hadn't been especially well thought-out. She'd had the conversation dozens of times in college.

What's your major?

English.

Oh. You want to be an English teacher?

No. A writer.

Oh, like a newspaper reporter?

No. Probably something in marketing . . .

That had been vague enough to shut them up.

She'd been told what a versatile major English was for going into anything from marketing to the legal field. Somehow she'd believed it. What she really wanted, she supposed, was a solid day job so she could pursue something more creative on her own time.

Chloe knew what she was good at. She excelled at writing, and she loved it. She just didn't know how to make a living at it. Especially in Tall Pine. So, six months into her stint as a waitress, when the *Tall Pine Gazette* had advertised for freelance reporters, she'd cracked. As it turned out, she enjoyed it far more than she expected. But writing a few stories a month certainly didn't earn enough for her to quit the Pine 'n' Dine.

Now she had this, while it lasted.

Ten stories a week for the next three months. Including interviews and research, as well as writing them. Not to mention coming up with enough story ideas that would pass muster with her new boss.

She could do this.

It was this, or back to waiting tables.

Bret closed the door of McCrea's office behind him and resisted the urge to lean back against it and bar out the outside world. With glass walls, that wasn't an option. So, keeping his back straight, he closed his eyes and pinched the bridge of his nose.

He'd been wrong about one thing: her eyes weren't blue.

There was some blue in there, but they were more of a deep gray, with a hint of green if you looked long enough. Like the ocean on a stormy afternoon. Especially when he'd asked her to make coffee. And now he remembered her snarky joke about the Unabomber. So, not a china doll.

But she still didn't look much like a reporter, unless you counted the ones you saw on TV shows, with that bright smile and that shiny briefcase. Pretty enough to make him wonder, again, if McCrea had been thinking straight when he hired her.

He wouldn't invest much time in her—couldn't afford to—until he knew whether she was going to last beyond the first two weeks. He'd set the bar pretty high. But no higher than McCrea had set for Bret when he started here.

She'd pan out or she wouldn't. And he wouldn't let a pretty face sway his judgment.

Chapter 2

Chloe landed on the well-worn plaid couch, clunked her stocking feet on top of the cheap wooden excuse for a coffee table, and closed her eyes. She wouldn't have the apartment to herself long.

But it shouldn't be hard to doze for a few minutes, after the two days she'd had. On the inside of her closed eyelids, she saw her computer screen at the office, with its eccentric news editing software and square gray cursor blinking at her. Until the cursor started moving by itself. Backward, over the words she'd just typed, their meaning unintelligible. The letters blurred and faded away . . .

And the front door opened, jarring her halfway out of her skin. Kate came blustering in with Tiffany right behind her, both still dressed in the obligatory pink Pine 'n' Dine uniforms. How had they *both* pulled the day shift the first week Chloe was gone?

"Hey, sunshine." Kate held out a narrow white box. "Dick Rickard misses you."

Chloe sat bolt upright, this time not because she was startled. Dick was one of her nicest customers, an older gentleman who loved the Early Bird dinner special. And if Chloe wasn't mistaken, that white box contained candy from Sue's Sweets on Evergreen Lane. It might not be a heaping plate of her mother's mashed potatoes and gravy, but it would do for comfort food tonight.

Not worried about spoiling her appetite for her frozen dinner, Chloe took the box from Kate and snatched the lid off. She scrutinized the chocolates. A lot of times, the oval ones had maple filling, her favorite. She picked one up and bit into it.

"Orange." Oh, well. The candy was a gift, and chocolate was chocolate.

"If you look inside the lid, there's a diagram that shows you which ones are which." Tiffany perched on the arm of the sofa on Chloe's right.

"That's cheating." Chloe contemplated the rows of candy in their little brown paper nests. Was it her imagination or did it seem a little roomy in there? She tilted the box, and the candies slid, exposing quite a bit of the white cardboard bottom. She cast a distrustful look, first at Tiffany, then at Kate.

Tiffany looked a little shame-faced. Kate shrugged. "We taste-tested a few."

Chloe tried to muster the energy to glare at her roommates. Tiffany, with her short, dark hair and passion for punky eyeliner, probably had the softest heart of anyone she knew. And Kate, with her straight, shoulder-length brown hair, always speaking before she thought. Chloe had known them both all her life, even though she and Kate hadn't really been friends until their junior year of high school. Kate had spiked a volleyball that smashed straight into Chloe's face, Tiffany had rushed to her defense, and Kate had apologized profusely while the three of them tried to stem the flow of Chloe's bloody nose. Somehow, out of that messy experience, the three had forged a bond that had lasted through all the comings and goings of Chloe's college years.

There was no point getting mad at them. After all, it wasn't reasonable to expect self-control when chocolate was involved.

"Thanks for saving me some." Chloe tried for a little sarcasm, just on general principles, but she knew it didn't convince anyone.

It would have taken a sledgehammer to get through to Kate, anyway. "How was Day Two with Simon Legree?" Kate plopped onto the couch on Chloe's left, suspiciously close to the box of chocolates.

"Ask me tomorrow." Chloe gestured weakly toward the open box of candy. After her roommates each grabbed a piece, she closed the lid. "I don't think I have any words left in me right now."

Even from across the newsroom, Bret's presence had hung over her like a vaguely disapproving shadow, and she couldn't dispel the feeling he was just waiting for her to screw up. For the past two days he'd barely gone near her, except to drop more press releases on her head. How she was supposed to get any work done on the three out of five article ideas he'd approved, Chloe didn't know. But at least she had an interview scheduled for tomorrow morning. She'd better be able to speak English again by then.

Maybe Bret was God's way of trying to cure her of her weakness for smart, quiet guys. The kind who had never approached her in high school, either because they were too shy or they just plain weren't interested. Bret was like one of those guys grown up—just take away the quiet and shy and add in a healthy dose of terror. It sounded like the perfect vaccine to Chloe.

"You could come back to work with us," Tiffany said.

"Or we could break his legs," Kate chimed in.

Chloe huffed out a weak laugh in spite of herself. But the laugh and the chocolate were just what she needed. She didn't plan to jump ship for the Pine 'n' Dine, at least not until this fill-in gig was over. And when McCrea got back, there was always the chance it could turn into something permanent. After all, unless you were planning a career in restaurant management, no one wanted to wait tables for too long.

Through her bleary eyes, for the first time, Chloe saw this apartment for what it was: a way station. The lumpy couch, donated by one of Tiffany's ex-boyfriends. The coffee table, a discarded woodshop project from Kate's older brother. And the brick-and-board bookshelves Chloe had thought were so ingenious the first time she'd constructed them in college. By her senior year, they'd looked a little tacky and tired even back in the dorm.

This place was temporary, and in most ways, that was a good thing.

But for right now, it was nice to know that either of her friends stood ready to beat Bret to a pulp—at least metaphorically—on her behalf.

There was just one thing. This town was small, and words had echoes. "I didn't call him Simon Legree," she murmured weakly.

With that pronouncement, she vowed she was officially done talking for the day. She slumped silently, flanked by her roommates, who eyed the candy box like two sparrows on the prowl for a dropped sandwich crust in a parking lot.

Chloe gave up and pulled the lid off the box. "Okay, have at it. Just save me some of the oval ones."

And she let her head drop onto the back of the couch.

Wednesday morning, and it was shaping up to be a long week.

Bret's newly inherited office felt more and more confining, its glass walls cutting him off from the newsroom more than letting him see into it. It was unexpectedly hard to write in here. Somewhere along the line, he'd not only mastered the art of working with activity around him; it felt strange trying to work without it. He closed the window of the article he'd been working on—he was spending *way* too much time second-guessing his own prose—and returned to editing some of the material for tomorrow's paper.

Chloe came back into the office, lugging that impractical briefcase, and plunked into her chair. Without wasting any time, without opening her briefcase, she jiggled the mouse to wake up her computer screen and started to type. She hadn't worn her hair pulled back since the first day, but now she paused long enough to twist the shoulder-length locks into a hasty bun, as if it were an annoyance.

It was an annoyance to Bret. It was distracting. The

tumble of blond hair kept catching the corner of his eye, reminding him of the new presence in the office. Qualified or not, a pretty female shouldn't have that effect on him. He had better concentration than that.

As for her qualifications . . .

He redirected his focus to his screen, which displayed Chloe's latest news brief. She was, at least, a competent writer. There was one problem, and it was setting his teeth on edge a little more with each edit. He finished going over the article and closed it, biting his tongue once again.

But as he started on her next piece, a detailed list of weekly events, a sound escaped from him that bordered on a growl.

He'd been putting it off, but it wasn't going to get better on its own. He had to deal with this. He didn't give himself any more time to hesitate. He picked up his phone and hit the intercom button.

"Chloe. Can I see you in my office? Now?"

The summons hit Chloe like ice water down her spine. Whatever it was, it didn't sound good. She saved the three lines she'd written so far and went to the editor's office, remembering to grab a notepad and pen on her way.

Bret waited for her behind his desk, the wide expanse of oak between them making him look even more formidable. All business, despite the fact that he didn't wear the traditional power suit. In fact, Chloe realized, he wore the same simple gray sport jacket he'd worn since the day she started—casual, but versatile, and above the curve for day-to-day business in Tall Pine.

He barely waited for her to settle into one of the little straight-backed chairs across from him. "We have a problem," he said without preamble.

Her stomach, which hadn't felt great all week, lurched. *Don't show fear. He can probably smell fear.* Chloe sat tall in her chair. "Yes?"

"Your copy's okay. Your punctuation's decent. But if you're serious about this, there's something you need to work on."

If you're serious about this. She stiffened, if that was still possible. "What's that?"

"Style." He tapped his monitor, which faced away from her, so the gesture didn't do much good. "On your calendar of events, you have 'p.m.' abbreviated three different ways. The accepted form is lower case, with a period after each letter. Those details may not seem important to you, but they are. Your AP style leaves a lot to be desired."

She kept her steady posture, but her heart pounded. She didn't have a bluff for this one. "What's AP style?"

His features went utterly still.

"Associated Press," he said slowly, as if speaking to someone who'd recently arrived from Minsk. "Remember? From Journalism 101?"

"I never took journalism."

In the flood of silence that radiated from Bret, Chloe realized for the first time that McCrea had a clock on his desk, and that it ticked. Deafeningly. She didn't move her eyes to look at it, though. For better or for worse, she held Bret's disbelieving stare.

He spoke without inflection. "I'm sorry. What?"

"I never—"

"I heard what you said. I'm just trying to wrap my head around it. You have a degree in English, and you never studied journalism. What did you *take*?"

"Literature, composition, creative nonfiction—"

"Creative nonfiction." He pinched the bridge of his nose, just above his glasses, his eyes closed.

"I knew I wanted to write." Now that his eyes weren't fixed on her, Chloe found her tongue and a bit of conviction. "I love words and I'm good with them. I just didn't know what kind of writing I wanted to do."

He opened his eyes. His stare remained expressionless. "I've got a reporter who doesn't want to be a reporter."

"Not then. But things change. Not everybody knows what they want to be when they're in college."

"I knew when I was ten."

Bully for you. She kept that immature thought to herself. "That's great," she said instead. "For some of us it takes a little longer. I've been writing for the *Gazette* for over a year and a half—"

"And McCrea's been cleaning up after you. But I don't have that luxury. He had two seasoned full-time reporters, and you were turning in, what? A couple of stories a week?"

More like three or four in a month. "Something like that."

"Well, you're one-third of our writing staff now. It's time to step up your game." He opened a desk drawer, brought out a chunky, spiral-bound volume, and tossed it onto the desk in front of her with a *thunk*. "Here's the

AP Stylebook. That's where you get your standardized forms of abbreviation, word use, you name it. Learn it. Love it."

"Pie." Chloe spoke as soon as Sherry reached the corner booth at the Pine 'n' Dine. "I need a piece of Hal's peanut butter chocolate pie. And coffee. Please."

If she survived these next three months, she'd probably gain thirty pounds. At least the peanut butter had some protein in it.

"Okay." Sherry made a show of jotting down the order on her pad, but she studied Chloe with brown eyes that missed nothing. "Tough morning?"

Chloe expelled all of her breath with a helpless shake of her head. She was out of words for the day already. And it wasn't even eleven-thirty.

She'd brought along her briefcase with the notes from her interview inside. Half an hour ago, when she first returned to the office, her head had been buzzing with lines for her article. Now she couldn't even muster the enthusiasm to look at her notes. She brought out the style guide instead. It must weigh about ten pounds.

"Hey, sweetie." Kate appeared beside Sherry. "Simon Legree giving you a hard time again?"

"Don't call him that." Chloe cast a hasty glance around the diner, where early lunch patrons were starting to drift in. "I never called him that."

"Ebenezer Scrooge, then." At least Kate remembered her literary references from school.

Sherry skittered away with her order pad, only to be

replaced by Tiffany. Didn't *anyone* work the night shift anymore?

"Hi," Tiffany said. "Is he giving you a bad time again?"

"Stop. Stop." Chloe leaned forward, elbows on the table, hands pressed to her temples. She didn't come here for sympathy. She came here for pie. Except she'd come to the place where everyone knew her. Because the pie was here. But they had pie at The Foggy Notion, too.

Okay, she wanted some pity, and she'd known where to get it. She couldn't have it both ways. Venting had to take a backseat. She was practically drawing a crowd, and anyone within earshot might tell Bret she'd been in here griping about him.

She raised her head. "I don't want to talk about it," she said, her voice low. "Not here. I don't want everyone to—"

"What's this?" Tiffany fingered the well-thumbed stylebook on the table.

"My homework. Did you know there's a right way and a wrong way to abbreviate 'p.m.'?"

"You're kidding," Tiffany said.

"Who cares?" Kate added.

Chloe found she *did* care. Even if Bret thought she didn't. That phrase stung her again: *If you're serious about this . . .*

Chloe pulled the book toward her and cracked it open. It was learn this stuff or run away screaming, and she couldn't do that without finding another job. Coming back to the diner with her tail between her legs, she resolved, was not an option.

"Excuse me, ladies." Sherry sandwiched her way between Tiffany and Kate to slide a plate of pie in front of Chloe. "You guys had better get back to your stations before Hal kills you. Kate, turn around the 'Please Wait To Be Seated' sign. We're starting to get the lunch crowd."

When they left, Sherry turned Chloe's coffee cup right side up and poured, remembering to leave plenty of room for cream.

"Thanks," Chloe said. Sherry would know it wasn't just for the coffee.

"No problem." Now that the other girls were gone, Sherry stared at Chloe with naked curiosity, but offered no comment. Which was unusually restrained for Sherry. Then again, she'd worked at the Pine 'n' Dine longer than any of them, so she probably realized the walls had ears.

"What's that?" Sherry nodded toward the style guide.

Chloe stared at the table of contents and fingered the two inches of pages beneath it. "It might be my tombstone."

Chapter 3

Chuck stood in the doorway of Bret's temporary office, shrugging into his coat. "Need anything else before I go?"

Bret leaned back from McCrea's desk. This was almost too rare to pass up. At five o'clock on Friday, Chuck usually took off fast enough to leave his chair spinning in a puff of smoke.

"Let's see." Bret squinted in thought. "I don't suppose you'd care to help me get a head start on Sunday's layout."

"Seriously?" Chuck froze, car keys already in hand.

In all fairness, Bret had never known Chuck to say "no" when he was needed. But Chuck had two small girls to get home to, so he wasn't one for staying late unless it was absolutely necessary.

"No, I'm not serious. Or crazy."

"This place would burn down without me and you know it."

Bret did know it. "Yes. Probably shortly after you left the building with the matches." He gave Chuck a nod. "Have a good weekend."

With that, Chuck was out the door, leaving Bret to

the article on his monitor. Chloe's third real story for the week, not counting all the press releases he'd given her to write up. She'd turned it in about half an hour ago. Looking back on the week, Bret realized Chuck had probably filed more stories than Bret and Chloe combined.

Bret ran his cursor over the text of the lighter-than-air piece about a local woman who'd turned her talent for metal lawn sculptures into a self-sufficient business. They'd been short on freelance photographers—Ned had stayed home this week with Debbie and their new baby boy—so Chloe had shot some decent-resolution photos using the camera on her phone. Bret's mouth quirked upward. He'd never seen a lawn flamingo with a coffee can for a body before.

And the writing was . . . okay, it was more than just passable. What could have sounded like something out of a school paper was executed with nicely chosen quotes woven neatly through the story. And with only two AP style errors. He suspected she'd gone over every word until she felt it gleamed. That seemed likely, considering how long it had taken her to write it.

But he decided McCrea wasn't so crazy after all.

Bret sent the piece over to the night editor's in-box and got back to work on the article he'd started writing this morning.

A clattering sound down the hall from the newsroom told Bret that he and the night editor weren't the only ones left in the building. He glanced at Chloe's desk and saw her coat still draped over the back of her chair. No real surprise there; she'd stayed after office hours every night since she started here.

Bret rose, stepped outside his door, and listened. A distant whir of machinery came from the room that housed the photocopier. The whirring was cut off by another clattering noise.

The copy machine was an ancient, temperamental beast that jammed at the drop of a hat. He wouldn't wish it on his worst enemy. Bret started down the hall to see if she needed help.

As he reached the door to the copy room, he heard a colorful four-letter word he wouldn't have expected from his new reporter. One that definitely wasn't printable.

Chloe pulled her hand out of the jaws of the copier, her fingers flying to her mouth. She tasted blood. And toner.

"What happened?" a now-familiar voice said behind her.

If she hadn't had her fingers in her mouth, she probably would have sworn again.

She turned to face Bret, putting herself between her boss and the open door of the front of the copier. Belatedly she pulled her fingers from her mouth, cupping her wounded right hand in her left. It was still bleeding. Great.

"Hey. Let me see that." He reached for her hand and she flinched, aware now that her hand was not only bleeding, but it *hurt*.

She pulled her hand back. "I'm okay."

"No, you're not," he said matter-of-factly. "You're bleeding like a stuck pig. And swearing like a sailor. Let me see it."

"I didn't—"

"Hush." He didn't give her a chance to argue. He took her hand. Before she knew what was happening, he'd pulled a handkerchief from out of nowhere and wrapped it loosely around her fingers.

A handkerchief?

"Don't worry," he said. "It's for the glasses. When they get smudged it drives me crazy."

With deft fingers, he cradled her hand and dabbed at it with the handkerchief, trying to determine where she'd been cut. Chloe realized she hadn't been this close to Bret since she poured him that refill for his coffee at the diner. She held still and tried not to breathe too loudly as she took in the fact that he was taller than he seemed, that his fingers were surprisingly gentle, and that she was now oozing red blood onto the clean white fabric of his handkerchief.

And the cut still throbbed. Chloe pulled in a deep breath and held it, trying to remember if she'd ever met anyone in real life who carried a handkerchief.

Biting her lip, she sneaked a look up at Bret, but his head was bent to assess the damage. It looked like she'd sliced her third finger on whatever piece of metal wouldn't let go of the jammed paper.

"I wouldn't have thought there was anything that sharp inside the copier," he said.

"It felt like a corner," she said. "I was pulling out the paper and I guess I yanked pretty hard. It was the third time the thing jammed and I was—frustrated."

"It's a prehistoric monster," Bret agreed. "Corporate isn't really into spending money on us here in the hills. Come on. Let's get this cleaned up."

He started down the hall, and since he still held her

fingers wrapped in his handkerchief, she didn't have much choice but to go along.

At the far end of the hall was a break room Chloe had visited a couple of times to heat up some ramen noodles. It boasted a vending machine, a microwave, a bunch of mostly empty cabinets, and a kitchen sink. Bret brought her to the sink and rinsed and soaped her cut with calm efficiency. Somehow, without ever releasing her hand, he replaced the handkerchief with a paper towel torn from the dispenser over the counter. She resumed bleeding, more slowly, onto the towel.

His eyes met hers over her wounded hand. Up close, his stare felt even more penetrating than usual. She wondered if he could see how nervous she was, or if he felt her hand tremble.

Her fingers still cupped in his, he said, "Have you had a tetanus shot?"

That brought a smile out of her. "Please. My mom's a retired nurse. There's no way I could dodge that bullet."

"Really." He reached up to the cabinet above their heads and unerringly, with one free hand, retrieved a little plastic first aid kit. "Where did she work?"

"Tall Pine Hospital."

"Mm. What part?"

"Labor and delivery."

Well, he was getting her mind off the cut, and somewhat off the fact that he'd been holding her hand for about five minutes. "Sounds like a pretty cheerful department, as hospitals go."

"Usually. It gets pretty dramatic, though."

He gave a faint chuckle. "Ned—the photographer

with the new baby—told me his wife said, 'Get this thing out of me.' Ten minutes later she was ecstatic."

"I hear that's how it usually goes."

He managed to open the first aid kit one-handed. "Here, hold on to that for a minute." He released her hand, and she held the paper towel around it. "Iodine or Neosporin?"

"Please. Neosporin. I'm not a masochist. You know, I can—"

But he already had her hand again. He spread the medication over her cut, then wound a strap of gauze around her finger. Not too loose and not too tight.

And then he returned her hand to her as if it were a book he'd borrowed, and put the first aid kit back into the cabinet.

"How'd you know where the first aid kit was?" Chloe asked.

"Because I put it there." Another slight smile. "Former Boy Scout. Eagle Scout, actually. 'Be prepared.'"

"Neither of my brothers did scouting."

"The nerd gene probably doesn't run as strong in your family."

"No, I'm the sole carrier."

Chloe cradled her bandaged hand, feeling it throb again. She bit her lip.

And they stood, face-to-face, in the fluorescent glare of the break room. For a minute or two, he hadn't felt like her boss. He'd been downright human. But now that her moment in Bret's urgent care ward was over, Chloe wasn't sure how to close the transaction.

"Thanks," she said finally. She took a step back. "This was really nice of you."

"Don't sound so surprised." He flicked another brief smile at her. "It's not like I'm the kind of guy who kicks puppies, you know."

Chloe felt her cheeks flush. "I didn't say that."

"I know. But just for the record, I love puppies. It's kittens and babies I can't stand."

That was a closing line if ever she'd heard one.

Chloe returned to the copy room and scooped up her copies, remembering at the last minute to take out the original. She peered into the belly of the photocopier and didn't see anything left of the jammed paper, so she closed the plastic door in front. The machine belched out a series of chugging-whirring noises, and it didn't beep at her. It must be satisfied. She went back to Bret's office and found him fixed on his computer screen. "Bret?"

It felt strange to say his first name. Maybe that was why he raised his head so sharply, as if she'd startled him. She realized that so far, she'd avoided calling him anything at all.

Now he looked at her with barely a trace of recognition. Certainly not as if he remembered bandaging her finger five minutes ago. Maybe you had to be bleeding to hold the guy's attention.

She shouldn't have poked her head in. "I just wanted to say . . . I'm headed out. I think the copier's okay now."

"Okay." He was virtually expressionless. "No more bloodshed?"

So he did remember. "No, I'm fine. Thanks again." She ventured a smile.

He didn't give one back. "No problem. Rest up this weekend."

Okay, then.

34

Chloe left, the cumbersome AP style guide weighing down her briefcase.

Once Chloe left, Bret dropped his head forward and clasped his fingers at the back of his neck, trying to stretch away the tension. The words he'd read for the last ten minutes had barely registered. He would have liked to blame it on an exhausting week. But he kept remembering the little hot and cold flashes he'd felt while he was holding Chloe's hand.

He'd be back in the office tomorrow; that went with the territory. He'd taken plenty of calls from McCrea on a Saturday afternoon, asking about some fine point on one of Bret's stories for the Sunday or Monday edition.

Pace yourself had been McCrea's last words of advice to Bret before he left last Friday. For tonight, maybe the smart thing for Bret was to go home and get some food and a good night's sleep before he tried to put together two more days of news. He could take copies of the layouts home with him and glance over them before he went to bed. Give his brain a chance to process them while he slept.

So he took the layout sheets to the copy room. When he hit the button to make the first copy, the photocopier revved up, whirred, and beeped in annoyance.

Bret sighed without surprise. Finding every source of a jam on this machine was a lot like trying to find an itch in the middle of your back. He opened the front of the copier and looked. Nothing in the middle of the machine, the site where Chloe had sliced her finger. He tried another lever, pulled a latch, and fished out a sheet of paper. It was curled, half-torn, and smudged with toner. He glanced at it.

Chloe's résumé.

And suddenly, he recalled the way she'd stood in front of the machine when he walked in. Concerned about her hand, he hadn't questioned it. Note to self: Chloe wasn't too bad at subterfuge. He'd have to remember that.

Better than remembering the pretty gray-green eyes that had looked at him so uncertainly, or the way she'd bitten her lip to try to hide the obvious fact that the cut hurt. Or how small her hand had felt in his. How he'd liked the chance to take care of her. Just for a few minutes. You'd think, by now, he would have had enough of taking care of people.

More to the point, after one week in this office, she was already updating her résumé. Either a slacker, or she really didn't like it here. Maybe it wasn't hard to imagine why that would be.

He glanced over the résumé, printed on smooth ivory-colored paper that was thicker than the photocopier's standard stock. He'd never seen Chloe's résumé before, since McCrea had hired her before he told Bret about it. Like the résumé of most people in their early twenties, there was basically nothing on it. Waitress at the Pine 'n' Dine for two years, plus the recent addition of her job here, vaguely dated from the current year to present. Just as much space was devoted to her college years. B.A. in English with an impressive grade point average, graduated summa cum laude, volleyball team.

Volleyball?

He wondered if she had any prospects. Tall Pine wasn't

exactly rife with job openings. Maybe she'd try to take her vast journalistic experience down the hill. A few days ago, that wouldn't have sounded so bad to Bret. But if she left, he'd end up doing more writing himself, or trying to find someone else with some ability. And train them.

As green as she was, her writing skills were good, and she took direction pretty well.

That lip-biting, though . . .

Bret crumpled the tattered résumé and threw it into the waste paper basket next to the copier.

Chapter 4

She was late. Or, more precisely, she wasn't here.

Through his windowed wall, Bret eyed Chloe's vacant desk, felt steam rise between his ears, and tried not to jump to conclusions.

It didn't mean she was off on a job interview or, more irresponsibly, that she'd simply decided not to show up. Chloe seemed more conscientious than that. But then, he didn't really know her, as her clandestine copying attested. And no matter how you sliced it, late on a Monday morning didn't look good.

He tried to be patient. He didn't even count her as late until Chuck rolled in at his usual ten minutes after eight. That, Bret had learned to expect long before he stepped into McCrea's shoes. Chuck always made up for any lost time while he was here. But now it was eight-twenty, and with Chuck's presence, Chloe's absence became glaring.

Bret did a recount of the stories filed last week. Chuck had turned in a whopping fifteen articles, stepping up his pace without breaking a visible sweat, while Bret had completed a measly six. McCrea's warning was coming true. Bret couldn't write nearly as much as he normally did—not while he was editing everyone else's work, chasing photographers, choosing from the national stories that came off the wire, and laying out the paper. He was putting in a lot of extra hours, including most of his Saturday to get the Sunday and Monday editions put together.

Three reporters, twenty-four local stories, counting Chloe's three, plus all those press releases he'd had her write up. If you took out Chloe's share . . .

Bret passed a hand through his hair and glared uselessly at her empty desk again. *No point in living out every scenario,* McCrea would have said. After all, she'd left her cat coffee mug on her desk, along with the custom-printed mouse pad she'd brought in. Somewhere she'd scared up an image of the now-retired comic strip reporter Brenda Starr with a speech bubble that read, "I didn't go into journalism for money or fame."

Bret gritted his teeth. A job interview at this hour on a Monday, he reminded himself, wasn't likely.

He'd almost succeeded in getting focused on his plans for the day when she pushed through the door from the lobby at high speed, just shy of eight-thirty. She wore a skirt, not the best choice for a November day in Tall Pine, but if she'd been on a job interview, it had ended pretty quickly.

Dropping into her seat, Chloe shrugged her coat onto the back of her chair and cast a surreptitious look toward Bret's office. *Yep. I see you.* He averted his eyes and tapped at his keyboard.

Patience, he reminded himself. *Give her the benefit of the doubt.* After all, there were all kinds of reasons for being late. And hadn't he made up his mind last week to be nicer?

She was here. For the moment, he'd take it.

He waited a suitable amount of time before he got up to go to the lobby. Jen ought to have the weekend mail sorted by now, and it would give him a chance to stretch his legs. He'd been here nearly two hours already.

He passed Chloe with a nod, not acknowledging her tardiness one way or the other. Giving her the benefit of the doubt, the way he'd made up his mind to do.

In the lobby, Jen sat behind the reception counter, stacks of envelopes piled in front of her. She didn't look up as Bret entered.

"Hey, Jen. Have you got—"

She scooped up a pile of mail, reached over the counter, and slapped it into his hand. "Here you go. Sorry."

Bret sifted through the envelopes. "So how was your weekend?"

"Not bad."

Something off-key in the receptionist's usually placid tone poked through Bret's contemplation of the mail. He looked up to find her intent on the task of distributing envelopes in the vertical files on the left side of her counter. Her movements seemed brisk and just a little harried.

That wouldn't do. Jen wasn't quite old enough to be his mother, but she generally gave off a calming presence that was almost maternal. The sane front line of defense in the *Gazette*'s chaotic little world.

"Everything okay?" Bret asked.

"Oh." With a quick shake of her head, she looked up from her task for the first time with a distracted smile. Her hair was still shaped in its usual orderly brown waves, so nothing could be *that* amiss. "No big deal. Just running behind. My car wouldn't start this morning, and I had to get a jump from a neighbor. I'm just playing catch-up."

"Sorry. Not a fun way to start the week." Bret glanced back down at his mail, but then his brain processed a pertinent fact. "So you don't know if it'll start again."

"I'll figure it out after I catch my breath."

Bret folded his arms. "I'll give you a jump at lunchtime and we can run it over to Alex's Garage."

Jen raised a neatly shaped right eyebrow. "Since when do you go to lunch?"

"Not since McCrea left. See? You'll be doing me a favor. Don't give me any guff about it, or no cheeseburger for you."

He smacked the counter with the mail and started back toward the newsroom before she could argue.

Jen's voice stopped him. "By the way, when are you going to give that poor girl the key code?"

Bret turned back, feeling a prickle of premonition. "What do you mean?"

"The new girl. Chloe. She was waiting in her car in the front parking lot for me to let her in. She's beaten me here most mornings. Didn't you ever show her the side entrance, or the employee lot?"

It hadn't dawned on him. The twenty-four-hour employee entrance opened, not with a key, but with a code on a numeric keypad. He frowned. "You mean, give her the code? She's only been here a week."

"What do you think she's going to do, wheel out the printing press? Steal the silver candlesticks?"

Bret shot her a warning look. Jen didn't bat an eye, but her scolding expression looked more maternal than ever.

He shook his head at her. "You're lippy when you've had a bad morning."

He swatted the counter with the mail again and went back into the newsroom.

Behind her keyboard, Chloe tried to brainstorm three more story ideas to present to Bret. Last week he'd asked for five and turned down two of them. This week, she figured she'd better have no fewer than ten.

He returned from the lobby, mail in hand, and started past Chuck's desk and hers. Then he turned and leveled a look at her that she couldn't quite decipher. But it was milder than the veiled glare he'd given her when he passed by a few minutes ago.

"You don't have a key code?" He looked at her, arms folded, a stance she was beginning to learn was a common one for him.

"A what?"

"For the employee entrance." He inclined his head vaguely toward the hallway, in the direction leading away from the copier room.

"I didn't know we had one."

"You follow the hallway to the door at the end. The one that leads to the lot where the employees' cars are parked."

"I didn't know we had—"

"The code is one-eight-three-five."

She pulled her ever-handy notepad toward her.

"Don't write it down. Memorize it. It's Elvis Presley's birthday, if that helps. January eighth, 1935."

"McCrea's a big fan," Chuck chimed in, half-turning from his screen.

"If I have to change it before he gets back, I'll change it to something that'll really annoy him," Bret said. "Perry Como's birthday, maybe."

Chloe frowned. "Why would the code change?"

A pause filled the air, and she wished she hadn't asked. Chuck turned back to his screen. The answer was obvious: if an employee who knew the code quit. Or got fired.

Bret said, "Just stay away from the silver candlesticks."

Huh?

While she pondered that remark, Bret unfolded his arms. "Story conferences this morning," he said. "Chuck, nine o'clock. Chloe, nine-fifteen."

And he went to his office, leaving Chloe with about twenty-five more minutes to brainstorm.

"And there's a junior at the high school who makes money writing thank-you notes. She started her freshman year, and she's put away almost enough for a car."

Bret leaned back behind his desk, arms folded. Again. A faint smile quirked up at the corners of his mouth. "I'm detecting a theme here. That's three local entrepreneurs so far, plus the two other stories."

Chloe skimmed the list she'd printed out. "Mandy

43

Wyndham is holding one more of her craft workshops at The North Pole Christmas shop."

"That's more of a news brief."

She'd written plenty of those last week—little single-paragraph items that ran down the side column, with no byline. They didn't count as stories. And if she didn't get enough ideas approved, he'd probably drown her in press releases, and she'd probably never get a chance to meet her ten-story goal. Until last week, Frank McCrea had assigned the stories she'd written. Chloe bit her lip and reconsidered her list. She did know a lot of local entrepreneurs, thanks to small talk with customers at the Pine 'n' Dine. She couldn't think of much else to write about. Crime was low around here, and things didn't change much. She'd have to—

"Tell you what." Bret's voice broke in on her thoughts. "Go ahead with the thank-you notes—I know a lot of people who could use that. That gives you five stories to work on for now. Get started on those. Things are bound to come up during the week. When they do, run them by me. Look for local issues. The kinds of things that tick people off. I know Tall Pine isn't exactly a hotbed of controversy, but it's not all sweetness and light." He considered her with that level gaze of his. "How would you feel about covering the town council meeting Wednesday night?"

As a new hire, Chloe knew there was only one right answer to that. "Absolutely."

"Don't get too enthused. You'll probably wish you brought along a good book. But here's what you *don't* do. Tempting as it may be, *don't* read a good book, don't check your cell phone, and in this case, take notes by hand. Don't use a laptop. You don't want anyone to think you're browsing the Internet. The meeting has your rapt, undivided attention." Before Chloe could get any more insulted, his mouth quirked up a little higher. "I recommend lots of coffee beforehand."

Chloe brushed aside her indignation. "What's my deadline?"

"Let's say ten p.m. The meeting starts at six; it's usually out by eight. I know it's an evening-killer. But if you do have a laptop, you can stop somewhere afterward for a bite while you write it up."

And, for the first time Chloe could remember, his eyes shifted away from hers. Leading her to believe he might remember The Night of the Unabomber at the Pine 'n' Dine, after all.

Bret resumed, "You probably won't have Internet connectivity to e-mail it from where you are, so just bring it in on a thumb drive when you're done."

"You'll still be here at ten?"

"Please. I *live* here. For the next three months, anyway."

"Okay. Anything else?"

"That'll do for now."

Chloe stood, and Bret did, too, in what appeared to be a show of old-school manners. "Thanks," she said.

"Don't thank me. You haven't been to the town council meeting yet." As she started for the door, he added, "You'll want to look up the articles on the last couple of meetings before you go."

Annoyance prickled at her. Bret didn't seem to think she had the sense God gave a grapefruit. "Of course."

Like I wouldn't do that.

One dark eyebrow arched up over his glasses, and

Chloe almost wondered if she'd said it out loud. But she knew she'd watched her mouth, if not her tone. So she didn't back down from his steady dark stare.

McCrea's clock ticked on the desk between them. Bret gave her one of his brief nods. "Thanks."

The torrent of press releases slowed, and Chloe had the vague feeling she'd passed some sort of initiation, although she wasn't sure when or how.

Now that she had a key code, she started coming in earlier to get a jump on the day. Bret was always in his office by the time she arrived, even when she got there a few minutes after seven. And the coffee was already made. So it wasn't just women's work after all.

He still didn't have much to say to her, and he rarely left his office. Not, at least, until late Thursday morning, when he emerged, took a seat at the desk across from Chuck's, and unceremoniously started typing.

It was the desk he'd paused at frequently on her first morning here; it must be his spot when he wasn't filling in as editor. Rather than sitting parallel to Chuck's desk, it faced their row of desks at a ninety-degree angle, giving Chloe, who sat behind Chuck, a view of Bret's face above his monitor. He'd barely sat down, but his speed and concentration suggested he'd been pounding away for the past half hour.

Chuck looked up. "Decided to come down from Mount Sinai for a while?"

"Shut up," Bret said absently, with no visible sign of animosity. His typing barely slowed.

It reminded Chloe of the way her brothers talked to

each other. She supposed she'd have to be one of the boys for Bret to say anything that rude to her.

"Hey, if you're going to mingle with the mortals"— Chuck's eyes were already back on his computer screen—"you'll have to put up with our prattle."

"That's kind of the idea." Bret gave a shake of his head. "I can't get used to writing in there. Too quiet, or too boxed in, or something. I might save the office for when I'm wearing my editor hat."

And just like that, they were a newsroom of three.

Bret's fingers resumed their impressive speed, producing a steady, soft clatter of sound on the keyboard. It wasn't anything like Chuck's forceful hunt-and-peck jabbing. Or Chloe's own sporadic output, broken by long pauses for thought. She forced her attention back to her own screen and reread her last paragraph. But there was a leak in her concentration now. She felt her attention pulled toward Bret, sitting across from her, probably wondering why she wasn't typing. *Just write something. Good, bad, or indifferent. You can always fix it later.*

She wrote:

Millie Bond first discovered her passion for knitting when her two children were both away at college. "I guess you'd call it classic empty-nest behavior," she said. "And of course I started with one of the hardest things to master. Socks, that I could put in the kids' college care packages. I still have the first pair I ever made, because they wouldn't fit either my son or my daughter. One was too small even for me, and the other one was huge. A little lesson in humility."

There. A whole paragraph, even if most of the words were a quote from Millie. Verbatim, of course.

To her left, the unbroken sound of Bret's typing continued. Did he ever stop? Chloe listened. After a moment, she was reassured by a temporary pause, only to hear him pour on the speed again as if to make up for lost time.

She sneaked a look at him. Even in college, she'd met very few men who'd bothered learning to touch-type. Most of them typed with two fingers like Chuck, or they made big, sad eyes at their girlfriends and asked them to type their papers.

Clearly, that wasn't Bret. She couldn't help being fascinated by the relentless clamor of keystrokes, the fierce look of concentration as he studied his screen.

Okay, it was kind of hot.

She remembered a joke she'd read once in a women's magazine: *Any man becomes exciting if you think about him long enough.*

She just needed to get out in the daylight a little more. But she'd always liked the smart ones. Except that this one was her boss, not to mention the fact that he—

Bret glanced up suddenly, dark eyes locking on hers. "What?" he prompted.

Heat flooded her face. She stammered, "How fast do you type?"

He shrugged. "I'm not sure. Seventy, eighty words a minute?"

Chloe could type that fast. She just couldn't *think* that fast. And apparently Bret had never been through the indignity of a typing test. A few job applications had put her in a room with thirty other women, typing like drones for five minutes until a timer went off. It was like a cattle call. One of those things they pulled on women.

She managed another paragraph about Millie Bond, doing her best to shut out the presence of the typing dynamo across from her so she wouldn't get caught watching him again. *That* had been embarrassing.

And she needed to focus, because she needed to turn in two stories a day if she was going to make it to ten in a week. She'd only finished one Monday, so she was already an article behind. She'd started doing some of her writing on her laptop after she got home. Maybe that was why her mind was so sluggish today. That, and the fact that it was raining.

She stood and went to the coffee maker. She'd gone out on a limb and brewed a second pot before Bret came out of his office. She poured a cup, added the vitally necessary creamer, and allowed herself a moment to stand beside the little cabinet as she took her first sip. She closed her eyes and let the slightly stinging warmth and flavor flood her senses. There was nothing like fresh coffee.

She opened her eyes. This time Bret was watching her.

He remarked, "Our coffee consumption is up since you started here."

She raised her eyebrows. "I'll pick up an extra can."

"Not what I meant. All I'm saying is, if you drink more coffee than Frank McCrea, you just might have a problem."

"It's one of the other two major food groups." Chloe

cupped her hands around her mug's warm sides. "Coffee and chocolate."

"Coffee, I'll grant you. You can keep the chocolate."

"You're kidding."

She stared at him in what wasn't entirely mock horror, but his eyes were on his work again. What kind of person didn't like chocolate?

As she settled back into her chair, Chuck hit a key with a definitive smack and stood to stretch. "School board story coming your way." He nodded at Bret.

Barely glancing up, Bret returned the nod, fingers still in motion. Fascinating.

Chuck paced a slow circuit around the room. He showed no interest in the coffee. Were she and Bret the only ones who drank it? That *was* concerning. The pot she'd discarded had been nearly empty. Maybe one of them did have a problem.

"What is it about rainy days?" Chuck completed his brief stroll and returned to his desk. "We don't even have windows in this room, and I still feel restless."

"Back to work," Bret said brusquely. "You can get started on your dream story: EVERYONE GOES TO BED EARLY."

"Better than your dream story." Chuck settled into his chair. "TALL PINE SLASHER ON THE LOOSE."

"Hey, I told you. Just one lousy murder. Of a really evil tourist."

Chuck glanced at her over his shoulder. "What about Chloe? What's her dream story?"

She smiled a little. Chuck was always kind to her, but he'd remained as neutral as Switzerland between her and Bret. She'd probably never make it into the boys' club, but the question felt like a conscious effort to include her.

Bret studied her briefly. "That's easy," he said. "FIREFIGHTER RESCUES KITTEN FROM TREE." His eyes glinted. "AGAIN."

And he went back to work without missing a beat.

Chloe laughed, because it *was* funny. If there was one thing she'd learned growing up in her family, it was how to take a joke.

Then her eyes went back to her article about Millie Bond's knitting.

By the time her son and daughter finished college, Bond had branched off into crocheting. She discovered she could make an eye-catching purse out of old plastic grocery bags. "I got all kinds of compliments on it," she said. "So I whipped up a few on consignment for Linda's Crafts. . . ."

Maybe Bret's headline wasn't so far off.

By her story conference in Bret's office the next Monday, Chloe had a solid idea for an article that extended well beyond light and fluffy. She saved it for last.

Taking a deep breath, she said, "I'd like to do a story on hospice care."

"I'm sorry. What?"

It was exactly what he'd said when she told him she'd never studied journalism, and he wore virtually the same expression. Unreadable. She'd kind of expected it. And yet, somehow, she hadn't prepared a response.

Bret saved her the trouble. Sitting back in his chair,

arms folded, he asked, "How'd you come up with that topic?"

For that, at least, she had an answer. "November is National Hospice Month. The local visiting nurses' association has been running ads in the paper all month."

"Right." He stared at her. "It's a pretty heavy subject."

"Well, it's not exactly kittens in trees."

"Chloe." Had he called her by name before, if she wasn't twenty feet away? "That was a joke."

"I know." She held herself straight. "But there's a little truth in most jokes. You had a point. My stories *have* been pretty light. But that doesn't mean that's all I can do."

He surveyed her from across the desk, as if he were measuring her. He was about as physically distant as he could get without hitting the bookcase with the back of his chair. "Sure you don't want to try something a little lighter first? Like maybe global thermonuclear war?"

"It's timely," she pointed out.

His eyebrows dipped slightly, the only change in his near-blank expression. "Do you know someone who's been through something like this? Lost a family member?"

"No. But I've heard my mom talk about it. She worked with a lot of the visiting nurses, and she always admired people who worked in hospice. A lot of them are volunteers. She said it takes someone with a really special heart to see someone through the end of their life."

Bret nodded slowly and pinched the bridge of his nose above his glasses. "All right. Let's look at this for a minute. For this story, you'd be interviewing—who? Not a hospice patient."

"No." It had crossed her mind, but obviously that was

out. "I thought—a family member of someone who's passed away. Not last week or anything, but someone who's been through the process in the last year or so. And one or two hospice workers. I'd start by getting in touch with the visiting nurses' association, see if there's anyone they'd refer me to."

"Okay." Bret fixed her with one of his dark-eyed stares. "But go easy on this one. I wouldn't usually advise a reporter to be sensitive, but this is one of those times. You're going to be asking people about a difficult subject. I don't want my phone ringing."

"Understood."

"And this one's going to be more involved. Allow yourself some extra time on it, but don't make it your only project. Keep getting the simpler stories written while this one's in the works."

"Got it."

He inclined his head, still leaning far back in his chair. "You're sure you wouldn't rather solve nuclear war instead?"

"I'll be careful." Chloe stood. She'd gotten the go-ahead; better not to prolong the discussion and give Bret more time to raise objections. "Anything else?"

"No. We're good." As Chloe started to leave, Bret sat forward, elbows on the desk. "Get the door on your way out," he added.

Bret watched Chloe's retreating sweatered back through the glass door as she left.

Really, God? Seriously?

He didn't see any sign that Chloe's motives were

anything other than innocent. And she'd never struck him as a spiteful person. Still, what were the odds?

He didn't waste any time. He pulled the phone toward him and called the visiting nurses' association. He dialed the number from memory.

Some things, you didn't forget even when you wanted to.

"Paula? Bret. I wanted to give you a quick heads-up."

Chloe's first stop was the coffee machine. Good.

"Bret. How are you doing?"

"Good. Thanks for asking. You're going to be getting a call from a new reporter. She wants to do a piece on hospice. She'll want to interview a staffer, and ask for some contacts. Use your judgment," he said. "If you tell her it's not a good idea to interview family members, I'm pretty sure she'll back off. And I'm sure this goes without saying, but—don't mention my mother. I don't think she knows anything about it, and that's the way I want to keep it."

Chapter 5

At one time, Bret never would have envisioned himself standing over a hot stove, but it happened with great regularity nowadays. Especially Tuesday nights.

At least once a week, he went over to his dad's house for dinner. When he did, he made it a point to see that his father ate something that resembled actual food, rather than the processed stuff that lived in David Radner's kitchen. Stocked with preservative-laden canned foods, salty snacks, and powdered donuts, the inside of his dad's cabinets looked like the set of a game show called *Name That Carcinogen*.

He'd already lost one parent to cancer, and it wasn't going to happen again if he could help it.

The television droned from the next room as Bret leaned to check the steaks in the broiler. Baked potatoes were humming in the microwave, and he'd gone through the motions of bringing a bagged salad that would probably only get picked at. Bret's skills hadn't advanced beyond meat and potatoes—cooking was a necessity, not a passion—but properly prepared, they were at least somewhat healthier than the typical bachelor diet.

"Almost ready," Bret called into the living room. He wondered if the television set ever got turned off. At least it was generally tuned to CNN, not some brain-dead game show or sitcom. But still.

A few minutes later, his dad joined him at the dining room table—another part of the ritual that Bret hadn't let go of yet, although he knew his father generally ate in the living room or over the kitchen counter.

"So how about those clowns in Washington?" Bret asked. It was a running joke, because on any given week, it always applied.

"Don't get me started. If they ever start talking *to* each other, instead of barking *over* each other, maybe they'd get somewhere."

"Job security," Bret said. "If they didn't keep canceling each other out, probably half of them would be out of work."

"So I hear you gave up on the clowns on the town council." David reached for the saltshaker.

Bret winced. "Don't you think maybe you could taste it before you—"

"Winston said he saw some little blonde at the council meeting, scribbling away at a notepad."

Crotchety as Winston Frazier was, he got credit for his part in trying to keep his longtime friend involved with the human race. He dragged Bret's father out to the diner a couple of times a week for lunch or a cup of coffee, sometimes a game of chess.

His dad went on, "He said she looked like one of the waitresses from the Pine 'n' Dine."

Up to now, there was one thing Bret never would have pegged Winston for: a gossip.

"I told you about her," Bret said. "McCrea hired her right before he left. She's green as—"

"You didn't mention she was pretty."

Bret shrugged. "So? Does Winston want me to get him her phone number?"

"Don't play dumb."

"Tell you what. I'll start talking about blond reporters when you start a conversation with a woman your own age."

"You know the answer to that."

Bret did.

I already had the love of my life, his father had said once, in a tone that pronounced the subject forever closed.

Bret's mother had died a few days before Christmas seven years ago, and his father had never decorated for Christmas again. The place didn't just lack a woman's touch; it looked nearly *un*touched.

Getting his dad to move out of this house sometime in the years since Helena Radner's death might have helped. The place stayed fairly tidy, largely because not much got disturbed, and it didn't look substantially different from the way it had seven years ago. The neutral brown sofa and loveseat set looked a bit more faded; the family photos on the wall hadn't been updated since Bret's graduation. The television remote control rested on the coffee table, easily findable. Beside it lay today's *Tall Pine Gazette,* neatly refolded in the unlikely event that David needed to refer back to it. Bret knew for a fact that his father read the paper every day, because he always had something to say about one of Bret's articles.

Bret glanced across the table and had a disquieting

sensation he'd experienced before—that he was looking into an age-progression mirror and seeing himself at sixty-six. Similar hair, thick and disobedient, now more gray than dark brown. Similar glasses, although Bret had tried to change that the last time he'd gotten new ones, going with lighter-weight frames. And his father's questionable diet hadn't really added any extra pounds to his frame, probably because he didn't bother to eat often enough.

David Radner had retired from the town council when Bret started at the *Gazette*, saying he didn't want to cause any conflict of interest issues for Bret. In reality, the months of his mother's illness would have made it hard for him to concentrate. Afterward, his dad couldn't seem to muster interest in much of anything beyond armchair criticism of those clowns in the news. Even then, it felt more like he was trying to do an impersonation of his old self.

If this was what having a love of your life got you, maybe that was why Bret's relationships with women tended to stall at a certain point.

He'd try again to correct that. After he got past Christmas.

His father persisted, "I notice you didn't say she *wasn't* pretty."

Of all the subjects in the world, his dad had to latch on to this one. "It doesn't matter. She's an employee. Not going to happen."

Bret braced himself mentally, preparing to counter his father with reminders of things like business ethics and sexual harassment suits. But wisely, his dad let the matter drop.

Bret took another bite of his steak. It did need salt.

* * *

When Bret returned to the newsroom after lunch the next day, he noticed a tall aluminum can on Chloe's desk as he passed.

Chloe sat behind the canned energy drink, typing for all she was worth.

The drinks had begun appearing on Chloe's desk with increasing frequency over the past week or so. The phrase *performance-enhancing drugs* flitted through Bret's mind. Energy drinks might be different in degree, but not necessarily in kind.

She'd turned in eight stories last week, a shade below the goal of ten that he'd set for her on her first day. Maybe he should make sure she knew the quota was more of a guideline.

Let it go, he told himself, and kept walking toward his office. As he passed, he saw her forehead faintly creased in concentration.

He hadn't asked her how the hospice story was coming, and she hadn't volunteered. He'd told her to take her time on it; maybe she was taking that to heart. Or maybe the story would quietly fizzle. Bret wouldn't mind. Maybe she'd concluded that she'd bitten off more than she could chew.

Or maybe that was why she was pushing herself all the harder.

Unable to stop himself, Bret found himself backing up a step, then another, until he was alongside Chloe's desk again.

"How many of those do you drink in a day?" He nodded toward the energy drink.

She raised her head, and it took a moment for the

cloudy look to fade from those gray-green eyes. He knew that hazy feeling. She really *had* been engrossed.

Her gaze shifted to the can on her desk. "I don't know. Two, sometimes three?"

"Three is the maximum on those things."

"And I never drink more than that. And only sometimes." A grin slipped across her face. "You're looking at a veteran of college all-nighters."

Bret remembered those years. He held back a smile. "You should stick with coffee. It might not be great for you, but at least it's a known quantity."

"The coffee's pretty gross by the afternoon. And I wouldn't want to break McCrea's record."

"Make another pot. If you keel over, I don't want to be responsible."

Her brows descended in the most delicate frown he'd ever seen. "Are you some kind of a health fiend?"

"No. I just try to avoid things that can kill me."

"This?" She picked up the can and peered into it, one eye closed.

Then, to his surprise, she swung the can in a slow arc toward Bret. Then she swung it back toward herself. Then out again toward Bret, as though she were threatening him with some kind of supernatural wand. Her eyes gleamed. In another context, Bret might have thought she was flirting.

Bret took a step back. "You really *are* sleep-deprived," he said. "Or else the chemicals are kicking in."

Her smile widened, a dimple deepening below one corner of her mouth, and Bret's knees unexpectedly weakened.

Pretty. It wasn't as if he hadn't noticed before. His dad's report about Winston's remark shouldn't have any effect. It didn't take two elderly men to make him realize a woman was attractive.

She was undeniably pretty—lovely, in fact—but it took more than that to get to Bret.

It was her spark, her humor, her determination. And heaven help him, she was smart.

"I'm serious," he said. "I don't want you burning yourself out. And you can't live on caffeine and ramen noodles."

She looked a little startled. As if he wouldn't have noticed that, like Bret, she'd gotten into the habit of staying in the office for lunch most days, and that her lunch generally came out of a Styrofoam cup. More chemicals. But he couldn't go into a full-scale nutrition lecture. He'd said enough; he'd just have to hope that some of it took root.

For now, her eyes held his, the way they tended to do whenever he challenged her. Her chin tipped up just a fraction, and Bret's knees turned to butter.

"I'm a big girl," she said. "I can take care of myself."

"Make sure you do." He kept his voice brusque, but he felt a smile escape. "Can't have you falling over, or you'll miss your deadline."

And, as briskly as he could with faulty knees, he started back toward his office.

He's going to hate it, Chloe thought, seconds after she sent the hospice piece over to Bret Friday morning.

She reminded herself she'd felt this way before, whenever she turned in a paper to a demanding professor in college. The urge to second-guess herself, wishing she'd given her work just one more look. But she knew this story backward and forward by now; on the last pass, she'd found herself changing back changes she'd made earlier.

She knew the panic was normal. Up until she sent the article, she'd been sure it was the best thing she'd ever written. She'd *wanted* to make it the best thing she'd ever written—not just to prove herself to Bret, but because she owed it to the people she'd interviewed. She'd turned up uninvited in the lives of surviving families, asking them to reopen healing wounds and share a little of their grief with her. It had taken more of her heart and soul than she'd expected. One of the hospice workers had even brought her near tears when she talked about reading *Marley & Me* to a patient.

She *had* cried when she wrote it up. And if that wasn't the way a reporter was supposed to feel about a story—well, she didn't know any way around it.

She glanced at Bret's office, just the top of his head visible behind his computer screen, and had no idea whether he'd seen the article land in his in-box.

But it was literally out of her hands, and she had work to do. By the end of the day, thanks to the late-night hours she'd been putting in at home, she'd be able to finish her tenth story of the week.

Bret got the e-mail from Chloe late that afternoon: Did you get the hospice piece? Sent it over this morning.

Well, at least she was getting the hang of communicating by e-mail within the office. The first time he'd e-mailed her from across the room, she'd been bewildered. But it was the best way to communicate quickly and keep interruptions at a minimum.

She was catching on to AP style and office communications, all right. Learning patience appeared to be taking a bit longer.

Of course he knew how it felt. Waiting to hear back from an editor on an important article could feel like hanging from a rope over Prospect Lake, not quite able to get the rope swinging enough to put you back over the shore. He knew how it felt because he'd been there. Chloe would just have to learn, the same way he had, that it went with the territory.

But it was only humane to e-mail her back: Got it. Working through the stories I'll need for the weekend first.

A few minutes later, he watched Chloe take one of her frequent strolls to the coffee machine. He admired the resolute set of her shoulders, covered in a slate-blue cardigan sweater. She must have a cardigan for every day of the week, and each one looked just a little softer than the last.

Bret could use some of that coffee himself, but he'd need to walk past her to get to it.

Instead, he pulled himself up straight and opened the file Chloe had sent him this morning. Her headline read: LEAVING WITH DIGNITY.

His throat tightened. He closed the file.

Maybe he'd look at it tonight. After everyone else was gone.

* * *

When Chloe came in Monday morning, instead of the customary one-on-one meetings, Bret announced a meeting of the newsroom staff. Which meant herself, Bret, and Chuck. Bret stood facing them, arms folded, leaning back against the desk where he did his writing.

"This is Thanksgiving week," Bret said, "which means we have five days of holiday weekend to cover, including next Monday, before the office closes Wednesday. That means we go into what McCrea calls 'crank' mode. We need to generate as many stories as possible, to fill the days when the office is closed. So we start now. Let's look at the articles we can work on ahead of time. Chuck, what have you got?"

Chuck seemed prepared. "Holiday traffic projections. Ski conditions up at Mount Douglas. I'm interviewing the church that does that annual Thanksgiving dinner. And I got some quotes last week from the kids at the elementary about what's on their Christmas wish lists."

"Okay. A good start." Bret gave a spare nod, and Chloe wondered if that was as effusive as praise from him ever got. He picked up a yellow legal pad from the desktop behind him. "I jotted down a few to dish out. A rundown of the restaurants in town that serve Thanksgiving dinner—I'll take that one. The annual toy drive at the town hall—Chuck. Turkey tips to run Wednesday—Chloe."

"Why me?" Chloe interrupted before she thought.

"I'm sorry?" Bret's eyes shot to her. His glare seared like a laser.

Pick your battles, she reminded herself. But the female-centric assignment rankled. She tried to hold her ground gracefully. "I mean, that sounds like something we could get off the wire."

Bret's eyes stayed fixed on hers. From her peripheral vision, Chloe caught a glance from Chuck. She had the feeling that, if he'd been able to, he would have been waving his arms over his head in warning.

"That's a wonderful idea," Bret said crisply. "The more we rely on the wire, the less local we are. The less local we are, the more likely the corporate office is to start thinking about all the money they could save if they got rid of some of the human beings around here."

That deadly look didn't release her, and Chloe wondered why she hadn't transformed into a puddle of sizzling goo by now.

"Turkey tips," Bret concluded quietly.

Adjusting his glasses, he returned to his list.

By Wednesday afternoon, Chloe had a vivid understanding of what Bret had meant by "crank" mode.

She'd whipped out fourteen stories in three days, if you counted news briefs taken from press releases. But with five days of newspaper to fill, those seemed to be fair game.

All through the week, Bret had never said a word about the hospice article.

A few minutes after four, Chuck stood and shrugged into his coat. "I'm headed to the airport. Wish me luck."

"You're kidding." He'd mentioned he and his girls were going to visit family; she hadn't realized he was flying out of town tonight. "You're a brave man."

"Brave or foolish." Chuck grinned at her on his way out. "Have a happy Thanksgiving."

Must be nice, she thought, but she couldn't begrudge him his early freedom. Besides the fact that he was a nice guy, she knew by now just how much of the paper Chuck wrote.

So now the newsroom was down to Chloe, her monitor, and one more story to finish before she left. While Bret sat in his editing cage. *Mount Sinai,* Chuck had called it.

It had been a busy week. She knew that. But was Bret going to run the hospice piece or not?

Every fiber of her being warned her not to nag him, especially after their face-off Monday. But the waiting and wondering was driving her nuts.

Concentrate. The article refused to come together. Maybe because her brain was starting to fizzle out. Chloe eyed the coffee maker, but that seemed wasteful this late in the day. She'd finished her last energy drink a couple of hours ago, trying not to notice the way Bret's eyes lingered on the can, almost imperceptibly, as he passed. Even the way he *didn't* comment on it amounted to a comment.

She pulled herself straight and took a couple of long, deep breaths, trying to pull in extra oxygen to revive herself. Then she started slogging at the article again. If she could just stop moving words around and *write* the darn thing . . .

"Chloe." Bret's voice jarred her like an alarm clock going off way too early in the morning.

Her head jerked up. How in the world had he managed to sneak up on her in plain sight? He stood in front of her, arms folded, and she wondered what it meant that he hadn't e-mailed her as usual.

He asked, "What have you got left for tonight?"

"Just finishing the interview with Arnie Jacobs about the goose problem at Prospect Lake."

She willed him a telepathic message: *What-about-the-hospice-piece?*

If Bret was telepathic, he showed no sign of it. "So, you've got about half an hour, forty minutes left?"

I wish. "Something like that."

He passed a hand through thick dark hair that already looked mussed. Appealingly mussed—if it had been anyone else. And if it had been anyone else, she might have said he looked just a tad uncertain.

Then Bret spoke, squelching any fatigue-induced delusions before they could take root.

"There's still a lot of work backed up." The words came out quick and flat. "Can you come in on Friday?"

Chloe's mouth went dry. In a flash, she saw her shopping plans go down the drain.

She'd planned to hit the big mall out of town with Tiffany and Kate first thing Friday morning, gunning for the kind of after-Thanksgiving doorbuster sales that didn't exist in Tall Pine. But when your brand-new boss made a request, it wasn't really a request.

"You don't have to come in first thing," Bret added. "Ten o'clock is good. And I'll feed you. Breakfast and lunch."

Breakfast *and* lunch. Which meant she'd be here quite a while.

It wasn't really a request, and she didn't really have a

choice, even though he was trying to make it seem otherwise.

She squared her shoulders and kissed her bargains good-bye. "Okay."

Ten o'clock. Not a minute sooner. And you're getting me as-is. Jeans, no makeup. I may not even brush my hair.

As if he'd notice.

Chapter 6

"Don't let Chloe burn the salad, Mom." Her older brother, Todd, paused by the kitchen island to steal a handful of walnuts from the stack she was chopping.

"Hey," she said, "don't mess with me when I've got a knife in my hand. I don't see *you* doing any of the cooking."

"Be careful what you wish for," her mother said. Jan Davenport stood at the kitchen sink on Chloe's right, carefully spooning stuffing into the turkey. "You don't really want either of those lunkheads in the kitchen, do you?"

Her mom had a point.

Raising her eyes past the kitchen island, Chloe watched Todd saunter into the adjoining family room. From the back, he looked like the sturdy, broad-shouldered twenty-eight-year-old man most people probably saw him as. Somewhere along the line, Todd had grown up, gone to school, and opened a practice as a veterinarian. She still couldn't wrap her head around it. If the good people of Tall Pine could only see him the way Chloe did. Moments after stepping into their parents' house, both of her brothers reverted to adolescence.

Todd joined their younger brother, Joel—the second lunkhead in question—on the couch with their dad to watch a pregame something-or-other. Except for the size of her brothers, it looked like every Thanksgiving at home since Chloe was a kid.

It smelled the same, too.

She turned toward her mother. "The turkey's not even in the oven, and the stuffing already smells good."

Jan upended the turkey, lightly shaking it to allow the stuffing to settle inside the bird. "Tell me about it. I should have had a bigger breakfast before we got started."

Chloe walked over and popped a walnut half into her mom's mouth. "Here. Instant protein."

Her mother accepted the walnut without question, probably remembering all the times she'd done the same thing for Chloe.

Retirement looked good on her mom. Jan's hair was still the same ash brown it had always been, although Chloe knew she colored it. Middle age may have thickened her mother's waist a bit, but her movements were quick and decisive, with the kind of efficiency that came after twenty-five years of being a professional nurse. A professional who, nevertheless, had always seemed content to make Thanksgiving dinner without any help from the males in the next room.

Not that there wasn't an art to it. Which was why, each year, Chloe was a little more inclined to help out in the kitchen.

Now, Jan slanted a frown Chloe's way. "You're looking a little skinny yourself."

"I'll make up for it today. Believe me."

She didn't want to talk about her wonky work schedule and the resulting wonky eating habits. Not today. Chloe squeezed her mom in a one-armed hug. Jan, still holding on to the turkey with both hands, couldn't very well hug her back, but she shrugged a shoulder against Chloe in response.

Chloe returned to the kitchen island, glancing once more at the three male heads poking over the top of the couch as she got back to chopping walnuts and celery for the Waldorf salad. Naturally, Todd hadn't stolen any of the celery.

She scooped up a big piece of walnut and popped it into her mouth.

Once the turkey was in the oven, her mother went to change clothes before the rest of the family arrived. Chloe went out to the backyard, where her father and brothers tossed a football around in the chilly gray afternoon.

She breathed in, refreshed by the bite of cold air after the hot kitchen. She hoped they'd get their first snow soon. Tall Pine was low enough in the mountains that snow never came until late November, but anytime after Thanksgiving was fair game.

"Think fast." Her younger brother, Joel, sent the ball spinning her way. Unprepared, Chloe still caught it in her arms with a satisfying *thump*.

"Is the halftime show over?" Todd asked.

"Beats me." She lobbed the ball at Todd. She'd tried, once, to watch televised football with her dad and brothers. All the time-outs had driven her crazy. At least, in the backyard, the football *moved*.

Ball in hand, Todd took a step back, then another, his eyes on Chloe. Her dad stood by several yards to Todd's left. As her brother held the ball cocked and ready to throw to her, Todd glanced over her head with a nod, and suddenly Chloe had a bad feeling about this.

The next thing she knew, Joel grabbed her from behind, pinning her arms alongside her as he picked her up off the ground and spun her around. Fast. She shrieked in protest. She should have known. She should never trust her brothers.

Joel deposited her on a big pile of leaves under the old oak. At least it was a soft landing. She grabbed for some leaves to hurl at her attacker, but that didn't do much good as Todd rushed in. Both brothers scooped up double handfuls of leaves, raining a steady barrage down on her.

"Hey!" Chloe remembered to cover her face with both arms to keep from getting a mouthful of leaves. At least it hadn't rained in a while, so the leaves were dry instead of mucky. She tried to reach for a foot to yank, or some other defense against the sneak attack, but she could barely see anything beyond the dry, crispy shower of brown and gold.

At last it was Joel, the accomplice who'd dumped her on the leaves to begin with, who grabbed her by the arm and pulled her out. Two years younger than Chloe, Joel was never the mastermind; ever since they were kids, he went along with Todd's schemes and then made nice with her afterward. She whapped Joel with a quick backhand on the arm before she launched at

Todd with the best nonlethal weapon she had on short notice: lowering her head, she charged at him like a goat and rammed him in the stomach.

After all, she could revert to childhood, too.

"Oof!" Todd was half laughing, but the rush of air that came out with the *oof* filled her with satisfaction.

Her dad's voice came from behind Todd. "You'd think after all these years, you boys would learn to play nice."

"She loves it." Todd mussed the hair at the top of her head as if she were a spaniel. Leaves fell around her face.

"Yeah, right." Chloe brushed more leaves off her sweater and tried to glare, but then Todd grabbed her in a one-armed hug. She gave in and laughed, still catching her breath. Behind her, Joel was picking leaves from the back of her hair and sweater.

Some things never changed. Then again, maybe she didn't want them to change too fast. What would she do if she came home one holiday and Todd was respectful and polite? She wouldn't be sure he even remembered her.

"Come on." Todd gave her hair one last rumple as he spoke over her head to Joel. "Let's go see if the game's back on."

He led Joel inside, and Chloe shook her head. Boys' clubs. It seemed like they were everywhere these days. Granted, the one at the office was more civilized.

And that thought ended the longest amount of time she'd gone without thinking about the paper.

Her father approached her, the abandoned football in hand. "Ready?"

"Always." Chloe ran forward and stole the ball before her dad could toss it. She kept running farther across the brown grass of the yard, then turned and threw it to him.

Yeah, he *could* have intervened on her behalf. But around here, you fought your own battles, especially the silly skirmishes. She wouldn't have liked being defended like some little flower. Not since she was four, anyway.

Bill Davenport grabbed the ball out of the air and sailed it back at her. She grinned as she caught it, took a few steps farther away, and chucked it back to him.

It was nice to get a few minutes alone with her dad. And it felt good to get outside and move around, including the obligatory hazing by her brothers. She spent a lot of time stationary and indoors these days.

"So, how's the job going?" her dad asked across the twenty feet of space between them.

Chloe made a face. "Ask me tomorrow. I'll be there."

"You're working the day after Thanksgiving?"

She hadn't planned to talk about it, but her father's surprise gave Chloe a little sense of vindication. Even her dad thought working the holiday weekend was above and beyond.

She shrugged offhandedly. "I didn't exactly have a choice."

"That's why they call it a job."

Hey. Come back over to my side. Chloe threw the ball again, a little more forcefully. "I already crammed five days' worth of work into a three-day week. I turned in fourteen stories." *Counting press releases.*

"I'll bet that made an impression."

"You'd think so, wouldn't you?" *I would have thought that about the hospice piece, too.*

"Are you still hoping it turns into a permanent job?"

Chloe hadn't thought that far ahead since the week she started. She was too busy trying to keep her head above water. But if her job ended when Frank McCrea came back, she'd be high and dry. Or back at the Pine 'n' Dine. If they had an opening for her.

"Maybe," she said. "We'll see when the real editor gets back. The guy who's filling in now . . ." She searched for words to explain Bret. She settled for, "Don't get me started."

This was her day off. No point bringing Bret into the conversation. But the wheels in her head had already started to spin again, and she knew they'd been humming in neutral all along, just waiting for the slightest flip of a switch.

"Not easy to work for?" her dad prompted.

Chloe bit her lip. When she searched her brain for tangible grievances, she came up short. "It's a lot of little things," she said. "Or maybe it's an attitude. Nothing I do seems to be good enough."

"Hm." Bill Davenport threw the ball again. Chloe knew he wanted nuts and bolts. Something he could work on.

But hey, he was listening. She knew he'd always been a little at a loss for what to do with a daughter. Hanging out with her brothers was easier for him; he knew how boys worked because he'd been one himself. From the time Chloe turned twelve and got her ears pierced, he seemed to feel she was just a little bit alien to him.

Hence, the football-throwing. A way to connect that was refreshing in its simplicity.

It was physical, external, and tangible. And, she had to admit, the activity helped her think in more concrete terms.

"I didn't even know I was working tomorrow until almost five o'clock last night." There. That was concrete.

"What did you tell him?"

"I said 'yes.' Of course."

Her father nodded. "You remember what I taught you to say to say to a police officer when he pulls you over?"

Chloe caught the ball. "You call him 'sir.'"

"And why is that?"

"Because a lot of traffic cops are little Napoleons on a power trip?" She snapped the ball back.

"Simpler than that." Her father threw the football a little harder this time. It landed in her arms with a thud.

"It's his ball," he said. "You're playing on his field. And in this case, maybe he knows a little more about the game than you do."

"I don't deny that. But he—"

"So for now," her father pressed on, "assume he's right. If you don't agree with him, *pretend* you assume he's right. Learn to play the game his way. Then, later on, if you have other ideas, you've earned his respect."

"But I've tried to—"

"How many times? Once?"

Once? Her tongue was practically sore from biting it.

"You've been there three weeks, Chloe."

"Three and a half." She heard her sulky tone and

grinned reluctantly. Admittedly, it didn't sound like much.

All right. She sounded childish and impatient. But it was more than the extra hours. It was slaving away without the slightest acknowledgment. It was writing the best thing she'd ever written, only to have it roundly ignored.

Chloe could foresee her father's answer to that: *What do you want, a gold star?*

If she wanted to find someone to side with her a hundred percent . . . well, that was what her roommates were for.

She took a step back and set the ball sailing higher on its way to her dad, arcing across the blue sky in a smooth spiral. It was a beautiful throw, and her dad gave a nod of approval as he caught it. Chloe felt her spirits lift again.

This new job was *her* ball, and she needed to own it. So she'd sift through her parents' advice, accept her friends' sympathy, and glean what she could. Ultimately she had to find her own way to deal with a guy who could rake her over the coals one day, and hold her injured hand like a baby bird's wing the next.

The next morning, Chloe caved in and put on makeup after all. Might as well, since she'd even worn mascara to eat turkey and throw a football in the backyard with her father.

At the newsroom, she found bagels and coffee waiting, and Bret already at his keyboard. Sitting at the desk he'd designated for writing, he looked as if he'd been there quite a while.

Easy enough if you didn't have a life, she supposed. But it was hard to maintain a shell of cynicism with a tempting array of bagels laid out on one of the unoccupied desks in the newsroom. There were a dozen or so. She identified plain, poppy seed, possibly onion, either egg or cheese—and was that one jalapeño? "These are for us and what army?"

Bret shrugged. "I like choices. Plus, there'll be more people in the building later on. They won't go to waste."

Of course. Despite all the doors and hallways, the newsroom usually felt like an island unto itself. Chloe seldom thought about the fact that someone had to run the press and get the papers out after she went home.

She picked up a sesame seed bagel. "Thanks," she said belatedly as she smoothed on cream cheese with a little plastic knife.

The ever-typing fingers were in motion. "No problem."

Bagel in one hand, she scooped her coffee mug off her desk with the other and went to the coffee maker. "So, what am I doing today?"

"Well, a motorcycle gang started a reign of terror on Evergreen Lane about ten minutes ago. That's your first priority."

Chloe actually turned before she thought. Bret hadn't even raised his head. *Sucker.* She turned back to the coffee maker, set her mug down, and poured. "Like you'd let anyone else cover *that*."

"Got me there." Bret leaned back in his chair, hands clasped behind his head. "If you could chase down the weather and touch base with the public information officers at the police and fire departments, that'd be great. Not that they're likely to have much. Later in the day, you can get happy quotes from a couple of the stores on Evergreen Lane."

"Those bikers do like to spend money."

The corners of his mouth quirked up, and she felt absurdly flattered. "Exactly."

For a day she would have rather spent Christmas shopping, decorating, or sleeping, it wasn't so bad.

The newsroom felt different today. Chloe had quickly learned that although it was usually quiet in here, it was also *intense*, with the constant silent presence of deadlines to be met. Today the atmosphere was less urgent. Bret still didn't say much, still seemed absorbed in his work, but there was something more companionable in the silence.

Better yet, she saw that the hospice piece was scheduled, at last, to run on Sunday. Bret had never commented on it, and she concluded he probably never would. But at least her labors would see the light of day.

Late in the afternoon, Bret asked, "Could you look over a couple of Chuck's stories for me? I'll send them over to your in-box."

Chloe's fingers froze over her keyboard. "You're asking me to edit?"

There was that faint smile again across the ten feet that separated them. "I never said there was anything wrong with your grammar skills. Give the stories a first pass, and I'll do the final polish. It'll save me time, believe me."

Two minutes later, she knew what he meant.

The stories were well written, but Chuck's punctuation was . . . hit and miss. She remembered all the times, in college, when she'd helped friends make their papers more presentable. A sharp mind could miss a lot of the subtleties of the English language.

But she couldn't stifle a groan. "He's got *its* with an apostrophe when it should be—"

Bret nodded sympathetically. "I know, I know. That's one of his trademarks. It's irritating, but you learn to look for it."

Chloe forced herself not to hyperventilate and focused on fixing the mistakes. She shouldn't be badmouthing a coworker and friend. "Chuck's a good guy."

"Yes, he is. If he was any more laid-back, he'd be horizontal. But he's fast. While you and I are polishing away at a story, he's on to the next one. Sometimes productivity is as good as art. And nobody's perfect. That's why we have editors."

Chloe finished the edits and sent the stories back to Bret, eyeing the time displayed in the corner of her screen. A quarter to four. She was supposed to meet Tiffany and Kate for the town Christmas tree lighting at five. The town square was just a couple of blocks from the paper. She should be able to make it with no trouble if—

"Speaking of 'Nobody's perfect,'" Bret said, "could you take a look at these last two pieces of mine? I can't see my own words anymore."

She frowned. "Seriously?"

"Sure. You can't catch everything in your own work." Bret shrugged. "Don't mess with my deathless prose or anything. Just check it over. Sometimes a fresh pair of eyes makes all the difference."

Moments later, she was scrutinizing one of Bret's

stories on her screen, not surprised to find it was a study in clean, spare writing. She wondered what sorts of flaws Bret, or Frank McCrea, would find in it.

On the second story, to her initial glee, she caught one. He'd used capital letters on *p.m.*, one of the mistakes he'd called her on a couple of weeks ago.

And left out the periods?

Wait a minute.

She smelled a rat.

She looked over at Bret, intent on his screen. This was Mr. Meticulous. No way had he made *two* style mistakes on the same word.

Now on high alert, she went back to the first story and scoured it more carefully. This time she concentrated on the punctuation and words more than the meaning. She found two more. *Web site* instead of *website. Back yard* instead of *backyard.*

She opened her mouth to call him on it and bit her lip instead. There was always the chance—however remote—that he'd really been that mentally fatigued.

She didn't buy it. He was *planting* mistakes. The day after Thanksgiving.

She stifled her aggravation, remembering her father's words: *It's his ball.* If this was some kind of test, she was determined to pass it. She bit her tongue, fixed the errors, and sent the stories back to Bret without comment.

That should do it. She still had time to get to the tree lighting.

She opened her desk drawer for her purse.

"Chloe?" Bret said. "There's snow in the forecast for tomorrow night."

She smiled. She'd been telling Chuck she hoped

they'd have snow to kick off the Christmas season; Bret must have heard her.

In a tone as close to apologetic as she'd ever heard from him, he asked, "Could you write it up?"

She felt her smile drop.

Then she went online, checked the information, and started to write up the weather, vowing not to make any style errors.

If she left in the next fifteen minutes, she could still make it to the tree lighting on time.

Bret ran his cursor over the stories Chloe had sent back, feeling gratified.

She'd caught them all.

He wondered if it had been hard for her not to gloat. The errors had been fine-tuning things, the kind she would have made herself a couple of weeks ago. She was a quick study, no doubt about it.

And passionate about misplaced apostrophes.

She sat across from him, hammering on her keyboard as if she were breaking the rocks that would release her from San Quentin. She'd put in a good day's work without complaining, but he could feel the impatience starting to radiate from her now. She was visibly anxious to get out of here.

Bret was in no hurry. Outside, the Christmas lights on Evergreen Lane would be coming on at any moment. Shopping, tinsel, and *'tis-the-season*. He avoided it out of habit.

He still had one more day of paper to lay out, but

after Chloe's short weather piece, the editing was done. He stood and stretched.

"Well, that does it for me. Be sure to lock up on your way out."

She glared at him. Twin gray-green daggers. Her expression provoked twin reactions in Bret. Number one, he wouldn't want to really mess with her. Number two . . . was something he didn't dare examine too closely. Something tantalizing. He thought of the silly cliché about women who looked pretty when they were mad. He'd never seen it until now.

Yet, for some reason, he let her glare at him for a few extra seconds.

See Number One, he reminded himself.

"Kidding," he said. "I'll be here a couple of hours after you."

He thought she might smile, one of those smiles that crossed her face so quickly most of the time. Instead she bit her lip and returned her eyes to the screen.

Bret crossed the room to the coffee maker, considered making a fresh pot, and settled for the dregs instead. His eyes and back needed the break more than his body needed the coffee. At this point, any more caffeine would be redundant.

He turned back to Chloe, who, after one of her trademark pauses of contemplation, started typing again. He'd pushed her hard today, and he knew it. He didn't want the afternoon to end on a sour note.

He lingered by the coffee maker. "You never did tell me what kind of writing you were interested in before you started here," he said.

She didn't answer.

He thought of the way she'd written the hospice piece, infusing it with notes of emotion that managed not to be overly sentimental. She wrote with more color than the typical journalist, but more restraint than the typical amateur.

"Let me guess," he said. "You're slumming here until you write the Great American Novel."

Her fingers froze fractionally over the keyboard, then went back to typing.

"Nailed it, didn't I?"

She bit her lip. "I am writing a book, yes."

He took a guess. "Romance or children's book?"

Her fingers froze again, then started pounding harder.

"Well?" he prompted.

Typetta. Typetta.

"Nailed it again, didn't I?"

Typetta. Typetta.

By now, he really wanted to know. "Tell me," he coaxed. "Which is it?"

Typetta. Typetta.

"I'm on deadline," she reminded him.

"I'm not going anywhere," he said. "Seriously. Tell me about your book."

The typing slowed a little. "You're just trying to be polite."

"When have you ever known me to be polite?"

Her typing resumed its former steady pace, minus the violent mashing of the keys. "I want to get this done," she said. "I want to make it to the tree lighting."

Of course. The annual Tall Pine Christmas tree lighting. Bret had covered it once or twice, but McCrea handed it off to someone else whenever he could. It hadn't occurred to Bret that someone might actually *want* to go.

To Chloe, white Christmases and jingle bells were still merry.

He opened his mouth, ready to offer to step in and finish the weather, but something about the set of her profile stopped him. She was biting her lower lip again.

With a decisive keystroke, Chloe stood, somehow managing to shrug into her coat in the same motion. "Done."

"Thanks."

In a flash she had her purse over her shoulder, car keys in hand. He'd never seen her ready to leave so quickly.

As she started to go, she looked back over her shoulder with some reluctance. In a tone that practically froze the room with its civility, she said, "I could write up a piece on the tree lighting if you want."

Was it his imagination, or had her eyes gone to pure, stainless steel gray?

"No, thanks," he said, "I've got Ned out there already for a photo. If I'd known you were planning on going—" He stopped himself. "Never mind," he said. "Enjoy it."

"I will," she said. "Good night." And she left.

Bret wasn't sure what he'd done wrong—*which* thing he'd done wrong—but one thing was abundantly clear.

Chloe Davenport had a limit, and he'd reached it.

Chapter 7

Chloe huddled between her roommates in the crowd at the town square, shivering under the tall pine tree the town was named for.

When she'd first arrived, she'd felt a little short on heavenly peace. Through the first few Christmas carols in the sing-along, she kept arguing with Bret in her head, finding clever, articulate ways to say the things she'd stopped herself from saying at the office. But eventually, the cold starry night and the songs worked their magic, and Chloe felt Christmas seep into her bones.

The series of traditional speeches from city officials came after the sing-along. "The first Tall Pine tree lighting was held in 1947," Margery Williams of the town council said, "the same year the town was incorporated. It was the day after Thanksgiving. World War II had been over for two years, and the new homes in the area were filling with families. The tree was dedicated by . . ."

She'd probably heard the same speech many times over the years. Until now, she'd never felt the urge to dig in her purse for a notepad. The mental hunt for the next story was getting to be a habit.

Stop it. You're off the clock.

It was pretty interesting material, though.

"I think they're just waiting till it gets even colder before they light it," Tiffany whispered in her left ear.

"At the end of the first tree lighting," Margery went on, "those in attendance were blessed with the first snowfall of the season."

Chloe wondered if that was true. It sounded like it could be a convenient piece of folklore. Maybe she could research it.

Winston Frazier stepped to the microphone, and Chloe felt the crowd's attention lift. As senior member of the town council, he'd been leading the countdown to the tree lighting ever since Chloe could remember. With his full head of white hair, and teeth that were just a little too straight to be true, he could have passed for anywhere from sixty to a well-preserved eighty. She did some math in her head and wondered which was older, Winston or Tall Pine.

After the countdown, the lights flared on, and Chloe felt the colors wash over her as voices around her joined in a chorus of "Silent Night." Yes, she'd needed this. She closed her eyes and drank it in.

When she'd left Tall Pine for college, she'd been eager for the independence, trading her small mountain town for a bigger beach town. But with each year of school, she'd found herself increasingly happy to come back home on school breaks. And she'd never missed a tree lighting.

"Silent Night" ended, and Kate and Tiffany each gave her a quick hug.

"Gotta go," Kate said. "We're due at the diner in ten minutes."

Right. Chloe remembered that now. Last year, the three of them had done the same thing—dashing off to work after the tree lighting with no time to spare. She didn't envy them.

Or did she? There had been a simplicity to it. You worked hard, but when the day was done, it was over.

"See you later," she said, keeping her tone bright.

And then she was alone, surrounded by the jostling crowd. Some headed for their cars, while others went to line up for Styrofoam cups of hot chocolate or a visit with Santa. Chloe pulled up the hood of her coat—suddenly the cold felt a whole lot colder—and started her lone trek to the parking lot.

"Chloe?" A woman's voice came from her right.

Absurdly glad to hear a friendly voice, she turned to see Mandy Wyndham in a red coat and blue scarf.

"Hey!" Chloe grabbed Mandy in a hug. "Merry Christmas!"

No other person could have been better, or more natural, to wish her first "Merry Christmas" to. Mandy and her husband Jake ran The Snowed Inn, Tall Pine's new Christmas hotel. Chloe had interviewed them for their June soft opening a year and a half ago. It had been one of her first assignments as a freelancer for the *Gazette*.

"Merry Christmas." Mandy returned the greeting and the hug warmly. "Are you here by yourself?"

"My friends had to leave for work. What about you?"

"We're shorthanded at the hotel tonight. Jake couldn't get away. In fact, I'd better get back pretty quick." Mandy inclined her head toward the parking lot. "Are you going this way?"

Chloe nodded and fell into step with Mandy, feeling just a little unmoored. Mandy, Tiffany, and Kate all had a place where they needed to be tonight. Chloe had already put in a day's work; she should be glad for the freedom. Instead, she felt a little lost.

"So, you're full-time at the paper now?" Mandy asked. "I've been seeing your bylines with 'Staff Writer' underneath."

"It's kind of a temporary-for-now thing. The editor's out of town for a few months, and they needed an extra writer, so I'm filling in. We'll see how it works out after that."

"How's it working out so far?"

"It's—" Chloe's tongue fumbled for an answer.

When most people asked how you were doing, it was pretty much a rhetorical question. When Mandy asked—although Chloe didn't know her all that well—it sounded as if she really wanted to know.

"It's—a little frustrating," she conceded, and she really intended to leave it at that.

But there was a hesitation in her voice, and Mandy heard it. She stopped, empathetic blue eyes focused on Chloe. And the next thing Chloe knew, the story of her day spilled out, about coming in on a holiday weekend and fixing mistakes that didn't need fixing and barely making it to the tree lighting. Probably half of it didn't even make sense. But Mandy stood in the cold and listened to the jumble of words until Chloe paused for breath, embarrassed.

"It'll work out. I can handle it," she finished awkwardly.

"Of course you can. You've *been* handling it. You're just a little worn out, and who could blame you?" Mandy nudged her elbow, starting them back toward the parking lot. "Follow me over to the hotel. I know just what you need. A cup of hot chocolate."

Bret had most of Saturday and all of Sunday laid out by the time Ned arrived with the camera card of photos from the tree lighting. All Bret needed was one picture to drop into the space he'd saved for it in tomorrow's paper. A quick caption, and Saturday would be done.

"How do they look?" Ned asked as Bret clicked through the image files on his computer screen.

"Good." Bret nodded as he contemplated the pictures. Ned had given him an abundance of choices, as always, but this was one time Bret wanted to make his decision as quickly as possible.

Fortunately, as would often happen, one of the shots simply popped out at him. Bret clicked through the rest to be sure, then unerringly went back to the photo of a toddler on her dad's shoulders. Ned had caught them in a profile shot that included the newly lit tree. What made the picture was the glow on the little girl's face—an expression of unguarded wonderment.

"That one," Bret said.

Ned smiled. "I liked that one myself."

Bret poised his fingers to enter the caption information. "Got their names?"

"Dane Davidson is the dad. The little girl is Gracie."

"Perfect." Bret typed the caption and glanced back over his shoulder at Ned. The *Gazette*'s resident new dad was sporting some reddish stubble these days. Bret wasn't sure if the photographer was trying for a style, or if having a newborn in the house just didn't allow much time for shaving. "That could be you and your boy next year."

"If someone gives me the night off," Ned said.

"Don't look at me. Next year you can talk to McCrea about that. Now, go home before I find something else for you to do."

Ned didn't need a second invitation. He slipped out, leaving Bret with the pictures still on his screen. He clicked idly through them one more time. A faint pang of envy surfaced at the general look of holiday cheer on the faces, although he had to chuckle at one photo: an eight-year-old boy, his head hunkered down between knit cap and his drawn-up coat collar, brows drawn down in disgruntlement. The little guy looked cold and ready to go home.

So not *everyone* was jolly.

As he skimmed the photos, Bret caught himself searching the crowd for a certain blond head. If Chloe hadn't covered it with a hood or a cap, she shouldn't be hard to spot. Of course, she was also fairly short, and Ned couldn't photograph everyone. It looked like she'd escaped his camera lens.

Bret finished adding the photo and moved on. Now that the tree picture was in place for tomorrow's paper, he just had Monday to finish. But as he worked, two images replayed in his mind: the flicker of Christmas tree lights, and the flash of annoyance in Chloe's eyes as she left.

Okay, he wished the day had ended differently. But what could he do about it?

Curiosity pulled him away from his work again. He opened the database of the *Gazette*'s archives. Not sure what he was looking for, he typed in Chloe's byline and the word *Christmas*.

She'd covered a couple of holiday fundraisers last year. Not surprising. She'd also written up the soft opening of The Snowed Inn a year ago last June. Chuck, he remembered, had covered the big grand opening at the start of last year's Christmas season.

Bret read over the article. Nice. With well-chosen quotes from Jake and even a couple from Mandy, it displayed Chloe's knack for capturing a mood without being too sugary. She did have a way with a feature story. If she left the paper before McCrea got back, his editor wouldn't be happy.

And she had been photocopying résumés a couple of weeks ago.

Yeah, *that's* what he was concerned about. Just a valuable employee. Nothing to do with her charm or her wit . . . or the way she looked when she bit her lip.

Bret finished reading and decided the last touches on Monday's paper could wait.

He'd learned to trust his hunches. And somehow, he had a feeling he knew where he'd find Chloe Davenport.

* * *

The moment Bret stepped into the lobby of The Snowed Inn, the scent of evergreen and the sound of carols engulfed him. Okay, what else did he expect? After all, he'd wandered into a Christmas hotel the day after Thanksgiving.

A dark-haired young woman smiled behind the front desk. Bret did a quick memory scan: Alyssa Chen. Tall Pine High. A couple of years behind him.

"Merry Christmas," she greeted him.

"Hi, Alyssa." Bret returned her smile, took a deep breath, and followed the sound of murmuring voices into the lobby.

A few months after opening the hotel, Mandy and Jake had started serving hot beverages in the lobby. You wouldn't have thought their clientele would have reached much beyond the hotel's guests, but word had spread. Except for the diner, Tall Pine didn't have anything like a Starbucks; chain restaurants in the little community were still taboo. But to hear people tell it, The Snowed Inn was a cozy gathering place with great hot chocolate, and even a small conference-type room for business meetings.

The next best thing to Starbucks . . . if you were into Christmas.

He ventured farther into the lobby, where people clustered around tables over their cups of coffee and cocoa. He knew local restaurants would be doing a good business after the tree lighting, but The Snowed Inn was definitely getting its share, despite its less central location on the highway leading out of town.

She might not even be here.

He swam through the sea of white mini-lights and

literal boughs of holly. He'd expected a riot of red and green, but there was nothing that garish. No elves on shelves peered at him anywhere, and the place gave off a warmth that Bret couldn't deny. If it weren't for past associations—

There she was. Sitting all by herself at a small round table next to the stone fireplace, hands clutched around her cup. At first glance, she looked lonely and plaintive, like the little match girl. But when Bret got a few steps closer, her expression was visibly content, her lips curled faintly upward in a half smile.

Until she saw him, at least. Then her eyes widened, and the mug she held stopped halfway to her mouth.

He stepped up and spoke quickly before he could hesitate. "I won't take up much of your time." He indicated the vacant chair across from her. "May I sit down?"

"Sure." Chloe nodded. She looked puzzled, but her eyes had lost the stainless-steel gray they'd had earlier. Bret dropped into his seat.

He'd barely landed in the chair when a woman spoke beside him. "Hi, Bret. Can I get you anything?"

Where had she come from so fast? He turned to see Mandy Wyndham. "Hi, Mandy. I'll have a cup of coffee, please."

Mandy's brows furrowed, her eyes wandering briefly from Bret to Chloe, before she replaced her frown with a sunny smile. "How about a hot chocolate instead? It's our specialty."

"No, thanks. Just coffee. With plenty of creamer."

"Are you sure you don't want to try—"

Jake appeared behind Mandy, resting a hand on her

shoulder. Bret fought the urge to look past Jake and see if the rest of Tall Pine was forming a line behind him.

"Remember, Mandy," Jake said, "the customer is always right." A look passed between them, some kind of unspoken married-couple communication, and then Jake's eyes went to their table. "Hi, Chloe. Hi, Bret. I don't think you've been in here before, have you?"

"There's a first time for everything." Bret gave a tight smile. He'd avoided the Christmas hotel the way vampires avoid the beach, but Jake wouldn't know about that.

"Good to see you," Jake said. "Let me know what you think." One hand still on Mandy's shoulder, he drew his wife away from their table.

"They're nice," Chloe offered.

"Extremely." It was true. He didn't think there was a kinder person than Mandy. He'd interviewed Jake once, before the hotel got off the ground, and in the past few years Jake had beaten him at racquetball half a dozen times. In spite of the latter, yes, he was nice.

"So," Chloe said carefully, "what brings you here?"

It felt like an invitation for him to apologize. *Just do it.* "I know I'm probably the last person you want to see right now. I'll keep it quick."

As Jake steered her into the kitchen, Mandy had the feeling she was living in an *I Love Lucy* rerun. Or one of those other old sitcoms, where the husband was always scolding the wife. He stopped her beside the refrigerator, his arm curved around her. They were as far as they

95

could get from earshot of Angie, who was pouring a cappuccino at the counter.

"Mandy." Jake spoke in a near whisper. "What are you trying to do in there? He ordered coffee. Twice."

"You don't understand," Mandy said urgently. They'd left Chloe alone with Bret. She had to get back in there. "If anybody ever needed a hot chocolate, it's Bret."

It had been a weird discovery, and Mandy didn't understand it herself, but her hot chocolate seemed to have a way of making people more . . . mellow with each other. She and Jake had seen it happen too many times not to believe it. And it sounded like Bret had given Chloe a heck of a day.

"It'll be okay," Jake said. "Bret's a decent guy."

Mandy sighed. Bret had been two grades ahead of her at Tall Pine High. Back then, she'd only known two things about him: he was quiet and wickedly smart. Certainly nothing like a bully. But from what Chloe said, maybe the power of running the paper had gone to his head.

"They're not evenly matched," Mandy protested. "She's had one and he hasn't."

And she's already had a long, hard day. Because of him.

"Mandy," Jake coaxed. They'd been together three years now, and his direct brown eyes were still every bit as hard for her to resist. "I can't tell you what to do. But you don't want to manipulate anyone. Giving Chloe a pick-me-up after a hard day is one thing. Trying to turn your hot chocolate into Love Potion Number Nine is another."

Was *that* what he thought she was trying to do? "That's

never happened! It couldn't make anything happen if they didn't already—"

Jake was nodding at her significantly. She turned her head in the direction of Chloe and Bret's table, but the kitchen wall stood in the way.

She frowned. "Really?"

"Those two? Oh, yeah."

Jake was pretty intuitive, for a guy. He was rarely wrong about people. Had she really missed that?

Her eyes lingered, wishing she could see through the wall into the next room, trying to imagine the pair of them at their table. A smile played at her lips.

Jake sighed. "I said the wrong thing, didn't I?"

"Excuse me." With a gentle nudge, Mandy moved away from Jake to join Angie at the kitchen counter. "I have an order to fill."

Chloe had already made up her mind that Bret wasn't going to spoil her good mood. After a little time cozied up by the fire with a cup of hot chocolate, the world looked a lot better. And now that he was outside his domain of the newsroom, Chloe thought she even detected a faint discomfiture from him. It was enough to make a girl feel charitable.

Elbows on the table, she took another sip from her cooling drink, savoring the rich cocoa.

Bret raked a hand through his hair and met her eyes dead on. "I know I haven't made things easy for you."

"Really?" She lifted her eyebrows. "'PM'?"

Bret may have balked, but he recovered quickly. "Résumés in the copier?"

It was Chloe's turn to balk. "On my own time. With my own paper."

"And company toner." Bret shook his head. "Never mind. Not the point. The point is . . ." He shifted back from the table, assuming the familiar arms-folded stance. "I know I've been tough on you. There isn't a lot of 'please' and 'thank you' in this business. If McCrea ever said anything nice to me, I'd probably have a heart attack. If things were different, I might say, 'If you can't stand the heat, get out of the kitchen.'"

If she'd been hoping for a sugar-coated apology, this wasn't it. Chloe took another sip of cocoa, clinging to her feeling of peace on earth. "But?"

"But under the circumstances, I really need you to stick around. For one thing—I'm up against it. Filling in for McCrea is a lot more work than I expected. He warned me I'd need extra help, and he was right. For another thing . . ."

Chloe kept her mouth shut and waited. And waited.

"You're good," he said finally. The two words were low and quiet, as if it cost him something to say them. "You're green, but you learn fast. And you have talent. Your hospice piece was excellent." Bret lowered his eyes and traced the edge of the table. She didn't think she'd ever known him to break eye contact before. "That's why I held it for this Sunday. Which—since you're green—you might not realize is the most-read edition of the week."

She was going to fall over. If a kind word from McCrea would have given Bret heart failure, Chloe was one step away from a slab in the morgue.

Mandy returned, buying Chloe a moment to recover.

Mandy set two mugs in front of Bret. He looked up at her questioningly.

"There's your coffee," she said. "And I made a hot chocolate by mistake. Habit. It's our most popular item. That one's on the house, of course."

"Mandy." Bret's eyebrows lifted in an *I-don't-buy-it* expression.

Mandy straightened, both hands raised. "Sorry. I can't take it back once it's on the table. Food service regulations."

"Okay." A smile twitched at Bret's lips, his tone milder than usual. "Thanks."

Mandy walked away with a light, brisk step. Bret looked after her bemusedly, and Chloe remembered what he'd said in the newsroom: he didn't care for chocolate. But he eyed the mug for a moment, shrugged, and took a tentative sip.

He sniffed the drink. "Cinnamon?"

Chloe nodded. "She puts in some vanilla, too. I asked her how she makes it, but she wouldn't tell me exactly."

"Not bad." Bret took another drink and set it down, regarding the two mugs in front of him. Then looked at Chloe. "I should go," he said. "I said my piece, and I promised I wouldn't keep you. See you Monday?"

"Of course. I'm not going anywhere. But—"

She cut herself off as Bret started to rise. When she broke off, he hesitated, halfway out of his chair.

"—But you have two drinks," she said.

"Thanks to our generous hostess, yes." His eyes flicked to hers; it wasn't quite the usual incisive stare.

"Hanging out with the boss probably isn't quite what you had in mind."

Chloe shrugged. Manners aside, she found she didn't really want him to go. Maybe because he'd actually said something nice for a change. "We're off the clock." She smiled a little. "Just don't tell me what to do and we'll be fine."

Bret settled back into his seat. "You can have the coffee, if you want."

"That works."

Bret slid the coffee cup across the table to her. Mandy had added the creamer, per Bret's specifications; he drank it the same way Chloe did. She eyed her near-empty cup of cocoa and saw the solution. Picking up the coffee, she upended the cup and poured most of it into her remaining cocoa. Bret flinched in alarm, but the coffee went safely into her mug without spilling.

She grinned. "When you're a waitress, you learn how to pour."

He relaxed visibly, sat back, and took another sip of cocoa. And suddenly they were in uncharted territory.

"So," Bret said, "tell me about your book."

"Seriously?"

"I asked before. I wasn't kidding."

Chloe hesitated. She didn't talk about her writing much to anyone—largely because she didn't get much of it done. Especially these days. And hardly anyone ever asked. Bret was asking, and he looked as if he might even be listening.

She took a sip of cocoa-tinged coffee and confessed, "It's a murder mystery."

His eyebrows lifted, but it wasn't quite the astonished reaction she'd expected. "And?"

And it would help if I could decide who did it. She bluffed, "A good mystery writer never reveals her plot."

"Oh, not fair." Bret smiled—actually smiled, a real smile—over his cup. It sent an unexpected warmth through her. Or maybe it was the coffee. "Do you go home at night and try to think up new ways to kill editors?"

"Not yet. Although that's an idea." She fingered the handle of her mug. She liked this new version of Bret, and her mouth got ahead of her brain. "Can I say something? Without fear of reprisal?"

This wasn't safe. She shouldn't bring it up. But sitting by the fire in the middle of The Snowed Inn, for some reason, she *did* feel safe. And of course, now that she'd started, Bret wouldn't let it go.

He nodded. "You said it before. We're off the clock."

He might remember this Monday, when they were back on the clock. But it felt too late to turn back, so Chloe forged ahead. "You can be . . . a little . . . sexist."

He blinked. "You're kidding."

He looked honestly surprised.

In for a penny, in for a pound. "When I told you I was writing a book, you immediately assumed it was a romance or a children's book. Why is that?"

"Because you write stories about Christmas hotels and nice old ladies who knit?"

"Those are the kinds of stories McCrea assigned to me."

"They're also the kinds of stories you've been proposing, except for the hospice piece."

She considered. "Well, I don't exactly know where the bodies are buried in this town. I know the people I meet at the Pine 'n' Dine. So, a lot of the stories I have material for are . . ."

101

"Soft." Bret shrugged. "There's nothing wrong with that, really. Nice, human interest stories about nice people—there's no shortage of those in Tall Pine. And you do them well. Not because you're a girl. It's just part of who you are. You like positive things, and most of those stories tend to be light. It's one of the reasons I underestimated you."

She raised her eyebrows. "So you're admitting you were wrong about me?"

"I thought I already did." Bret cracked another smile. "But cut me some slack. You walked in your first day smiling like Mary Poppins. Complete with magical bag."

"Briefcase."

"Still. What was I supposed to think?" He shifted forward. "Can I give you an honest piece of advice? If you want people to take you seriously, don't put volleyball on your résumé."

She blinked. So he'd actually read her résumé. "It's a highly competitive sport. And I was good at it."

"Chloe." A glint of humor lit his eyes. "Think about it. A Southern California blonde. Who plays volleyball. Who went to college in Long Beach."

"And that's not sexist?"

"All I'm saying is, the world isn't a fair place, and you do fit a certain stereotype."

She frowned, feeling a little of her good will dissipate.

But Bret wasn't looking at her now. He was gazing down as he swirled the remaining cocoa in his mug. For someone who didn't care for chocolate, he'd managed to go through more than half of it.

When he raised his eyes, their serious expression caught her completely off guard. "What I'm really trying to say is: never let anyone underestimate you."

Bret regarded her, dark eyes solemn, giving Chloe the feeling he was really *seeing* her. The sensation was hard to define, but it made her feel warm, and she felt color fill her cheeks.

Or maybe the combination of cocoa, coffee, and the fireplace beside her was more potent than she'd realized.

It felt like a good time to shift the conversation over to Bret. "Meanwhile, what *you'd* like to write about is a *real* murder mystery."

"Not exactly." Bret rested his elbow on the table, leaning his head against his hand. "Chuck and I joke about it all the time, but that's not what I had in mind when I went into journalism."

I knew when I was ten. He'd said it her first week. Chloe asked, "What did you want to write about?"

"You'll laugh."

Her? Laugh at Bret? She shook her head.

"When I was ten years old," he said, "my dad left a copy of *All the President's Men* lying around, and I read it. I'd read anything." That, she believed. "But when I read it—*that* was what I wanted to do. Other kids wanted to play cops and robbers. I wanted to crack a story like Watergate." He gave a self-deprecating grin. "Of course, that's not what all reporting is. I know that now. But the idea of finding the dirt, righting the wrongs . . . I wanted to be the next Woodward and Bernstein. To expose a corrupt president, or something else important. The kind of story that makes a difference."

His eyes had drifted past her, and Chloe wondered what he was seeing. Some imaginary time and place, maybe, taking anonymous phone calls, meeting informants in an alley. It made her wonder why he'd stayed in a place like Tall Pine—where, as far as she knew, there weren't any bodies buried. Admittedly, she liked it that way. It was why she'd moved back here after college. But from Bret, across the table, she felt a wistfulness that pulled at her.

She thought of an answer. "Maybe those aren't the only stories that make a difference," she said. "Maybe the soft stories make a difference, too. Maybe positive stories about everyday people really need to be told."

"And *you're* writing a murder mystery?" Bret shed his pensive look with a shake of his head and a wry grin. "Come on, tell me. Who gets killed? How far along is it?"

"Oh, no, you don't." She folded her arms smugly, enigmatically. Bluffing again. "You'll have to find out when it's finished."

If that ever happened.

As she stared across the table at her complicated boss, keeping her Mona Lisa smile in place, Chloe realized how quickly Bret had deflected the topic back to her. He didn't like being the subject of conversation, she realized, and she suspected it had been some time since anyone had asked him any serious questions about himself. Perversely, it made her want to dig deeper. Maybe those reporter instincts really were becoming ingrained.

But she'd glimpsed a yearning underneath his customary crispness. And under that, maybe, something else. A melancholy, for lack of a better word. Whatever it was, the puzzle of Bret suddenly intrigued her far more than the mystery she'd been trying to write.

Chapter 8

Chloe crossed the employee lot of the *Gazette,* relishing the crunch of snow under her feet even as she took care not to lose her footing. The layer of white was thin and crisp from melting and refreezing the past few nights. But it still sparkled in the morning light, a cheerful herald of the Christmas season.

By February the snow would be old hat and no longer so welcome, but today, it was perfect. She didn't even mind the way the cold seeped into her on the short walk to the employee entrance.

She adjusted the cardboard box under her arm, entered Elvis's birthday on the keypad by the door, and stepped into the quiet building. At seven-thirty the Monday after Thanksgiving, all the doors she passed in the hallway were still closed.

The newsroom was dark and empty when she reached it, and she made short work of decking her desk. A swag of bargain-shelf garland across the front, a wooden stand-up MERRY CHRISTMAS sign on her desktop, followed by the pièce de résistance: her pre-lit, battery-operated mini-tree. It took just a few minutes to hang the little ornaments on it; after all, there were only a dozen of them.

Satisfied, she settled into her chair, booted up her computer, and started going over the list of story proposals she'd e-mailed to herself over the weekend. She felt refreshed, rejuvenated, and optimistic after two days away from the office. And Friday night had been an encouraging sign that Bret was fairly human, after all.

When the newsroom door swung open a few minutes after eight, she was surprised to see not only Bret, but Chuck as well. Early for Chuck. Late for Bret. Chloe had never beaten him into the office before.

". . . two feet of snow in Utah already," Chuck was saying. "We don't know what cold is around here."

"So I hear." Bret was already shrugging out of his overcoat. He hung it on the rack that stood near the door leading out to the lobby. "Jake's from Pennsylvania, and he says we have no idea what a real winter's like."

Chuck went to his desk, shook his own coat off to hang over the back of his chair. He greeted Chloe as he sat. "How was your Thanksgiving?"

"Great. How—"

"What's that?" Bret interrupted. He'd stopped on his way to the editor's office, his eyes on Chloe's miniature Christmas tree.

"Oh." Chloe sat forward, picking up a pen to point out the ornaments. "It's the twelve days of Christmas. See, the topper is a pear, for the partridge in a pear tree. There's a turtle dove over on your side—"

"I get it." Bret's gaze went from the tree to the swag

of garland across the front of her desk. "You're not going to get carried away with decorations, are you?"

Stunned, Chloe looked at her humble tree, then at Bret. If he had any memory of their conversation at The Snowed Inn, there was no evidence of it on his face.

As the silence in the room lengthened, he added: "It's . . . distracting."

"You know, you're right." To her surprise, Chuck stepped into the fray. He held one hand out in front of him as if to shield himself from the glare of the tree's tiny bulbs. He swayed comically. "I'm starting to freak out."

Bret's eyes darted to Chuck with a look that could melt lead.

Chloe held her breath, afraid that Mr. Neutrality had picked the worst possible time to chime in. She didn't want Chuck to get his head chopped off for sticking his neck out on her behalf.

Chuck switched on his computer, seemingly oblivious to Bret's stare. By the time Bret turned back to Chloe, his glower had faded.

He gave a faint shake of his head. "Just don't overdo it."

Without another word, he went into McCrea's office, closing the door behind him.

Okay, if she'd ever thought she and Bret were going to be pals, obviously that wasn't happening.

Chloe sagged and turned to Chuck, bewildered. "Thanks," she said. "But I hope I didn't buy you any trouble."

"Don't worry about it." Chuck pulled his keyboard toward him and started typing.

"I never thought—" She stopped. She didn't think she needed to apologize for Christmas decorations. Unless . . . "Did I do something politically incorrect?"

"Nah. He goes to Tall Pine Community Church, same as me."

"That's where my parents go."

"What about you?" His mildly chiding tone fell somewhere between that of a father and an uncle.

"I used to. When I came back up here after college and got my apartment, I kind of . . . got used to sleeping in on Sundays."

"It can be a bad habit." There it was, that faintly paternal tone, as he gave her the same mild rebuff she got from her own parents.

Then Chuck's glance drifted toward Bret's closed door. "Come to think of it," he said, "Bret gets into the same habit every December."

"Any idea why?" Suddenly the lights on Chloe's little tree looked louder to her, more conspicuous. Thank goodness she hadn't put them on the flashing setting.

Chuck started typing. "At this point, you know what I know."

Whether or not the newsroom was a boys' club, Chloe realized, boys didn't tend to tell each other much.

Half an hour later, Bret's door opened. "Story conferences. Chuck, nine o'clock. Chloe, nine-fifteen."

This time when he retreated back into his office, he left the glass door open, as was his usual habit. Chloe contemplated her list of story proposals. Maybe she'd better rethink this list of topics. Trouble was, she didn't have much time to brainstorm.

She joined Bret in his office promptly at nine-fifteen.

She started off by pitching two of her non-holiday stories, and he approved them. He also approved the story about a third-grade class that was making shoebox gifts for underprivileged children.

She had a feeling it would get harder from here. "Christmas tree preservation tips," she said.

"That's more of a news brief."

She nodded. She'd expected that. But she hoped it made a good segue to her next idea. "Speaking of Christmas trees, I got to thinking about the tree in the town square. I thought it might be neat to do a history—when the first tree lighting was, what kind of lights they used back then, find out if anyone knows how old the tree actually is . . ."

"Chloe." Bret was shaking his head. "The tree is lit. It's going to stay lit. If the tree goes out, *then* it's news. If we wanted to run a piece on the tree, the time to do it was before the tree lighting."

She didn't even allow herself a sigh. She forged on. "The Christmas parade on Evergreen Lane is this Saturday—"

"We'll run a brief this week." Now he wasn't even letting her finish her sentences. "And a stand-alone photo the day after."

"Okay." *Think of yourself as a turtle,* Chloe told herself. *Just let it bounce off your shell.* Because Bret obviously had a shell of his own, and whatever aberration had made him set it aside the other night, it was firmly back in place.

She skimmed her list. Bret had already approved two of her non-holiday topics; she only had one left. She should have spread them in between the others.

But when seven out of her ten story ideas had to do with Christmas, what could she do?

Against her better judgment, she ventured, "You don't care for Christmas much, do you?"

His face was expressionless. "It's not my favorite thing, no."

"Why?"

He barely lifted an eyebrow. "It probably goes back to that Christmas I spent working in a shoe-blacking factory when I was a kid."

"That was Charles Dickens."

"Oh. I knew it happened to someone." Leaning back in his chair, Bret let a faint smile get through. Maybe he was pleased that she'd gotten the Dickens reference. Not that it mattered. "Here's the deal," he said. "Not everyone loves Christmas, and in most cases, it isn't news. There *will* be Christmas events to write about, I promise, and I'll make sure you get your fair share of those. But we have to be selective. Things that matter to the community. Steer clear of puff pieces. All right?"

"All right." Chloe skimmed her list again. *Puff pieces.* That stung. And it also brought her way up short. She pitched her last remaining non-holiday article; when Bret approved it, that gave her four out of the ten she'd come in with, plus a couple of news briefs.

She stood with a rueful smile. "I'm afraid the rest of these were a little too—jolly. I'll e-mail you some more ideas by this afternoon."

"Okay. Don't forget, you have the next town council meeting Wednesday night. That gives you one more."

"Right." Chloe started to leave. Unable to help herself, she turned back at the door, trying to find some trace of the guy she'd seen at The Snowed Inn. "Bret?"

"Yes?"

What did it matter? She asked anyway: "Do you at least like snow?"

One hand went up to cover the lower half of his face, as if in thought. Chloe studied the upper half. Behind his glasses, something in his dark eyes may have glimmered. Could he possibly be trying not to smile?

He lowered his hand, and she saw no hint of merriment. "When I don't have to drive in it. When it's not blocking the roads and causing problems. Then it's okay."

He sat forward in his chair, as if waiting for her to leave.

Chloe got back to her desk. Nope, they *definitely* weren't pals.

No big deal. If anyone had suggested she and Hal, her old boss at the diner, ought to be pals, she would have fallen over laughing.

Put on your shell, she intoned in her head. *Be a turtle.*

She'd make that her new mantra.

Bret had managed to go a year and a half without ever setting foot in The Snowed Inn.

Now he was here for the second time in a week. Right when the holiday season was kicking off.

But the monthly chamber of commerce meeting rotated from one business to the next, and he supposed December was a logical enough choice for the Christmas

111

hotel. When Bret arrived, Angie Cleghorn from behind the front counter directed him to the Man Cave.

Bret blinked. "The what?"

Angie pointed the way to a set of double doors off the lobby, and Bret walked into a cross between a conference room and a den. Rustic and comfortable, it was free of Christmas trappings, except for a tall artificial pine tree in one corner of the room. Better. A long table against one wall offered a spread of coffee, doughnuts, and pastries.

Bret queued up in the short line for the coffee maker behind Diana Trask from the local pizzeria. Not everyone in the Man Cave this morning was male. Only about two-thirds.

"I was hoping for Mandy's hot chocolate," Ralph Kirkgaard said as he poured his coffee.

"Sorry." Jake stood back from the line, waiting for the chamber members to serve themselves. "That's a specialty item."

"Paying customers only, you mean?"

"Something like that." Jake had a rare ability to be diplomatic without being phony, a trait Bret admired.

Ralph Kirkgaard, on the other hand, he'd never cared much for.

"So, Bret," Kirkgaard said as Bret poured his coffee. "How's that little blond intern working out?"

Bret felt unexpected irritation prickle under his skin. He wasn't sure which word annoyed him the most: *little*, *blond*, or *intern*.

He disregarded his annoyance and focused on the facts. "She's not an intern, she's a full-time staffer." He kept his tone relaxed as he reached for the creamer. "I inherited her from McCrea when he went out of town. Turns out she's a heck of a writer."

"She can write?" It wasn't Kirkgaard's word choice that bothered him as much as the smarmy tone. The prickles under his skin grew into little flames.

"Sure, she can write," Bret said easily, stirring in the creamer with a steady hand. "Now if only you could read."

That brought a laugh from the half dozen people within earshot. Bret took a swig of coffee, ignoring the fact that it burned his tongue.

Sexism, Chloe had said, and he'd dismissed it automatically. But why else would anyone be so quick to assume a pretty little blonde couldn't write?

Hadn't he come darn close to assuming the same thing?

He took another drink of coffee, letting it scorch his tongue again.

"In fact," he said, "I thought her story on hospice was pretty impressive." He kept the same offhanded tone as he mentioned his other least-favorite subject.

There was a slight gap in the conversation, like a classroom full of kids who hadn't done their homework. Really? At the front of the Sunday "B" section, and no one in the room had seen it?

"I missed that one," Jake said. "I enjoyed the one about the snow plowers this morning, though."

Bret nodded gratefully and took a more cautious sip of the hot coffee. Yesterday, after he'd shot down most of her Christmas story proposals, Chloe had whipped up a nice profile piece about the Galpin brothers, who ran the local snowplow service. She'd praised the two men as Tall Pine's unsung heroes, giving credit where it was overdue. Clearing the roads was vital both to locals and the town's tourist trade.

"I saw that one, too," said Joe Velosa, from the recreation center. "It was cute."

Cute. The story had been written with wit and personality. But was it *cute*? Bret wouldn't have thought so. His own tolerance for fluff was pretty low.

As he was frowning into his coffee, Millie Bond arrived, bringing in a welcome breath of fresh air.

"The school provides most of the gifts that go into the shoeboxes," Patti Moreno said over the phone as Chloe scribbled onto her notepad. "And my students bring in what they can. Candy canes, yo-yos, stocking stuffer type things. It doesn't have to be much. But it gives the kids a chance to contribute, and it makes them more aware of kids who don't have as much as they do."

"That's nice." Chloe smiled, scrawling rapidly to keep up.

"And they get a big kick out of decorating the shoeboxes. I bring in all kinds of gift wrap, ribbons, stickers, and stuff. They're all so different."

"Sounds like a perfect photo op." Chloe eyed the clock on the wall. "You say the shoeboxes are ready to go. If I send a photographer over this afternoon, could we get some shots of the kids with the shoeboxes?"

"That would be great."

Chloe adjusted the phone on her shoulder again.

"Can you give me a time range, and I'll find out if we have someone available?"

As she finished jotting down the information, Bret walked in, sifting through a handful of mail. For the second day in a row, he'd come in later than Chloe; he'd texted her this morning about a chamber of commerce meeting. He still wore his overcoat, and today a charcoal-colored knit scarf was draped over his neck.

He paused in front of Chloe's desk as she hung up. "Remember," he said, "learn to type your notes."

Good morning to you, too. "The phone kept slipping off my shoulder when I used both hands to—"

"Headset. If there's not one in your desk, there ought to be one in one of the others. If you can't find one, let me know."

"Okay." She nodded, distracted. She couldn't remember seeing Bret wear a scarf before. Closer up, she saw the yarn was actually a blend of different shades of deep gray and black. With Bret's dark hair and eyes, it was striking. "Nice scarf."

He looked up from the mail. "Don't make fun."

"I'm not. It has a beautiful texture."

"Thanks." He shook his head. "I feel like Fred from *Scooby-Doo.* You know, the guy with the ascot."

Chloe tilted her head, trying to decide whether to ask the obvious question: *Then why are you wearing it?*

Setting the mail on her desk, Bret slid the scarf over his head and went to hang it on the coat rack by the door. "Early Christmas present. Millie Bond gave it to me at the chamber meeting. She used to cut my mother's hair."

Used to. Bret's tone changed, and Chloe looked up.

115

With his back turned, his expression was hidden from view. She had a feeling any questions wouldn't be welcome.

"No wonder it's gorgeous," she said instead. "I wish I had a Millie Bond scarf."

"Play your cards right, and maybe someday you'll get one." That sounded more like Bret. He took off his coat and hung it next to the scarf. "Sorry, but I need to hang on to this one. I'll need it for the next chamber meeting."

He didn't like it, and still he planned to wear it. *Interesting.*

Bret picked the mail up from her desk and paused again, studying her with level dark eyes. Appraising? Disapproving? Whatever he was thinking, he didn't say it.

Chloe fought to keep from shifting in her seat. "I'll look for that headset," she volunteered.

Bret nodded, tapped the mail on the edge of her desk, and went into his office.

"I'm sorry." Bret shifted the phone from one ear to the other and kept his tone patient. "But I'm not really sure how it qualifies as news."

"He's had it since last winter," Ed Hollingsworth insisted. "Now he says he hasn't got it. Now, when a man borrows a chainsaw from his neighbor, he has a responsibility to give it back. Am I right?"

"Of course." Bret pinched the bridge of his nose.

"So, it's a matter of personal responsibility. It's human interest. If we let this kind of thing slide . . ."

Bret let Ed run on for another minute. He had the gist of it. It was entirely possible that Mel Kruger still had Ed's chainsaw and couldn't find it. Or that Mel had returned it, and Ed had forgotten and lost it himself. Either way, it was hardly a matter for the *Gazette,* or for the local police. Which, thankfully, Ed hadn't brought into the discussion yet.

When Ed ran out of steam, Bret said, "I'll tell you what. My father has a chainsaw in his garage. If I bring it by Saturday, can you hold off on cutting your firewood until then?"

"Well—sure, I suppose. But—"

"Great. I'll bring it over. Say hi to Wilma for me."

Bret hung up, aware that he'd probably just committed half of his Saturday to cutting wood. It was just as well. He could use the exercise, and he'd stick to fallen branches, per town regulations. Ed might be tempted to hack into some of the living trees. A seventy-two-year-old man shouldn't be cutting firewood, anyway.

He turned his attention back to the e-mail he'd been contemplating before Ed called.

"Do tamales count as graft?"

Chloe's voice pulled him away from his screen again. She stood in the doorway of his office, holding a big, flat plasticware container.

"Graft?" he echoed.

"Bribes. Kickbacks. You know, the kinds of favors we're not supposed to accept as journalists." Chloe hefted the container, a gleam in her eye. "Patti Moreno's mother-in-law dropped these off in the lobby. They were really happy with the story on the shoebox gifts. This was a thank-you."

"I see." He wasn't sure if Chloe was kidding about graft, but she was clearly pleased with the thank-you. And probably tempted by the tamales. They were a

117

holiday tradition in a lot of Hispanic families, and from what he understood, a lot of work went into them. As a result, if you weren't a family member, they were hard to come by.

Bret leaned back thoughtfully, keeping a straight face. "When you conducted the interview, did you do it on condition of free tamales?"

"No."

"During the interview, were you offered tamales in exchange for a favorable article?"

The corners of her mouth tilted up slightly, showing that dimple just below the corner of her mouth. "No."

Bret folded his arms and paused as if to consider. "I think you're in the clear."

"Good." She broke into a full-on smile. "Because it's almost lunchtime."

She started away, then backed up a step, leaning backward this time as she peered in through his doorway. "Want me to heat up a plate for you?"

Bret hesitated. His ingrained reflexes told him to say no. But maintaining professional boundaries was one thing. Turning down homemade tamales was crazy.

He'd worked hard, especially since their chat at The Snowed Inn, to keep their relationship businesslike. He could hold his distance. Even if that smile of hers could light up a room.

"Yes," he said, just as her smile began to waver. "Thanks."

Kickbacks. Bret grinned to himself as Chloe walked away. Little did she know she'd be the recipient of a Millie Bond scarf by Christmas. At the chamber meeting yesterday, Millie had asked him her favorite color.

As if Bret would have any idea. He'd finally suggested a sea green.

"Like her eyes?" Millie had asked.

The woman didn't miss much.

A few minutes later, Chloe returned from the break room with two heated plates, and Bret cleared a spot on her side of his desk. He caught a flicker of surprise on her face. They both ate at their desks routinely, but sending her off to her own desk when she was sharing her bounty seemed just plain rude. And what could be more businesslike than sharing lunch with McCrea's battleship of a desk between them?

Chuck was out somewhere on an interview. His loss.

She drew up the guest chair to sit across from him and took a bite, then closed her eyes and clutched the edge of the desk.

Bret's fork stopped on its way to his mouth. "Whoa. Are they that hot?"

She shook her head, eyes still closed, until she swallowed. "No. That *good*."

Bret pulled his eyes away, took a bite, and understood her bliss. "We owe Patti Moreno's mother-in-law. Big time."

"I ought to save some for Ned, too," she said. "His pictures really helped make the story."

Bret remembered stacks of gaily colored boxes in one photo, a group of beaming kids holding some of the boxes in another. "He has a good eye. And that Santa-type box in the foreground—I'll bet Ned set it there."

"He said that one was Patti's favorite." The box had been wrapped in solid red paper, with a black strip of construction paper around the outside for a belt, and cotton balls around the edges to suggest the white fur lining of a Santa Claus suit. Pretty imaginative for a third-grader. Bret wondered if the teacher had coached him.

Chloe said, "About the little boy who made that box."

She paused, and Bret raised his head, afraid she might be about to tell him the child was critically ill or something.

Instead, she said, "Patti says he told her he saw Santa Claus last year."

Bret's fork froze again. "I take it you don't mean at the department store."

"No. I mean, like Mandy."

He drew a deep breath. And took another bite.

Long before she was Mandy Wyndham, when she was nine or ten, Mandy had told a local television reporter she'd seen Santa Claus in her living room. To this day, she'd never backed down on her story, and it was now the stuff of Tall Pine legend.

Chloe forged ahead. "Patti says she had two students last year who told her the same thing. Do you think maybe I could—"

Bret covered his face with his palm, trying, for just a moment, to wish this away. His hometown was turning into Christmas Central, bit by bit, year after year. And apparently Chloe was as infected as anyone. Because she sounded serious about this story idea.

When he lowered his hand, of course, Chloe was still there.

Bret shook his head. "I think that article's been done pretty definitively around here, don't you?"

"Don't you think there's kind of a human-interest thing here? Maybe sort of a Tall Pine tradition?"

"Mass delusion? Like the Salem witch trials?"

She let out a long, slow breath. "No. The opposite. Like—maybe faith is contagious. Or hope."

He kept his tone even. "Okay, so you do realize that those kids probably talked to Mandy when she worked at the Christmas store. And she must have told them the story about how *she* saw Santa Claus."

"Sure."

"And children are highly suggestible."

She bit her lip. "But I'm not sure that detracts from—"

"And kids are also fond of telling tall tales."

"But—" It took a moment for Chloe's next words to come out. "What if they really do believe it?"

"Let's say that they do." Bret struggled once again for patience. "I remember what happened with Mandy. I was two grades ahead of her in school, and I heard about it. People gave her guff about that story for years. She never did live it down."

"She lived *up* to it instead."

He shrugged. "She stuck to her guns, I'll give you that. But maybe she's tougher than other kids. The teasing she went through, I wouldn't wish on any fourth grader. Have you thought about that?"

"But it's happened more than one time. And we wouldn't have to quote the kids by name."

"You think their classmates wouldn't know?" He leaned back in his chair, reluctantly abandoning his tamales. "I understand what you want to do. A nice, heartwarming story. But you could be causing some kids trouble for years. And we deal in facts, not fiction.

Your stories already skew a little bit"—he uttered the troublesome word—"cute."

Bret saw indignation flash in her gray-green eyes, saw the defiant thrust of her chin. And saw the set of her jaw as she tamped down her reaction. She had an impressive amount of self-control, even if she wasn't good at hiding her reactions.

He hadn't made her angry intentionally. But watching her temper flare, then watching her pull it back in, was a sight to behold.

"Okay," she conceded at last. She returned to her tamales, but he could tell she was far from blissful now. "Bret?"

He took another bite. "Hmm?"

"You don't think Mandy was telling a tall tale. Do you?"

"Mandy? No." His tone softened. "I know she really believes—whatever it was she saw."

Chloe's eyes locked on his, as if she were measuring him. "You like her."

"Of course." He blinked in surprise. "I never said I didn't. Everybody likes Mandy. In fact, between you and me, she and Jake are two of my favorite people." He frowned. "Just don't quote me on that."

"Why?"

"Journalistic objectivity. It's my job to be impartial." He inclined his head. "You ask a lot of questions."

"Journalistic training. It's *my* job to ask questions, right?"

"Yeah, but you can't interview me. That would be unethical."

Besides, I'm the guy who asks the questions. Having the shoe on the other foot felt more than a little uncomfortable. Why did she keep trying to get under his hide?

Chloe Davenport just needed to learn about professional boundaries.

One little thing needled at him. He had a question of his own. "Chloe?"

Uncharacteristically, her eyes were on her plate. "Hmm?"

"*You* know Mandy didn't see Santa Claus, right?"

She hesitated long enough to make him wish he hadn't asked. *No. No. No.* This was the *Tall Pine Gazette,* an island of rationality in this sentimental town. Until Chloe walked in, with her bright smile and her Christmas decorations, at his toughest time of the year.

"I don't think so," she said finally. "But it's nice to think about."

It wasn't the reassurance he'd hoped for.

Chapter 9

Chloe finished her lunch in silence, trying to savor the treat, wondering why she repeatedly felt the urge to knock her head into the brick wall that was Bret.

Something about Christmas really bothered him, and it wasn't some childhood experience in a shoe-blacking factory.

Not my problem.

Do the job.

Be a turtle.

When she stood to clear their plates, Bret surprised her by taking her plate from her hand as he picked his up, too. "I'll get it."

Nice manners. But if he wanted to get on her good side, he should just let her write the darned Santa story.

Instead, he said, "Before you go, there's something I've been meaning to run by you."

Warily, she eased back into her chair as Bret discarded their empty plates in his trash can, then set the trash can away behind him. "What?" she asked.

"A story assignment. If you're up to it. But it's a hundred

and eighty degrees from what we were just talking about."

Aside from press releases, he'd never suggested a story to her. Chloe waited.

"Someone e-mailed me a lead this morning," he said. "We have a twenty-year-old local veteran. He came home about four months ago with his left leg amputated at the knee."

Chloe scraped up the name. "Aaron McNamara." She'd heard about it at the Pine 'n' Dine.

"That's right. Someone you know?"

"No, I just heard about it." Chloe hesitated. She shouldn't hesitate. She should be up for anything. "And you want me to ask him what it's like living with half a leg?"

"There's a little more to it. He's had some hassles with the Veterans Administration. Bureaucratic red tape. They still haven't worked out the approval on funding for a prosthetic leg."

Chloe winced inside. She knew she shouldn't hem and haw. But he'd caught her completely off guard. "Does he even want to be interviewed?"

"Don't know yet. That's where you come in. Start by talking to his old high school advisor. She's the one who sent the e-mail. I'll forward it to you." Bret gave her a challenging look. "If you're up to it."

He'd said that already. This time, it sounded like a double-dog-dare.

"Why me?"

"It's not exactly rescuing kittens from trees, is it?"

He held her gaze, unflinching. Was this some kind of a test?

125

Of course it was. Because apparently she still hadn't proven herself. This was a job, she reminded herself. She couldn't take it personally.

It's his ball, her father's voice echoed. *Learn to play the game his way.*

And stop thinking you'll ever be buddies, she added on her own. The camaraderie they'd been enjoying a few minutes ago was a fluke. It showed up now and then, but she had to give up and regard it as a passing phenomenon. Like Halley's Comet, but not nearly as reliable.

Meanwhile, Bret's inscrutable dark gaze across the desk waited for an answer.

"Okay," she said. "Shoot me the e-mail. I'll start right away."

Having taken up the gauntlet, she stood. She didn't know why this sounded so much harder than talking to grieving families, but she didn't dare back down. She just had no idea how she was going to go about it. As Chloe left Bret's office, she knew only one thing.

She was going to write the hell out of this piece.

Aaron McNamara shifted in his wheelchair. "I'm luckier than a lot of people," he said. "Some guys who step on one of our own explosive devices don't live to tell about it. At least I got to come home."

They sounded like words he'd repeated to himself often. Chloe bit her lip as she scribbled on her pad, keeping her eyes on Aaron as much as possible. They'd been talking for nearly two hours, and it had taken half that time for him to forget he was being interviewed.

The guy was four years younger than Chloe, two

years younger than her brother Joel, and his life would never be the same. The girlfriend who'd waited for him through his deployment had, bit by bit, stopped coming around after he came home with the injury. Thanks to a computer spelling error, the processing on his doctor's request for a prosthetic leg was still tied up in red tape.

And their living room was decorated with Christmas lights and pine branches, and his mom had brought in milk and cookies. It all felt so wrong.

"I hope the claim gets worked out soon," she said awkwardly.

"It will eventually." Aaron's long fingers rubbed the head of his golden retriever, who hadn't budged from his spot alongside his master's wheelchair. "I've spent a lot of time on the phone, and everybody wants to help, but it's the humans versus the computers. We keep going in circles." Aaron shrugged, and a swatch of sandy brown hair fell over his eyebrow. His mother had apologized—actually apologized—for his hair when Ned arrived at the beginning of the interview to shoot the photo. She said they'd been meaning to get it trimmed for weeks, but simple errands had gotten a lot more complicated.

Everything about him seemed so ordinary. If Aaron hadn't enlisted, Chloe knew exactly who he would have been: one of a group of guys at the Pine 'n' Dine, killing time before or after work, maybe flirting with her as they ordered. Skiing at Mount Douglas in the winter, driving down to the beach in the summer.

All that had changed now. Maybe there'd be skiing

eventually, once they got the prosthetic leg worked out. She didn't know if he'd ever want to go to the beach.

Chloe wished she could tell him anything was possible, but advice and platitudes meant nothing coming from her, because she hadn't walked in his shoes. *Shoes.* She winced at how easy it was to stumble on the wrong word.

"I'm still not sure why I'm going to be in the paper," he said.

For that, at least, Chloe had an answer. "This is your town," she said. "What happened to you matters to people. Even people who only knew you a little bit."

"Yeah," he said, "I wish a few more of them would drop by."

Through the interview, he'd maintained a wry, upbeat attitude. Occasionally a glimpse of sadness got through, but mostly he'd kept his game face on. This was the first time she'd heard an edge of actual bitterness.

And Chloe recognized the truth of it. People wanted to be a step removed from things that were tragic, things that were uncomfortable, things that couldn't be fixed. *People mean well,* she almost said, and that might be the worst platitude of all.

"People don't know what to say," she said softly. The pen was in her hand, but the interview was over.

"I get that, too," Aaron said. His head lifted slightly, his sportsmanlike veneer back in place. "I don't know if I would have been coming around, either, if it happened to someone else. It's just—different from this side."

She could only nod. She tried to think of a way to end their meeting on a positive note. Thanks to her, he'd spent the last two hours reliving what he'd gone through, and she didn't want to leave him feeling worse off than he had before she arrived. How could anyone keep from getting emotionally involved in a story like this? But she knew it wasn't her job to change the story, or help him resolve it. Only to write it.

And that killed her.

As if on cue, Aaron's mother came back into the room, ostensibly to clear the plates from their milk and cookies. Wherever Mrs. McNamara had come from, Chloe suspected she'd stayed close enough to hear when it sounded like the interview had come to an end.

"Well, I won't take up any more of your time." Chloe rose, hating the false bright tone in her voice. She tried to make up for it by meeting Aaron's eyes with as much frankness as she could muster. She extended her hand, glad when he took it. "Thank you."

She made it to her car, made it out of the driveway, made it around the corner, before she pulled over to the curb and let the tears go.

She stayed up late to write the article. She handed it in the next morning.

An hour later, Bret called her into his office, told her to cut the story in half, and to contact the veterans' office for their version of the story. "We have to report both sides," he reminded her.

Chloe set her jaw, didn't argue, and got to work on it.

When she filed the revised story the next morning, he called her into his office again. "You're closer," he said. "But you've got to cut it down before it can run. It's still over forty inches long. Get it down to thirty."

"The hospice piece was longer."

"Which may have kept it from being read. One thing that'll help you? Drop the adjectives. Don't tell me how to feel. Make me feel it."

"But—"

"No adjectives."

Chloe shoved her way through the heavy glass door of the Pine 'n' Dine and headed straight for the booth by the corner window. Usually she sat on the side facing the other tables. Today she faced the wall.

"Pie?" Sherry's voice reached her as she sat with her fingers pressed over her eyes.

Chloe didn't take her hands down. "Apple," she said, her voice muffled by her hands. Her eyes felt hot. She wasn't sleeping a lot these days, but that wasn't the only reason.

She'd tried so hard. The story couldn't be maudlin, couldn't feel like a call for pity. She'd weighed every word. She thought she'd gotten it right. Twice.

And now she had to do it again.

You go write a story about a twenty-year-old amputee, she wanted to tell him. But in point of fact, Bret had done stories every bit as hard. She knew, because she'd searched the paper's database to see how he did them. Bret wrote them eloquently, sparely, letting the facts speak for themselves. The guy was freaking Hemingway.

I can't do that. She'd tried.

And it wasn't enough.

She fought the tears. She didn't cry over work. Ever. Not when tourists were rude to her. Not when Hal yelled at her for breaking dishes. She was never going to please Bret, and for some reason Bret's opinion mattered way, way too much.

She heard a plate slide onto the table in front of her, followed by the quiet sound of a coffee cup being set beside it.

Then she heard another sound: a person settling into the booth across from her. Quickly, she blinked hard and lowered her hands to see Sherry. Who else had she expected?

Who else indeed? *You dope.*

"What's wrong?" Sherry asked.

Chloe took in her surroundings for the first time. At eleven a.m., most of the tables were empty. "I'm going to kill Bret. If he doesn't kill me first."

Sherry frowned. "You had a fight?"

"No, it's not like that." Chloe slumped against the upholstered booth. She had to stop whining to people. After this. "I'm just tired. And there's no pleasing him. Every time I think I'm on the right track he shoots me down." She rubbed her eyes, feeling them start to swell again. "Every. Damn. Time."

"Bret's not so bad."

Sherry's voice held an odd note. Chloe raised her head and tried to fathom her friend's enigmatic expression. "How would you know?"

Sherry shrugged. "We went out for a while. Back in high school."

That dried up her tears. Her mind was too busy reeling,

trying to re-imagine a universe where Bret and Sherry ever would have dated.

"How did that happen?" Chloe stared at her friend unabashedly, but she still saw the same Sherry. Compassionate brown eyes, standard pink Pine 'n' Dine uniform, hair tugged up into the obligatory waitress's bun, currently dyed a deep shade of wine red. A different hair color every month. Sherry and *Bret*?

"It was a long time ago," Sherry said. "The point is—"

The front door opened with its familiar chime. Sherry broke off and stood as if ejected by the booth's cushions. Eyes on the door, she fished her pad out of her pocket and pantomimed writing on it. "Can I get you anything else?"

Something flickered in Sherry's eyes as they looked past Chloe to follow the newcomer's progress into the restaurant.

Chloe didn't turn around. Voice lowered, she said, "Bret just walked in, didn't he?"

"Mm-hmm." Sherry scribbled on her pad, tore off a ticket, and slapped it on the table at Chloe's elbow. With the polite friendliness waitresses used on total strangers, she said, "Let me know if you need anything else."

"This isn't your station," Bret said as Sherry walked up.

"Yeah, well, your usual table's taken."

"I noticed." Bret saw the back of a blond head in the coveted corner booth, facing away from the rest of the room. Unless someone else had the seat across from you, it ran contrary to human nature to sit with your back to a restaurant. "She's not back there crying, is she?"

"No." Sherry widened her eyes. "Why would you think that?"

"Because I'm trying to turn her into a journalist."

"And that involves what? Floggings?"

He should have stayed in his office, as usual. But the latest revision session with Chloe had left him unsettled. He was putting her through the wringer and he knew it. But the story had to be good. So good it couldn't be missed by even the laziest reader.

He glared at Sherry. "Constructive criticism."

"Your constructive criticism never made *me* cry."

"Yeah, maybe that's why you only got a C plus in English composition."

"It was all I needed."

And that, Bret concluded, was one of many reasons he and Sherry remained on good terms but could never have been soul mates. Settling for good enough, especially when words were involved, was beyond his comprehension. But Sherry had more horse sense than most people he knew, one of many reasons he was glad to count her as a friend.

Most of the time, anyway.

Sherry cocked a hand on her hip. "Is there the *slightest* possibility you're being too rough on her?"

Enough was enough. "What happened to taking a guy's order around here?"

From the corner of his eye, he saw Tiffany approach the table, get halfway across the room, and wheel back around. Tiffany was Chloe's roommate, he'd sat in her

133

station, and now his long-ex-girlfriend was taking his order. Could Tall Pine get any more interconnected?

Sherry held her notepad poised, looking over it with a reproachful stare.

"Coffee," he said. "Lots of cream."

"Want to pay for Chloe's pie?"

"Sherry." He did his best to send daggers from his eyes. "Let it go."

She spun away and went back to Chloe's table.

It was Tiffany who brought his coffee.

After the week she'd had, Chloe didn't even want to look at the *Gazette* that weekend, but she couldn't stop herself.

The Aaron McNamara story ran on Sunday's front page. Not the front of the "B" section. The *very* front page.

Chloe shut herself in the bathroom of the apartment, although Tiffany and Kate weren't up yet. Half afraid to look, she read the article to see how much of her third revision had survived Bret's final edits. Like all of her stories, she practically knew it by heart. This time it had been through so many revisions, it was hard to tell. But hadn't she deleted that paragraph?

She read it again. Every word was hers. But two of the paragraphs she'd sacrificed on the last go-round were restored. He'd even put a few of her adjectives back.

She sagged against the bathroom door with relief. But she wasn't prepared for what waited for her when she went out.

"Chloe," the grocery checker said when she went out for milk. "When did you start writing for the paper?"

She passed her old volleyball coach in the parking lot. "Great article. Congratulations."

"Good job," Kate said when she came home from the store. "You made me cry."

She made *Kate* cry?

No, of course not. It was Aaron's story that made Kate cry, and she couldn't forget that. She'd only told the story; Aaron had lived it. Was still living it.

She had a call from her parents, which shouldn't surprise her, because she already knew they were proud of her. But she'd written so many articles for the *Tall Pine Gazette* by now, they weren't usually a topic of conversation.

When she stopped at the Pine 'n' Dine to pick up some takeout chicken, it happened again.

"Congratulations."

"Beautiful article."

"How long have you been writing for the paper?"

She'd spent so much time steeling herself against Bret's criticism, convinced she was never going to measure up, that it took a few hours for full comprehension to sink in. He hadn't been trying to torture her, or even just using a harsh method to teach her.

He'd made her shine.

"Bret."

He'd just settled behind his desk Monday morning when Chloe showed up in the doorway of his office. "I wanted to thank you."

He didn't pretend not to understand. "Don't thank me. You earned it. And then some."

She smiled. But there was a reserve to her smile, and that wasn't like Chloe. "Okay." She shifted in the door. "Nine-fifteen for story conference?"

"Sure."

She turned to go. A cloud seemed to hang over her. Maybe she hadn't gotten over the grinding he'd put her through, but he didn't think that was the case. After all, she'd just thanked him.

"Chloe?" He let his voice come out softer than usual.

She turned back, eyes shimmering with what looked suspiciously like unshed tears. "What?"

"Are you all right?"

She leaned against his doorjamb, arms hugged around today's rust-colored cardigan sweater. "I feel like I'm benefiting from someone else's problem," she confessed. "Aaron's stuck in a wheelchair. And people are congratulating me. It doesn't seem right."

Dear God. He knew he'd given her a hard subject to tackle. But he hadn't expected this. Looking at Chloe now, he wondered why he hadn't seen it coming. It was her empathy that made her so good at writing stories like this one.

He struggled for some balance between moral support and professional neutrality. "You can't fix everything. You told the story. You told it honestly and you did it well. That's not nothing."

"I wonder—" Her shoulders drew up as she pulled in a breath. "I wonder if I'm cut out for this. I don't know if I can be—objective enough."

He tried to ignore the unshed tears. The fact that

they made her eyes brilliant, that at the moment they looked more blue than gray or green.

He couldn't acknowledge the tears, but he couldn't ignore them, either. He sat forward, trying for once to minimize the amount of space the desk put between them.

"I don't quite understand," he said. "What made this harder than the hospice piece? You asked for that one. And you were talking to bereaved families."

Her eyes drifted somewhere past him as she considered. "Maybe because when I talked to those families, the worst thing had already happened to them. It was over, and I guess they were already starting to heal a little bit. I mean, I didn't talk to anyone whose mother died last week or anything."

Bret flinched inwardly. Once again, if he didn't know better, he would have pegged Chloe for a closet sadist.

But he did know better.

"With Aaron—" She paused. "Maybe the worst thing's already happened to him, but he hasn't had a chance to start healing. He's been going through it for four months. And I couldn't make it better. I know that's not my job. But I kept wanting to change the story."

"I understand," Bret said quietly. "You wanted to make a difference."

She nodded, biting her lip.

He'd set her up for this. Maybe *he* was the closet sadist. Professional relationship or not, he needed to make it right. But he needed to do it from this side of the desk, even though he found it increasingly hard to stay here.

He asked, "Do you know why I assigned that story to you?"

She hesitated. "To help me make an impression?"

"That was part of it," he admitted. "I wanted to show people what you could do. But the other reason was—you were the right person for the story. I knew Aaron McNamara was in good hands. I knew you'd treat him right, and you did."

Her arms wound tighter around her sweater. "I just hope I didn't make it worse."

He shook his head. "He wanted to tell his story. Otherwise his family never would have let you in the door. And you treated him with respect. Don't feel guilty because you wrote an article that moved people."

The shadow of a smile appeared at one corner of her mouth. "With your help."

"In your words. And don't lie. I know you wanted to shoot me dead at least seven times."

She didn't deny it. At last her lips curved up in a smile. It was small, but it was real. Her eyes were still shining. He shouldn't be noticing, but in that moment he'd never seen anyone look more beautiful. Not because of her face, which was lovely enough, but because of the heart behind it.

Bret ignored the lump in his own throat.

"It'll be all right," he told her. "It gets better. You'll see."

With visible reluctance, she pulled away from the doorjamb to leave.

"Also," he added, "if you quit this job before Christmas, I'll kill you."

That got a shaky spurt of laughter out of her. Good.

Bret didn't say any more, but if he knew Tall Pine the

way he thought he did, things would look better sooner than she expected.

Chloe returned to her desk. The weight she'd been carrying since yesterday afternoon felt a little bit lighter. Not gone. But lighter.

She sat down and checked her voice mail. Several messages had come in yesterday and this morning, complimenting her on the article, most from people she didn't even know.

Then the e-mails. Two of them asked if there was anything they could do to help Aaron and his family. *That* was better, although she didn't have a ready answer. Maybe she could call his mother and ask. She put her hand on the phone and hesitated. It was still relatively early in the morning. And frankly, she wasn't sure what to say.

She took a fortifying drink from her coffee—coffee that Bret had made before she came in—and got busy polishing up her weekly list of story proposals. She made sure to include some cheerful ones. She wanted to write about kittens and puppies and babies and—

"Morning." Chuck's voice came from her right. She hadn't heard him come in. "Good job on the Aaron McNamara story."

She smiled faintly. "Thanks."

Just before lunchtime, she got another phone call.

"Miss Davenport? This is Wayne Schallert from Tall Pine Community Bank."

In what had become reflex, she grabbed her pen and notepad. "Yes?"

"We've had several calls this morning about your story on Aaron McNamara. People read about the problems he's been having with his insurance claim, and they're looking for a way to contribute."

Chloe sat up straighter.

"We wanted to let you know we're setting up an account for contributions. If you'd like to run something in the paper to let people know . . ."

She wrote down the information, started to e-mail Bret, and called his extension instead.

"Write up a news brief." His tone was as clipped as ever. Then he added, less brusquely, "It's all you'll need."

With the response she'd been getting from the town, she was beginning to believe that. What she no longer believed was Bret's terse, clipped tone. He had a heart. He just didn't want anyone to know it. She'd heard it in his voice this morning, when he talked about making a difference. The same words he'd used at The Snowed Inn. He'd been so much less guarded that night. She wondered what had gotten into him, and if she'd ever see that side of him again. Why did he work so hard to keep himself under wraps?

She shook herself. But at least she was thinking about something besides Aaron in his wheelchair.

Chloe worked through her lunch, taking calls about the story, referring readers to the bank when they asked how to help, all while trying to get this week's articles off the ground.

It was almost five, and she was finally almost done writing her first story for the week, when another call came through from Jen at the front desk. Chloe picked it up.

"Miss Davenport? This is Rita McNamara. Aaron's mother."

As if she could forget. "Call me Chloe. Please."

"Chloe." There was something strained in her tone; Chloe hoped it wasn't a bad thing. "I wanted to say thank you. I would have called sooner, but things have been so hectic."

She didn't know if Mrs. McNamara knew about the bank account yet or not. "You don't have to—"

"We've had calls all day long," Mrs. McNamara went on. "We've found money in the mailbox, under the doormat . . . But the best thing of all is, Aaron's friends have been coming out of the woodwork. They've called, they've dropped by—it's like Christmas came early."

Chloe found herself nodding, even though it was a phone conversation. "Just as long as they don't all come in one day."

"I finally told a few of the ones who called that it might be better if they came by in a few days, or next week. I think they understood."

Chloe clutched the phone. "Good."

And I'm dropping by again, too, she decided. *Before Christmas.*

As she hung up, she felt her heart lift, and she realized that was the call she'd wanted to get all day. She returned to her article, but she had trouble seeing the letters on her screen. She was crying again.

But this time, for a better reason.

Chapter 10

Chloe had never seen so many of the *Gazette* staff at once.

An e-mail from Bret had pulled them into the newsroom from the various departments throughout the building. She'd come to think of this place as the house M. C. Escher built; it didn't seem possible that a structure that looked so unassuming on the outside could hold so many departments. But the newsroom, in her mind, was the kernel of the enterprise—not just because the stories generated from here, but because it seemed to lie in the center, judging by the doors and hallways that led away from it on every side.

Most of the thirty or so faces in the room weren't familiar. She'd chatted with a few people in the break room now and then while she heated her ramen noodles, but most of them seemed in as much of a hurry to return to their own departments as she was to get back to her next deadline.

Bret stood against the door frame of the editor's office, as if loath to leave his post, and Chloe suspected that was the case.

He'd called the meeting for two p.m. Despite the murmur of voices as people continued to drift in, he started at five minutes after.

"Okay, everyone, I'll keep this short." Although he didn't raise his voice much, it carried easily, and conversation died off. Chloe had a feeling meetings like this were a rarity. "We have a Christmas surprise, or at least it came as a surprise to me. I got word this morning that an executive from the corporate office is coming to town tomorrow. Just in time for the company Christmas party."

That brought a fresh murmur of voices. Once again, Bret silenced it in the simplest way possible: he kept talking.

"Executive Vice President Lloyd Mossel will be passing through our offices sometime tomorrow. It's a disruption we didn't expect. But he's pretty high on the food chain, so we need to make sure we give the right impression. In our eyes, we're the only paper this town's got, and I happen to think we do a pretty fine job."

A small smattering of applause started.

"But." Bret cut it off. "In the eyes of Liberty Communications, we are a very small piece on a very big Monopoly board. Their interest in us is limited to how cost-effective we are and how little hassle we are. We need to be viewed as an asset, not a liability. When Mr. Mossel drops in tomorrow, I want him to see an efficient little gem. That means—and I'm sorry about this—tidy desks. Make an effort to clean up your work area before you leave tonight, because we're not sure exactly what time our executive rolls in for his nickel

143

tour. Also, tidy personal appearances. Some of us do our best work in sweats. But not tomorrow. If that's you, dig something a little dressier out of the back of your closet."

That wouldn't be a problem for Bret. He stood before them today in his habitual gray sport jacket. He went on, "Most of all, at the Christmas party tomorrow night, let's all be on our best behavior."

"Define 'behavior,'" a male voice somewhere behind Chloe interjected.

"I was afraid of that." Bret didn't miss a beat. "It means common sense. We've all heard stories about company Christmas parties—not necessarily ours, mind you—but let's keep tomorrow night free of colorful stories. If you drink, drink responsibly. You know your limits. And this should go without saying, but Mr. Mossel is to be regarded as a visiting dignitary. Give him the utmost respect. He's the Pope, the President of the United States, and Paul McCartney all rolled into one."

"Paul who?" came a younger voice—once again, somewhere in the back, in the smart-aleck tones of someone who obviously knew better.

Once again, Bret didn't so much as blink. "Dave Grohl, then."

Another brief smattering of applause. Chloe was surprised Bret could whip out the name of the leader of the Foo Fighters at a moment's notice. Bret's lips twitched with what might have been amusement as he shrugged. "Enough said. We all have work to do, so let's do some quick housekeeping and get back to it."

With that, Bret turned away and went back into his office. Five minutes, start to finish. No Q & A.

Chloe considered the surface of her desk. She had a tendency toward clutter, and no matter how often she cleared it, the new piles of folders and scraps of notes started right away. She'd have to make some extra time to clear it.

Eyeing her miniature Christmas tree and decorations, she hesitated. She hated to even consider it. But if anyone in the newsroom ran afoul of the bigwig from the corporate office, it had better not be her.

She waited until Bret passed by on his next trip to the coffee machine. "Bret? What about Christmas decorations?"

Bret's eyes narrowed, regarding her tree once again. This would be a golden opportunity for him to play the Grinch. But after a long moment, the corners of his mouth twitched upward again. Just barely.

"As long as the twelve days of Christmas are all in order," he said, "I think you're okay."

Bret had never gone to the company Christmas party before, and he hadn't planned to attend this one. Now he was obligated to be here, serving as both host and babysitter.

He sat at a table in the banquet room of Barrymore's Steakhouse, passing the time with Ned and Debbie. They wouldn't be here long; it was their first night out without the baby, and Debbie kept sneaking furtive glances at her cell phone. Lloyd Mossel, the high muck-a-muck from Liberty Communications, was perusing the hors d'oeuvres at the buffet table, and for the moment Bret was content to leave him to it. Schmoozing could wait. If one of the guys from the press room started to dance on the table, that would be Bret's cue to create a diversion.

The banquet room was decorated for Christmas, but they'd gone for understated gold-and-silver elegance, rather than bright reds and greens. Bret had ordered a hot toddy—something he could nurse over a couple of hours without any real effects, but it carried a bite and a sting that had a certain Dickensian flavor.

He thought of his crack to Chloe about the shoe-blacking factory and how quickly she'd picked up on the Dickens reference. So far, he hadn't seen her here.

"You know," Ned said to Debbie, "if we leave now, we could stop by the tree lot on our way home. It'll be easier without the baby along."

Debbie gave her cell phone another glance to check the time. "You're right." She turned to Bret. "Everything gets a little more complicated with a baby. It didn't hit us until two days ago that we needed to set up a sitter."

Ned added, "And tying a tree to the car while you've got a baby carrier in the backseat—"

"In the cold," Debbie added.

Bret shook his head. "Go, go. You don't have to convince me."

They stood. Deb surprised him with a hug. "Merry Christmas, Bret." She pulled back and studied him. With a softness in her tone, she added, "Are you doing okay?"

Bret blinked. Plenty of people remembered Helena

Radner. Very few thought of the fact that she'd died shortly before Christmas. Millie Bond would remember, yes. But the photographer's wife?

"Never better," he said.

"Say hi to your dad for me."

And there was the connection. Debbie had interned at the town hall, taking minutes at the meetings, when Bret's mother got sick. His father had stepped down from the council shortly after her death.

Bret didn't know why he always forgot how intertwined everyone's lives were in Tall Pine. But he knew Deb's concern was intended as a kindness, not an unpleasant reminder. He needed to respond with some grace.

"Thanks. I will." Bret nodded. "Good night, Deb."

He'd just resumed his seat at the table when, across the room, Chloe walked in. But it wasn't quite the same Chloe he'd seen at the office a couple of hours ago. She wore a black dress with slender straps at the shoulders, making her look more delicate than usual. Gold hoops gleamed at her ears, and she'd done something different with her hair, creating blond curls that fell loosely around her face. From across the room, her eyes had a look that was somehow smokier.

At the moment, those eyes were directed at Mike from the press room, who'd crossed the room in three strides to reach her. She smiled a greeting, and her lips shimmered faintly.

She was . . . exquisite.

Bret prided himself on finding the right word, and that was the one that came immediately to mind. If he

147

wasn't smart, she'd catch him staring at her like some love-struck guy from the press room.

He turned away, took a drink, and nearly choked, caught off guard by the burn of the hot toddy. Coffee this wasn't. His glance skimmed over the room for someone else to chat with and found Randy, the night editor. That would do. Someone who wouldn't make him choke on his drink.

"Your new reporter seems to be making an impression," Randy remarked.

Not the conversation Bret had hoped for. "Is that so," he said, refusing to let his eyes drift toward Chloe and Mike.

"Is she kind of a flirt?"

If he wasn't careful, he'd end up choking on his drink anyway. "Not that I've noticed."

When Randy didn't reply, curiosity dragged Bret's gaze in the direction the other man was looking. No longer standing with Mike—that must have been a short conversation—Chloe now stood by the buffet table. Hugh from the classified section had sidled up next to her, and Chloe was trying to divide her attention between Hugh and the hors d'oeuvre platter in front of her.

She wasn't flirting. She was dishing up cubes of cheese. Bret turned away again and resolved not to worry about it anymore. Chloe wasn't doing anything wrong, and even if she was, it wasn't his business unless she started dancing on the table.

So, for the next hour, he concentrated on circulating. Working a room didn't come naturally to Bret, but thankfully, he knew most of the people, at least in passing. And thankfully, everyone did seem to be on good behavior. He'd better find Lloyd Mossel, in case their guest decided to make an early exit.

Where had the stuffed suit gone?

At last he spotted Mossel at a table by the back wall, a martini glass in front of him, seated across from a very cornered-looking Chloe Davenport.

She was pretty sure the guy was trying to look down her dress. Which would be difficult, because her dress didn't show much cleavage, and she didn't have much cleavage to show.

"Deregulation opened up a whole new set of opportunities in media," Lloyd Mossel was saying. "In the early nineties, the company expanded into broadcasting properties. . . ."

Heaven help her, he was only up to the nineties.

Chloe sat up a little straighter and held her chin with one hand, trying strategically to position her arm in front of her chest. She kept a smile in place and did her best to feign interest. Friendly, but not *too* friendly. The iron gray of his hair was streaked with black. Chloe suspected it came from a healthy dose of Grecian Formula. She wondered if he'd scheduled his midlife crisis to coincide with their Christmas party.

Awkward. This was the boss from corporate, the one Bret wanted them to make a good impression on. Offending him wouldn't do. But she didn't think Bret had meant to offer her up as an hors d'oeuvre.

On the other hand—where *was* Bret?

He hadn't gotten within ten feet of her all evening,

149

and at ten and a half feet, all he'd done was give her a brief nod. He didn't appear to notice the dress.

And that made her realize she'd worn it hoping he *would* notice. She knew better than that. Crushing on the boss was the most god-awful cliché in the book, and she wasn't going to do it. Couldn't afford to. She had her reputation, and her deadlines, to think about.

". . . and then I saw the opportunity to acquire more newspapers on the West Coast. . . ."

Not to mention, Bret had left her to deal with *this*.

"Chloe."

Suddenly her absentee boss spoke at her elbow, sending a wash of relief through her. She turned.

Bret had traded in the customary gray jacket she'd been eyeballing at the office for a sleek black dinner jacket. The black looked more than fine on him, emphasizing his dark hair and eyes, and she couldn't help but drink it in just a little bit. What was wrong with her tonight? All she'd had was a ginger ale.

Bad idea, she reminded herself. No, letting herself think about Bret that way was worse than a bad idea. If she made it obvious, it would be a great way to keep people from seeing her as a professional. Bret included.

"You don't have cell phone reception in here, do you?" Bret asked in his usual blunt, cut-to-the-chase manner.

She frowned. "No."

"Didn't think so." He handed his phone to her. "Someone sent a text for you. On *my* phone."

That didn't seem likely. Cell phone reception was notoriously spotty in Tall Pine; the *Gazette* was one of the few places she knew of with decent reception.

Chloe read the words on Bret's screen: He probably wouldn't do more than bore you to death. But if you want, now's your chance to make a break for it.

A smile started to curl at the edge of her lips. Quickly, she pulled it down and took her cue.

"Holy cow." She rose to her feet. "What time is it?"

She met Bret's eyes. He returned her look with a perfect deadpan.

"About nine-thirty," he said.

She closed Bret's message, handed the phone back to him, and turned apologetically to Lloyd Mossel. "I'm so sorry. I totally lost track of time," she said, as if she'd been rapt at his every word. Now that she was making an exit, she could afford to give him her widest smile. "My boyfriend's down the hill, and he told me he was going to call at nine. After his kickboxing match." She backed up a step. "He gets *really* possessive."

Bret caught her eye. She usually had trouble reading his expression, but this time she was pretty sure she heard him loud and clear: *Don't overdo it.*

"Excuse me." She smiled at them both this time.

Bret took possession of her freshly abandoned chair. "No problem. I've been needing to catch up with Lloyd anyway."

"Thanks." She started her escape, then remembered her alibi. She rested her hand on the shoulder of Bret's jacket. "Where *would* I be able to get cell phone reception around here?"

Bret's mouth tipped up in a faint smile. "Probably the parking lot."

The fabric of Bret's jacket felt smooth under her

hand, and a little volt raced up her arm. What the heck had been *in* that ginger ale?

"Right." She turned away for good this time. "Have a nice evening."

With nowhere else to go, she retreated for the parking lot.

As Chloe departed in all her splendor, Lloyd Mossel asked, "How is it you have cell phone reception in here?"

"It wasn't easy. Tall Pine is full of cell phone dead spots, so I finally found a carrier that works most places in town. I ran into too many incidents when I needed it for work when it was important."

Mossel's expression looked both sour and dubious, as though Bret had taken his candy away. *Sorry, bud,* Bret thought. *We don't provide* that *kind of business entertainment.*

On that note, as Bret tracked Chloe's progress toward the exit, he noticed good old Mike from the press room drifting in the same direction.

Chuck came to their table, either to brown-nose the exec or to share the chore of keeping him entertained. Knowing Chuck, Bret bet on the latter.

Mike was still halfway across the room from Chloe, but his strides put him on a direct course toward her path. That one, Chloe might not mind so much. Bret wasn't sure. But . . .

Bret asked Chuck, "Could you do me a favor? It looks like Mike's headed for the parking lot. Would you check and make sure he hasn't had too much to drink?"

Chuck gave him a quizzical frown. "Mike?"

Bret nodded in Mike's direction. "Over there. Navy blazer. He doesn't look too steady on his feet to me."

Chuck tilted his head hard, and now it was his turn to give Bret a dubious look. But he said, "Okay."

Fortunately, Chuck had long legs. Bret watched his colleague catch up, then turned back to their guest of honor.

"Who is it?" Mossel asked as Chuck accosted a puzzled-looking Mike.

"Mike Pellegrini. Nice kid. He just might not—"

"No. Your cell phone carrier."

Oh. That. "I never tell anyone. Tall Pine may have lousy cell reception, but in a lot of ways, that's a good thing. Not only does it force tourists to stop being hyper-connected for a while, our teenagers have the best test scores in San Bernardino County. I did some research and found out there's a direct correlation. Students who live in areas like this tend to do better in school."

"How's that?"

"Less distraction, better attention span. I wrote an article about it."

As if to vouch for him, Bret's phone sounded with a text notification.

Once she got outside, Chloe hugged her arms against the December cold. It hadn't snowed in over a week and the weather had been mild, so she'd decided to forgo lugging a coat around for the brief walk to and from the restaurant. She just hadn't planned quite so abrupt an exit.

Bret had bailed her out, but where did she go from here?

She strode toward her car, heels scraping against the asphalt. She could wait a suitable amount of time and go back inside. But for what? Given the way she'd been thinking about Bret tonight, it was probably just as well. Tomorrow she'd put on her work clothes, and she could go back to business as usual. Without even a memory of how he'd looked in that sleek black dinner jacket, or how warm and solid his shoulder had felt under her hand.

She slid behind the steering wheel of her little white car, started it up, and turned on the heater. But before she drove away, she had to satisfy her curiosity on one point. She pulled her cell phone out of her little black bag and sent a text to Bret.

So, do you really get cell reception in there?

As she turned up the volume on the Christmas CD in her car, Bret texted her back:

Yep.

With Bing Crosby and David Bowie for company, she drove away.

* * *

The next day, Bret stepped out of his office to brave a cup of late-afternoon coffee. He had the place to himself, so he hadn't bothered making a fresh pot. He took a sip, grimaced, and added more creamer.

As Bret stirred in the powdered stuff, Mike Pellegrini came in from the lobby entrance and sauntered oh-so casually toward the rear door that led to the press room. It was far from the most direct route, and he'd certainly never cut through the newsroom before.

Bret sipped his nasty coffee and watched with a touch of wry amusement as Mike surveyed the half dozen desks, all unoccupied at the moment. "Can I help you?" Bret asked. "Or don't you have something to press?"

Mike responded with a sheepish grin. "I came in early. Do you know where Chloe is?"

The guy wasn't exactly leaving tongue marks on the carpet, but his intentions were pretty clear. "Out on an interview, I think."

"Oh." Mike shifted his weight from one foot to the other, his wheat-blond hair hanging a little over his ears in a careless look that made Bret think of the cool kids in high school. "Do you know if she's seeing anybody?"

Bret fought the urge to say he'd heard Chloe mention something about an intensely jealous kickboxing boyfriend. It wouldn't even be a lie.

Bret shrugged. "You'd have to ask her."

But he didn't like where this was going. For no reason, really. Based on limited observation, Mike seemed like a good-natured enough sort, although Bret suspected he wasn't the brightest crayon in the box.

He gave Mike a brief nod and went back to McCrea's

155

office before Mike could ask him any more questions, like Chloe's favorite color. And when Bret glimpsed a blond figure coming into the newsroom from the corner of his eye, he closed the door behind him. *Stay out of it.*

Intending to do just that, Bret settled behind his keyboard and pulled up the file he'd been working on. But of course, the door of the editor's office was glass, which gave him a perfect view of the silent movie playing out in the newsroom.

Chloe walked in. Smiled at Mike. And had to step around him to get to her desk, where she stashed her purse in the drawer.

Bret busied his fingers typing. Chloe hadn't sat down, but stood talking to Mike with what Bret would have described as a diplomatic smile. He took stock of the nonverbal cues: Mike's shifting feet, Chloe's straight posture, then a slight tilt of her head. The dimple below her smile deepened. *No, don't encourage him. Just send him on his way.*

At least, that was what Bret hoped was happening. Not that it was any of his business. Yet something in his chest felt strange, like a wet rag being wrung by invisible hands.

Still smiling, Chloe backed into her chair, and Mike backed away in the other direction. With a nod and a smaller smile of his own, he made his way past Bret's office toward the door that led down the hall to the press room.

Nothing in the universe had really changed. Just another afternoon at the *Gazette*.

But while Bret couldn't be a hundred percent certain

of the outcome, he relaxed slightly after he witnessed Mike's exit. He sat back and read what he'd just typed:

Zyjr wiovl znptem gpc ki,[rf pbrt yjr sxu fph.

Chloe pounded out the story, her seventh of the week. With all the interruptions—like the reactions to Aaron's article, straightening up for Mr. Bigwig's visit, and now, the drop-in from Mike—she'd been running behind. Three articles tomorrow would get her caught up. If she did some writing tonight at home, she could make it.

Mike. She felt a little bad about turning him down, but she couldn't work up much interest. He seemed nice enough, probably lighter on the ego scale than most good-looking guys. But when someone asked her out before he knew anything about her, it tended to go the same way: they just didn't have a lot to talk about. She didn't have time for that right now. With her current workload, she couldn't afford the distraction.

She filed her story on the local real estate market and glanced over at Bret's office. He sat behind his screen, a familiar sight. They hadn't really talked since the Christmas party last night. She had something to pass on to him, and she decided now was as good a time as any. After all, she wouldn't be second-guessing every trip to Bret's office if he was Frank McCrea, or Chuck, or Hal from the diner.

The glass door was closed. A little unusual.

She nudged it open and stepped inside. "Got a present for you."

He raised his head. Chloe held up the ledger-size booklet. "This lovely desk planner from Robert Quinn at Bluffs Mortgage."

She handed him the brown faux-leather ledger, helpfully emblazoned with the mortgage company's name and logo. Other than that, it was pretty nice, really.

"Thanks." Bret took the book from her, hefting it in his hand. "I actually do use these." He riffled the pages. "I have seven more just like it. Stack them all up, and you'd have a condensed version of my career at the *Tall Pine Gazette*."

He looked bemused. To Chloe, seven years sounded like a long time to be anywhere. Bret looked as if he might be thinking the same thing.

"I imagine you got one, too?" he added. "He's pretty liberal with those. I think it's eighty percent of his marketing budget for the year."

"I did." Chloe hesitated. She should go. But before she did, she said, "Thanks for bailing me out last night."

Bret shook his head. "Sorry about that. I hope he didn't have you buttonholed for too long."

"No. It only *felt* like three years."

He grinned faintly, his eyes going back to his screen. "For a minute I wondered if maybe you could use another rescue today." When she didn't answer, he glanced up. "Looked like you might have had a visitor from the Chloe Davenport fan club."

"Oh." Her face warmed; she tried to cool it with a deep breath instead of fanning it. "No. Mike's a sweet guy. He wasn't being pushy or anything. Just—" She groped for a short-form explanation. "Maybe a little young."

She lowered her eyes to Bret's desk, wondering why

she found herself trying to explain when Bret hadn't even asked.

Or had he? He'd certainly been the one who brought it up. Any reason?

Her glance landed on an oversize postcard on Bret's desk, with a photo of a familiar face, upside down. With a quick intake of breath, she picked it up. "This is my freshman composition professor."

"Do you mind?" he asked dryly.

Her face flushed hotter as she realized she'd grabbed a piece of mail right off Bret's desk. Fighting the urge again to fan herself, she held it out to Bret instead. "Sorry. I didn't think." She pointed to the square black-and-white photo. "Elizabeth Macias. She taught my freshman comp course at Long Beach. She kept telling me I ought to take her journalism class."

Bret took the postcard and studied the paragraph next to the photo of Dr. Elizabeth Macias. He nodded, as if to confirm she was telling the truth. "Impressive. She's the keynote speaker at a journalism awards luncheon this Saturday."

"That's great."

"So why *didn't* you take her journalism class?"

"I was going to save my writing skills for something creative, remember?"

"I think you've figured out by now that news writing can be pretty creative." He'd sounded teasing a moment ago. Chloe searched his face, but he looked serious now. "I'm sure she'd be proud."

Holy moly. If there was one thing she knew by now, it was that compliments didn't come easily to Bret.

He surprised her further by adding, "Would you like to go?"

That sounded like an invitation. Or maybe he was just offering her a ticket. "Are you going?"

"I have to. I'm speaking at it. One of McCrea's parting gifts. He was scheduled as a speaker before he got called to Chicago. He had them put me in his spot."

She stood in silence, trying to focus on Bret's practical words instead of the absurd step-up of her heart rate. An awards luncheon wasn't a date. He didn't mean it that way. But it would be good to see her old professor. . . .

"It's in Barstow." Bret pulled her away from her thoughts. "About a two-hour drive. It'd kill your Saturday. But if you'd like to come along, I'm allowed one guest. And you could let your old prof know what you've been up to."

Okay, that made it clearer. She weighed the question. Bret's eyes looked perfectly direct and matter-of-fact. In other words, pure Bret.

She remembered her silly disappointment when Bret hadn't paid any attention to her at the party. She had nothing to worry about. Bret was a level-headed individual.

That made one of them.

What could it hurt? They were colleagues. It was a business event. She'd just remember to think of it on that level, no matter what her heart rate told her.

She smiled. "I'd like that. Thanks."

* * *

After Chloe left his office, Bret stared down at the postcard. Printed up before his boss's surprise assignment, it still had McCrea listed on the lineup, along with two other guest speakers.

He couldn't remember his mouth getting so far ahead of his brain in—well, maybe ever.

He suspected the visit by Mike-from-the-press-room had a little to do with it. Or a lot. Bret had gotten territorial, which wasn't like him. And it wasn't smart. Now, suddenly, he'd booked himself an entire day alone with Chloe. Outside the office.

Where he'd have to remember to maintain those professional boundaries.

But hey, he'd gotten good at keeping people at a distance, even when he wasn't trying. As his recent dating record could attest. No reason to believe he'd break form now.

Still, he'd be lying to himself if he pretended he wasn't looking forward to it.

Chapter 11

Chloe stepped outside her apartment, a lidded travel coffee cup in each hand, and started for the front of the building. Knowing Bret, he'd be here to pick her up promptly at nine-thirty, if not earlier.

Sure enough, she met him halfway down the steps leading up to her floor. At his quizzical look, she said, "Tiffany's still in bed. I didn't want to wake her up."

More to the point, she didn't want to answer any questions. Kate had already gone to work the breakfast shift at the diner, but a knock from Bret might be just enough to rouse Tiffany, who had the late shift, in time to provoke some unwanted curiosity. She'd told her roommates she was going to "a work thing," trying to make it sound as tedious as she could.

It *was* a work thing, after all. Nothing to get excited about, other than the chance to see Dr. Macias again. Chloe had admired her in college—a woman in her mid-forties with a PhD, who'd challenged Chloe to work so much harder than she'd been required to do in high school.

That was why she was giving up her Saturday. It had

nothing to do with a man who, a couple of weeks ago, had been her nemesis. So she'd dressed much the same way she would for a typical day at the office. Okay, the blue silk blouse she wore under her sweater was a favorite, but they'd been having warmer temperatures lately. And Barstow *was* in the High Desert.

Bret, who'd gone back to his trusty gray blazer, nodded at the two cups in her hands. "Is one of those for me?"

"No. I'm a two-fisted drinker."

For half a second he hesitated. Chloe couldn't hold back her grin. *Gotcha, Mr. Deadpan.* She handed him one of the coffees. "Leaded. Lots of cream."

"Perfect. Thanks."

She figured Bret wouldn't turn down caffeine. For her, it was essential. She was perennially behind on sleep these days.

He took the cup and led her to the curb, where a vintage black Mustang convertible waited. Chloe couldn't conceal her surprise.

"I didn't know this was yours," she said as he pulled the passenger door open for her.

He lifted an eyebrow, but didn't comment. She supposed it should have been fairly obvious. The employee lot was sparsely populated most mornings, but there were always *some* cars there. She just didn't know which ones belonged to the overnight crew and which belonged to early arrivals. The Mustang had caught her eye, but—well, it didn't seem like Bret's type of car. Sleek and sporty, it came from a time when cars were built for style and speed, instead of practicalities like fuel efficiency.

Inside, it was free of the type of clutter that littered most cars, her own included. No scraps of notes, no junk mail, no candy wrappers. *That* didn't surprise her.

He got in beside her, started the engine, and turned to her. At her puzzled look, he prompted: "Seat belt."

"Should I be worried?"

"No. Just a good habit. You never know."

"In my own car, I always do." In friends' cars, she'd found, the safety belts were usually stuck somewhere in the seat cushions, if she could find them at all. Not the case here. She clicked her seat belt into place and gave him a nod: *Proceed.*

Bret pulled away, and their unlikely adventure had begun. Within a minute, Chloe found herself racking her brains for words. What was it about being alone in a car with someone that magnified every silence? She fished through her mind for topics: *Nice weather we're having. Boy, your car sure is clean. So, how's that coffee?* If that was the best she could come up with, the two-hour drive would pass by in dog years.

Bret must have had the same feeling, because a couple of blocks into the drive down Evergreen Lane, he pressed a button on the car stereo. Crunchy electric guitars blared out at a volume that made Chloe jump. Immediately Bret hit another button, and the snarky rock was replaced by the drone of a commentator. National Public Radio, probably.

He turned the volume down and gave her an embarrassed glance. "Sorry."

"Don't be. Nobody's NPR all the time." She nodded at the console, intrigued. "What was that?"

"Weezer. They started out in the nineties—"

"Please." Chloe blew out a puff of air. "I know who Weezer is." Emboldened, not to mention curious, she pressed the button Bret had hit. The guitars returned. She listened a moment. "But I don't have this album."

"It's *Pinkerton*. Their second." He nodded at her feet. "There's a binder of CDs under your seat. If you like Weezer, you might like some of the other stuff, too."

Chloe reached down and fished out the folder. "I didn't think to bring CDs. I've got some music on my phone, though."

"This is a 1965 Mustang. It doesn't do MP3s."

"If you were being authentic, you'd have a cassette deck."

Bret shuddered. "Authentic is one thing. Cassettes are an abomination."

As they turned onto the highway leading out of town, Chloe flipped open the CD folder and felt a surge of delight. They had *overlap*. Not a hundred percent, but a lot. Bret's music had a surprising amount of bite: Green Day, Foo Fighters, Nirvana, Cage the Elephant, more Weezer. Holy cow, the Smiths. And, sure enough, the Beatles, a must in any breathing human being's music collection as far as Chloe was concerned.

The trip ahead suddenly looked a lot shorter.

"You have taste." She flipped another of the plastic sheets. And squinted her eyes at him. "Wait a minute. Bon Jovi?"

He colored faintly. "Guilty pleasure."

She thought of the songs on her phone. She actually had a playlist labeled JUNK FOOD. "My biggest guilty pleasure is the Knack."

165

"The Knack? I'm surprised. Some pretty sexist stuff there."

"Yeah, but it's good-natured. You can tell they're kidding."

He shook his head. "That might be wishful thinking. I'm not sure they were kidding. Guys take a little longer to grow up."

"How much longer?"

He flicked her a grin. "What time is it?"

She couldn't resist saying it. Maybe she'd had a little too much caffeine. "That's not what Sherry said."

She watched Bret for his reaction. The car may have veered slightly, but other than that, he only chuckled. "That was so long ago, hardly anyone remembers. Sherry and myself included, most of the time."

She watched Bret, but his eyes stayed on the road, making any reaction hard to detect. He wasn't easy to faze, but between the two, he'd probably been more disconcerted when she found the Bon Jovi CD. She persisted, "I've got to admit, I'm still trying to figure it out. You and Sherry? How did that even happen?"

Bret sighed. "I was a senior, she was a sophomore. She needed an English tutor, I was available."

"Okay. Still. I love Sherry, but what did you have in common?"

"Hard to say." Another shrug. "Who are you when you're seventeen? Think back. What kind of people did you have crushes on in high school?"

And suddenly Chloe's face felt hot. Quiet, brainy types. Often with glasses. "I take the Fifth Amendment."

Bret nodded in satisfaction. "I rest my case."

While Bret's eyes were on the road, Chloe stole a

look at him, careful not to turn her head much. It was hard to say what made a face handsome, aside from a certain symmetry of features. With Bret, she supposed it would be the firm line of his mouth, and those almost fierce dark eyes. But he was undeniably good-looking, and she didn't understand anyone who couldn't look past a pair of glasses to see that. To Chloe, the glasses only added.

Still, she doubted that any of the guys she'd secretly crushed on in high school had ever grown into a Bret. Like the more popular guys in her high school and college years, he didn't seem to care much about what other people thought. Not out of conceit, like the jocks she'd dated in her teens, but simply because he had more important things on his mind.

She returned her eyes to the windshield, before he could catch her staring, and shifted the topic. "Okay. One more question." She folded her arms. "What color is Sherry's hair, really? She always tells us she doesn't remember."

"Light brown. The facts are never as interesting as the mystery."

Chloe contemplated Bret's profile again. *I don't know about that,* she thought.

"Your turn," Bret said suddenly, without turning his head. "I'm still trying to figure out you and volleyball."

"I told you. It's competitive, and I was good at it. What's to figure?"

"I'm not sure. It's either too obvious or not obvious enough. It seems like you'd avoid the expected. You *look* like a volleyball player. Except—"

She waited.

He said, tentatively, "Aren't you a little short?"

She laughed. "That's what the other teams thought, too. Every game, they'd start out aiming the ball at me. And I'd ram it down their throats."

Bret laughed. "Okay. Now I get it."

"I don't like being underestimated. But I *love* fighting back." She grinned, glad he understood. "Plus, it was something my dad could get into. My brothers had their sports, and I was off in my room writing. You can't exactly cheer a writer."

"Hmm." Bret glanced at her again.

"My dad's a bright guy," she added. "He's been a supervisor at the cable company for nearly thirty years. He just relates to things that are more—external."

Bret nodded. "Got it. My dad owes your dad a debt of gratitude, by the way. The TV's almost never off at his house. He leaves it on for the news." He paused. "And the noise."

Conversation paused, and Bret turned up the Weezer CD.

As they wound their way down the mountain, the pine trees grew more sparse. An hour later, they were passing through bona fide desert, with yucca plants and scrubby-looking dry trees, punctuated by suburbs. Victorville even had a mall, and Tall Pine didn't. As signs of civilization thinned out again, Chloe frowned. "I wonder why they decided to have the awards way out here."

"Two reasons I can think of. The event is at the Harvey House. It's a historical landmark, about a hundred years old."

"What's the other reason?"

Bret grinned knowingly. "It's only two and a half hours from Las Vegas. On a Saturday afternoon, I'll bet they figured a lot of people might keep going and make a weekend of it."

"Sin City, huh?"

"You've got it." Bret ejected the current CD from the player. "Could you grab the Foo Fighters, please?"

"Sure." Chloe pulled out the disc and put it in the player.

Eyes on the vacant stretch of road in front of him, he said, "This is the part of the drive I enjoy the most."

Chloe didn't see anything but blue skies, dry brush, and a ribbon of straight gray road. There weren't even any other vehicles in sight. "What's here?"

Bret advanced the CD a couple of tracks forward and slid a glance her way. "Absolutely nothing," he said.

He turned up the volume and stepped on the gas. The car surged forward while the music blared.

Chloe's heartbeat quickened at the sudden burst of speed. But there was, as Bret said, absolutely nothing in their way. Nothing but open road and soaring guitars as the Mustang opened up, smooth and sure, riding the dips and swells of the pavement. She loosened her hold on the door handle. Bret spared her one sly grin before returning his attention to the road.

For one song, the car sailed over the blacktop. When the next song started, Bret eased up on the gas, and they returned to normal highway speed. Seventy miles per hour felt slow by comparison.

"Now I know why you told me to fasten my seat belt," she said.

"No. That's for all the maniacs out there on the road."

"You're lucky we didn't get pulled over."

"Never had a ticket in my life," he said placidly.

Chloe frowned. Even in irresponsibility, Bret was carefully responsible. "There's something almost sad about that," she said.

"I don't know about that. I can't say I've ever lain awake at night because I have a clean driving record." A smile tickled at the corners of his lips, making her heart do those funny things it wasn't supposed to do. "Now, you. You strike me as someone who's talked her way out of a ticket or two in her life."

He looked at her just as she felt the temperature of her face rise again. "Maybe," she admitted.

"And how'd you get away with it?"

"My dad always taught me to call a policeman 'sir.'"

"Uh-huh. And maybe you made your eyes a little extra big?"

Her blush deepened. It was true. Although her father certainly hadn't taught her that.

"So you've been known to turn sexism to your advantage. Let's face it. If I tried that, the cop would have me hauled out in three seconds to search the car. Because he'd be sure I was up to no good."

"Talk about sexism. What if it was a she?"

"Mmm, I still don't think it would be smart for me to do the big-eye thing."

"Your point?"

"Nothing, I guess. Except that we grew up in different worlds. In my world, I had to get by on being a careful driver. So I'm careful about when I break the rules. Plus, I'm not interested in getting killed."

"That's something else most boys don't learn until they're about thirty."

"True."

They reached their destination ten minutes later, and Bret was almost sorry to get there. Being in the car with Chloe had felt like some sort of a safe zone—a desert oasis from real life. Away from other people, it had been easy to talk, even when it wasn't about anything important.

A vacation, he decided. That's what this was. At least, as close as he'd come to one in years, unless you counted taking time off for his dad's illnesses or repairs on the old house. Just for one day—or for several hours of it, anyway—not to be the boss or the reporter, the caretaker or the caregiver. To enjoy the way Chloe's eyes devoured the arches and bricks of the old Spanish-style building before they even stepped out of the car.

Not everyone got excited about twentieth-century historical sites, but as they walked toward the entrance of the Harvey House, Chloe grabbed her phone and started taking pictures.

"What is this place?" Ignoring the brisk wind, she stopped for another shot of the row of arches in front of the long two-story building.

"It was a hotel and restaurant for people traveling by train. There were a bunch of Harvey Houses in the late 1800s, early 1900s, when we were still settling the West. It's still a working train station."

Chloe's camera phone swung to include the railroad tracks that stretched behind the building.

She was equally enthused about the lobby—inevitably decorated for the holidays, with wreaths, garland, and a Christmas tree in the corner. Bret watched as she took in the period décor with her eyes, then documented it voraciously on her phone: the copper chandeliers overhead, the gleaming wood of the reception counter, the stairs leading to the second floor. "Can we go up?"

"Sure. It's not roped off."

Chloe started up ahead of him, her light steps taking the stairs at an impressive clip, while Bret followed at a more leisurely pace. He'd been here before; this time around, the real sight was Chloe's reaction to the charm of the place. The stairs made a ninety-degree turn at the halfway point; before she started up the second flight, Chloe turned around to photograph the Christmas tree in the lobby from her new vantage point. Still on the first flight of stairs, Bret stopped his own climb just to watch her. The phone covered half her face, but it couldn't completely obscure her smile.

She shifted, aiming her phone's camera again, and the flash hit his eyes. Bret flinched inwardly. He hated to be photographed.

"I'd better not be in that picture." His words sounded more abrupt than he intended.

Her smile dimmed as she lowered her phone. A guarded look returned to her eyes, one he hadn't seen since they left Tall Pine.

No. Not here. This day wouldn't last long, and he didn't want anything to disrupt it.

"You might break the camera," he amended lightly. He resumed his progress up the stairs to join her. Chloe's expression lightened again.

They continued up the stairs and down the hallway, peering into the roped-off rooms. They'd re-created the former stationmaster's suite with an office that included a vintage typewriter, and a bedroom with its original furniture. A plaque on the wall boasted that the bathroom included a tub reportedly used by Winston Churchill on a 1929 visit, but to Chloe's great disappointment, they couldn't see it from their side of the velvet rope.

They returned to the hallway and stopped at the landing that led back to the stairs. Her camera temporarily at rest, Chloe leaned her folded arms on the railing and looked down at the heads of reporters arriving for the luncheon.

She smiled at Bret. "Look. Those people down there look like . . . slightly smaller people."

Bret leaned his elbows on the railing alongside hers. "Think they'd like it if we tossed down breadcrumbs? Like ducks?"

It earned him a chuckle. And he wondered if, like him, Chloe felt a little reluctant to join the crowd.

"You've been here before?" she asked.

"The Harvey House? Sure. I like history, and I love obscure tourism."

"This place is amazing." There it was again—that unguarded smile. "But I meant the luncheon. Have you been to one of these before?"

"A couple of times."

"Are you up for an award?"

He hadn't thought to mention it. "I—yes." He felt his face redden. "A story I did last spring on school test

173

scores in Tall Pine, and why our students do better than the rest of San Bernardino County. It won't win."

"You don't know that."

He shook his head. That had sounded like a poor-me statement, or some kind of bid for reassurance. "Sorry, I wasn't fishing. Just stating a fact. It's not the right kind of story. You've heard the expression, 'If it bleeds, it leads'?"

Chloe nodded.

"Well, it's up against stories about gang wars in San Bernardino and the murder rate in Victorville. Those are just more—relevant."

Her smile gone, she was studying him closely. Too closely.

Bret sighed. "I joke about it, but you know I don't really want bad things to happen, right? It's just that they do, and it's important to write about them. Tall Pine is a great place to live, which makes it an awful place to write about."

So why are you still there? He could see the inevitable question forming. To circumvent it, he looked down at the thinning group of people filing toward the ballroom below. "We'd better get down there and find our seats."

As they turned away from the rail, he resisted an unexpected impulse to rest a hand on the small of her back. This vacation had unspoken rules, and he doubted Chloe was even aware of them. Today was his chance to enjoy being with her from a respectable distance, and maybe even pretend there was potential for something more. Just pretend. As long as he didn't cross the line to try to make it a reality.

174

Although where that line was, and how close he could come to crossing it, was getting harder to tell.

At the entrance to the ballroom where the luncheon was being held, a beige-haired woman behind a table took Bret's tickets in exchange for two adhesive name tags. Chloe grinned as she jotted her name on her tag with one of the black marking pens provided. "I always have the urge to write, 'If lost, return to 325 Hilltop Road.'"

She slapped the tag just below the light blue shoulder of her blouse. Bret, who'd been known to quietly disregard name tags, reluctantly followed suit. They continued into the banquet room, which was filled with reporters, about half of them seated while the others stood chatting in clusters.

"You're right," he said. "It looks like a luggage tag convention."

The room was more than half male, and memories of the Christmas party earlier this week surfaced in his mind. Bret wasn't anxious to deal with predators of either the executive or the Mike-from-the-press-room variety. He was glad when Chloe opted to look for seats right away, and he was equally pleased when she chose a seat next to a woman with a smart-looking gray pageboy haircut. Bret sat at her other side, figuring he'd precluded any wolf attacks.

That was, until a twentysomething guy with eager blue eyes and a snappy red tie landed directly across from Chloe. His name tag proclaimed that he was Tyler Shepperton from the *San Bernardino Sun*.

It seemed to Bret that he'd met a lot of shallow, self-serving guys named Tyler.

"I'm Anne Rueland," the woman on Chloe's left said. "Are you two together?"

Chloe's mouth formed an appealing "o." Clearly she'd been caught off guard.

"We're both from the *Tall Pine Gazette,*" Bret said. If that left a little ambiguity, he didn't bother to clarify it. He nodded past Chloe. "I'm Bret. This is Chloe."

Anne nodded back, her gray eyes keen but kind. If she'd been looking for personal details, she took the hint and let it go. "It's nice to meet you both. I'm with the *Mount Douglas Herald.*"

For some people in Tall Pine, mention of Mount Douglas—the bigger town up the mountain with enough regular snowfall to warrant a ski resort—brought out a sense of rivalry. Chloe only smiled.

"So we're neighbors," Chloe said. "I think you probably win the award for longest distance traveled."

While Chloe made small talk with their new friend, Bret noticed the kid across the table—sorry, you weren't a man until you needed to shave more than twice a week—kept eyeing Chloe. She had to be aware of it. But as beverages were served and conversation spread over the rest of the table, Bret noticed something else: the way Chloe managed to acknowledge Tyler Shepperton while limiting eye contact with him. Bret thought again of the Christmas party. It must be a constant for her, contending with male attention, whether it was from executives, coworkers, or the occasional traffic cop.

Traffic cops aside, it shouldn't be part of her job to deal

with admirers diplomatically. He needed to remember that, before he became part of the problem.

But today, away from the office, he still wanted to pretend.

As Anne got involved in a discussion with a man from Victorville, comparing notes on their weather challenges, Chloe lowered her eyes from her latest admirer and started reading the program left at the side of her plate. Idly, Bret picked up his program as well. Chloe's former instructor was the only one shown with a photograph, but below that, there were brief biographies of the other two speakers as well.

Somewhere along the line, McCrea had sent them updated information that included Bret's bio. He hadn't expected that. He skimmed the paragraph: born in Tall Pine, graduated from Georgetown University in Washington, D.C. . . .

He turned his own program face down and glanced again at Chloe. He knew she'd seen it when her eyes widened.

"Bret." Lovely gray-green eyes stared at him. "You interned at the *Washington Post*?"

Her words fell into a conversational lull at the table, and suddenly all eyes were turned on him. He fought off a sense of discomfort. While Chloe was used to being looked at, Bret preferred to recede into the background, which served him well in his work as a reporter. When necessary, it made it easy to be a fly on the wall, to watch and listen and observe.

"The *Washington Post*?" Anne echoed, and of all the people at the table, he would have guessed she'd be

177

the hardest to impress. Tyler looked relatively blank, and Bret tried to decide if he was jealous or clueless.

"It's not as big a deal as it sounds," Bret said. "They have a couple of dozen students go through there every summer."

"But it has to be awfully competitive," Anne said.

"What was it like?" asked a woman on Tyler's left who'd been quiet up to this point.

He drew a breath. He definitely wasn't used to being the center of attention, not like this. And although he didn't look at her, he could feel Chloe staring at him with a million questions.

"Really exciting," he admitted. "And hard work. The place is intense."

"So you walked where Woodward and Bernstein walked," the man on Anne's left said. Maybe that would clue Tyler in.

For the next five minutes, Bret fielded questions, and though the answers weren't hard, he was surprised at how foreign it felt. He was used to being the one to ask the questions. And he was acutely aware of Chloe's eyes on him, and all the questions she wasn't asking. Not yet. But he knew she remembered their conversation that night at The Snowed Inn, and he'd be hearing from her later.

It had been the most dizzying, exciting time of Bret's life, until it all came to a crashing halt. In the town of Tall Pine, the *Washington Post* might as well be on the moon. He never talked about it.

At last the conversation turned toward the film version of *All the President's Men,* and Bret exhaled. By the time their food arrived, conversation had moved on to the quality of the chicken. Chloe delicately picked at her meal while Tyler Shepperton pelted her with questions about snow in Tall Pine.

Bret marveled at the way Chloe controlled the wattage of her smile. Polite, friendly, but not too encouraging. The way she had with Mike from the press room. The way she had with Lloyd Mossel, until she was leaving the building. Another thing she shouldn't have to do. And then, on her way out, she'd felt safe enough to let the full brightness of that smile shine through.

He didn't remember eating his chicken. And when it was time for him to speak before the first award was presented, he didn't remember what he said. Thank God for preparation. He knew some people were terrified of public speaking, but for Bret, that came much more easily than dealing with a table of six.

His speech must have been coherent, because there was a decent round of applause as he made his way back to their table. At least they hadn't fallen asleep. What Bret remembered was Chloe's face as she made room for him to return to his chair.

And her smile was bright.

Chapter 12

As she watched Bret deliver his speech, Chloe couldn't help feeling proud. No, *proud* wasn't the right word. *Proud* implied that she played some part in his accomplishments, and that certainly wasn't the case. A month ago, she hadn't even known him.

"Some people say local newspapers are dying out," he began. "I'd say they'd be very alarmed at the number of walking corpses here today." A light chuckle went through the room. "But there's a reason we're here, even though the *Los Angeles Times* has regional sections for the High Desert, and the mountain communities, and the inland valleys." His eyes traveled the room, landing on different tables by turns. "A reason why our neighbors usually say 'no' when they get a call from those Los Angeles telemarketers."

Impressed was a better word, she decided. Bret had never struck her as an extrovert. But he could hold a room, the way he had at the impromptu staff meeting the other day. When he talked, people listened.

"My editor said something my first year that's stuck with me ever since: you can only truly serve one community. Reporters from Los Angeles can get on the phone and learn the facts, but they don't experience *our* freezes, *our* wildfires, *our* heat waves. They don't have the firsthand understanding of what it means when a certain school principal retires, or a favorite store closes, or a new business comes to town. They can't. They're not omniscient, and they can't teleport." He shrugged. "They're still working on the app for that."

Another general chuckle. As Bret stood behind the podium, delivering his words with conviction, Chloe tried to decipher the latest piece in the jigsaw puzzle. He seemed to mean what he said. Yet he'd given every indication that he wasn't happy in Tall Pine, that he wanted to do something more important. She looked down at her program again. He'd told her he'd always wanted to work for a paper like the *Washington Post*. How could he have never mentioned that he'd interned there? The bio couldn't be wrong—he'd looked too embarrassed when it came up—but it didn't make sense.

". . . So, until teleportation becomes a reality, keep doing what you're doing. Know your hometown. Know your neighbors. And tell their stories. Thank you."

Chloe applauded with the rest as Bret made his way back to their table. Halfway across the room, his eyes fell on hers, and she smiled. She couldn't help it: *proud* was what she felt, whether she was entitled to or not, no matter how much he baffled her.

"That was very good," Anne said as he reclaimed his seat.

"You have a knack for public speaking," Chloe said. "Where did you pick it up?"

"High school debate team." Bret grinned. "I liked arguing."

The grin vanished in an instant, but she'd seen more of them today than she had in the month she'd known him.

When the waiter arrived a moment later with a coffeepot, Bret quietly slid the little pitcher of creamer toward Chloe. It didn't mean anything. It was just consideration. It would be easy enough for Bret to remember she loved creamer in her coffee, since he took his the same way. But on some adolescent level, it touched her.

No crushing on the boss, she reminded herself. But Bret didn't feel like the boss today. He felt like—

She picked up her cup with both hands and closed her eyes as she took a sip, willing the caffeine to work its magic. And bring her back to her senses in the bargain.

The coffee had arrived in the nick of time. It kept her going through the next speaker, a Columbia graduate from a paper in Riverside who wasn't half as interesting, or succinct, as Bret. Then it was time for Dr. Macias to speak. She delivered her message with the same incisive wit Chloe remembered from the classroom.

Bret turned to her as they applauded at the end. "And you *didn't* take her journalism class?"

Chloe shook her head. "I don't know what I was thinking."

Even after only two and a half years, college seemed so long ago. And she hadn't seen Dr. Macias since her freshman year. She'd taken a position at another college after Chloe's freshman year. Dr. Macias might not even remember her. But chickening out wasn't an option. Seeing her old professor had been the whole rationale for her trip to this luncheon.

So, after the awards—true to his prediction, Bret didn't win—she stood with Bret in the small ring of people waiting to talk to the keynote speaker.

Dr. Macias finished a conversation with a blue-suited man and turned in Chloe's direction. A faintly puzzled frown formed over her eyes, nearly as sharp and dark as Bret's, and then her brows lifted in surprised recognition.

"Chloe!" She grabbed Chloe by the shoulders. "How are you? What are you up to?"

Chloe felt her cheeks flush as Dr. Macias released her. "I'm writing for the *Tall Pine Gazette*."

"Oh, you came around. I'm so glad." She looked past Chloe to Bret. "This girl was so smart. The last thing she needed was freshman composition, but it was a requirement. Her essays were wonderful. I kept after her to take journalism from me second semester. . . ." Returning her eyes to Chloe, Dr. Macias shook her head in a mock-scolding gesture.

Bret nodded. "She's written some great features for us."

Chloe didn't know if she wanted to melt into the floor or sail around the room like an escaped balloon. Then she remembered her manners. "Dr. Macias, this is Bret Radner, my editor."

"Acting editor," Bret put in, shaking Dr. Macias's hand.

"Elizabeth," she said to Chloe. "We're not in school anymore." Then, to Bret, "Your speech was terrific."

"Thanks. Yours, too."

Standing beside Bret as they chatted, Chloe remembered the question that only Anne Rueland had put into words: *Are you together?* They'd gotten curious glances quite a few times today, and Chloe could sense the speculation. In a roomful of people she didn't know, it hadn't bothered her much. In Tall Pine, it would have bothered her a lot. She'd gotten the job on her merits, and she didn't want anyone to think otherwise.

Not anyone that mattered, anyway.

She doubted Dr. Macias would think that about her. But when Chloe caught herself leaning slightly in Bret's direction, she shifted her weight to lean the other way.

Out in the parking lot, Bret opened the passenger door for Chloe. "I'm not sure she remembered you," he deadpanned, then got in on his side.

Chloe chuckled, resting her head back on the seat. The conversation with Elizabeth had been a wonderful capper for the luncheon. "Thanks for the nice things you said."

"Nothing that wasn't true." Bret started the car. When it came to displaying reactions, he and Elizabeth were nearly exact opposites. But Chloe knew he meant it. He wasn't one to throw compliments around.

Not Monday through Friday, anyway.

They started down the highway while Green Day picked up where they left off on the stereo.

"She was right, you know," Bret said. "You're talented. If McCrea doesn't have a slot for you when he gets back, you really ought to look into applying at papers down the hill."

"Trying to get rid of me?" she said lightly, although his suggestion didn't make her feel light.

"Not at all. But I know you went out on a limb when

you took this as a temporary job. Just know that you're good enough to grow into something bigger."

Thinking of the battle she had producing enough stories per week for the *Gazette,* she bit her lip. Bret didn't know about her late nights on the couch, hammering out first drafts to give her a head start on the next day.

"You will have one hurdle," Bret said.

Or maybe he did know?

"You need to be prepared for the fact that eventually, you'll have to say something bad about someone."

He had a point there. She'd written about painful subjects, but she'd always been on the side of anyone she'd interviewed. "You've never written anything bad about anyone in Tall Pine?"

"You've got to admit, we're pretty light on scandal. The biggest controversy that ever broke, I never wrote a word of."

"What was it?"

"Oh, nothing much. Just the time Winston Frazier was accused of embezzling town funds."

"What?"

Bret nodded. "About five years ago, one of the town employees came to me. He'd discovered a five-hundred-dollar shortage in city funds. They traced it down to a cash contribution from a couple months before. The last person to handle the money was Winston." He shrugged. "I didn't buy it. For one thing, I didn't think he'd be stupid enough to pocket five hundred dollars cash. But I've known Winston all my life. He and my dad are good friends, so I was too close to the story. I can interview Winston about day-to-day town business, but not something like criminal charges.

I took the information, gave it to McCrea, and he assigned it to someone else. Bella Graham. You're using her old desk. Well, McCrea told her to proceed with extreme caution. The article did run, a few inches at the bottom of the front page. But needless to say, people saw it, and needless to say, Winston was pretty riled."

"She gave him an opportunity to comment, right?"

"Of course." Bret fought a smile. "I didn't think even Winston used the word 'balderdash' anymore. But the town had to investigate, which meant a couple more articles."

He shifted his grip on the steering wheel. "Fast-forward about a week. Another town employee comes to me after hours. Me, again. And this one was in tears. Because *she* found the envelope of money between two folders in a stack she hadn't filed yet. She was going through a divorce at the time, and she was pretty distracted. So." He pinched the bridge of his nose. "You know how reporters are protected from having to reveal their sources? I went to McCrea. I didn't tell him who I talked to. And we agreed that we could run a story that completely exonerated Winston. And Bella reported the missing funds as a 'clerical error,' which, of course, it was."

"You don't think the woman stole the money and decided to—"

Bret shook his head. "No doubt in my mind. She was a wreck. But she was ready to face the firing squad. As it was—well, Winston knew what really happened, and he's not the world's most agreeable guy. Let's just say she found another job in town pretty quick. And that's the untold story of Tall Pine's biggest scandal."

"And the moral of the story is . . ."

"Tall Pine is a community," he said. "We have to stand behind what we report, but we also have to live alongside the people we report about. The story did Winston a lot of damage—short-term, because cantankerous as he can be, he really is a decent person, and he's lived here all his life. We had a chance to hurt someone else's reputation—another well-meaning, competent person. I didn't see any point in that, and McCrea agreed with me." He took a deep breath and blew it out. "Also, if you tell anyone else even that much, I'll have to kill you."

"Even McCrea doesn't know who she was?"

"Oh, he probably figured it out. You could, too, if you dug around enough. But again, no point. A nice person made a mistake she wasn't even aware of. That's not how they handle things in the big city, but there you go." A smile touched his lips. "And remember, you're sworn to secrecy. Because I really don't want to kill you."

She raised her eyebrows. "I think that's the nicest thing you've ever said to me."

She sat in silence for a moment, digesting Bret's story. And realized that he'd distracted her from the question she'd been meaning to ask him for the past few hours.

"Bret?" she asked. "What are you doing in Tall Pine?"

"Writing news stories. Remember? We just went to a whole big luncheon about it."

"Right. But if you think I could get a job in San

187

Bernardino—" She folded her arms. "Don't play dumb. You interned at the *Washington Post,* for heaven's sake."

"A lot of students intern there. You have no idea how huge that place is. It's hardly a guarantee of employment."

"Still. With that on your résumé, I'm sure you could have gotten on a paper in a major city."

His eyes were on the road, his mouth set in a firm line that discouraged further questions. Chloe's mind reeled with wild theories, each one more improbable than the last. He'd punched a senator. He'd gotten the president's daughter pregnant. He'd driven into a fountain in front of the Capitol. She was tempted to reel them off, just for laughs, but if any one of them was anywhere close to the truth, she'd hate to be sitting in this seat.

She tried for a direct approach instead. "You were so close," she said. "It was what you always wanted. How did you end up back in Tall Pine?"

After a moment's silence, his answer came, brief and clipped: "Life intervened."

She studied him as the desert scenery slid past the driver's-side window. The light was starting to take on the faintly gold color of late afternoon. His profile remained unmoving, like someone modeling to be the next face engraved on the nickel.

Then he turned toward her. "You know what?" he said. "We're wasting our last few perfectly good miles of *nothing*. Want a turn?"

She tried to follow his change of subject. "You mean, drive?"

Without a word, he pulled the Mustang to the shoulder of the road. Letting the car idle, he turned to face her. "One song. Your pick."

A faint smile teased at the edges of his mouth, but she tried like hell to read his eyes. They glittered with something she couldn't name. A challenge? A dare? Or just a warning that the previous subject was closed?

She couldn't read his eyes, so she went with the smile. "You've got it."

Stepping out of the car into the cold desert wind, they traded places. Chloe slid the car's front seat forward so she could reach the pedals, then fastened the safety belt before Bret felt compelled to remind her. The car felt different from the driver's side. Even in neutral, it felt more powerful than her little white compact. She curled her hands around the wheel in the ten-and-two position and turned to Bret, who sat beside her. With his safety belt fastened.

"The Killers, please," she said. "Track five."

While Bret obliged with the CD, Chloe pulled back onto the blacktop. The guitars kicked in, and she pressed down on the pedal.

The car shot forward, and she saw Bret clutch the door handle.

By the time his Mustang started the climb up the hill to Tall Pine, the light was fading from the sky.

Bret slowed the car as required for the winding switchback curves, but that wasn't the only reason he wasn't in a hurry. Earlier today, when the road stretched out wide and straight in front of them, the world had seemed filled with possibility. As the road narrowed, it felt as if the possibilities narrowed, too.

His vacation was coming to an end.

Coldplay music filled the car—Chloe's choice, a suitably gentle note for a day that was winding down. He glanced over at her in time to see her head drop slowly forward, then bob quickly back up again.

She darted a look at Bret and sipped her soda. "Almost home," she said.

Why was it such a universal reflex for people to deny they'd been falling asleep? It was a silly thing, but somehow endearing.

She'd picked up the soda when they stopped at a gas station halfway home. Bret wondered if she'd seen through the fact that the stop had been completely unnecessary. No one really *needed* a break halfway through a two-hour drive, not when the car had more than enough gas to get back to Tall Pine. But Chloe hadn't questioned it.

Maybe she didn't want the day to end, either.

It was after five o'clock. Suggesting dinner somewhere would certainly be an option. Except that once they reached Tall Pine, the game was over, and the possibilities ended. Dinner together in public would be the perfect fuel for the gossip mill.

No, once they got home, he'd go back to being her boss again.

Bret rounded another of the familiar tight hairpin turns and glanced over again as Chloe swayed, her eyes half-lidded. He'd seen her down a soda and four cups of coffee today, three of those after lunch. She must not be getting enough sleep. Not that it was any of his business.

After one more switchback, Bret turned onto the

main highway back to Tall Pine. Within a few more minutes, the road straightened, and they turned onto Evergreen Lane, which led through town to the residential area.

Evergreen Lane, with all its Christmas lights. They circled around light poles, stretched across buildings' rafters, and lined store windows. Several arches of lights stretched above the street from one side to the other: one with bells in the center, another with candy canes, another with a rather dazzling silver Christmas star.

Chloe looked fully awake now. "I think it gets prettier every year."

Bret doubted there was really any change in the lights from year to year, but then, he did his best to avoid the shopping section of Evergreen Lane during the holidays. He sneaked a look at Chloe as they passed under the silver star. He knew she'd been tired, but an unconscious smile touched her lips, and her eyes sparkled. Bret found room to hope that all her associations with Christmas stayed happy.

They turned up into the hills. Chloe's apartment complex—all right, the only apartment complex in Tall Pine—was a block off Evergreen Lane, just past the recreation center.

Bret parked at the curb and got out to walk her to her door, ignoring Chloe's protests that he didn't have to do that. He might be a lot of things, but he wasn't the kind of guy who'd let a woman out to walk to her door alone in the dark. There wasn't enough feminism in the world to convince him that would be civilized.

He followed a step behind Chloe as she led him up the slate stairway where she'd met him this morning, so many hours ago. Familiarity assailed him as they walked past one door after another, all of them painted a deep green. Evergreen, of course.

"I had one of these," he said, feeling a sudden urge to keep talking.

"You did?" Chloe stopped in front of a door and reached into her purse to fish out her keys.

He nodded. "Mine was downstairs."

"I think they're kind of a rite of passage around here when you move out of your parents' house."

"Something like that."

She hadn't put her keys in the door. And Bret became aware that his pulse had started racing.

It was a classic scenario, and he suspected Chloe realized it, too. He didn't feel like an editor and an employee. He felt like a boy walking a girl home after a first date. Her door didn't face the street. No one would see. Except that he was her boss again and he needed to start remembering that.

No matter how tempting it was to pretend he wasn't, just for a few more minutes.

Professional ethics, he reminded himself, and took half a step back. Just half a step. "Thanks for coming," he said. "Today would have been just an obligation for me. You made it a lot better."

Chloe's face softened into a smile, and God help him, it was one of *those* smiles, its glow soft and genuine. "Thank *you*," she said. "I had a wonderful time."

She hesitated a fraction of a second. Then she stepped toward the door, and Bret turned to go. Mission accomplished. He'd gotten through the day without crossing the boundaries, professional ethics intact. And doing the right thing had never felt so stupid.

A voice in his head said, *Screw professional ethics.*

The moment was almost gone and it would never be here again, so before it was over, before he could stop himself, before Chloe could get her keys in the door, he wheeled around, pulled her into his arms, and kissed her.

Chloe stiffened, and for a millisecond Bret was sure he was going to get his face slapped.

Then he felt her relax, and her arms, caught awkwardly between them, worked free, tracing their way up his shoulders to wrap around his neck. Her head tilted, angling so their lips connected fully, and then she was kissing him back. He drew her closer, tunneling his fingers into the soft tumble of her hair. Her lips parted to his.

He felt lightheaded, almost dizzy, as he deepened the kiss, his fingers curling lightly around the tendrils of her hair. His other arm encircled her waist, pressing her closer, and for a moment he went for broke, kissing her with everything he had.

And now that he knew he wasn't going to get his face slapped, he slowed down to take his time and do it right. The outside world simply ceased to exist. There was only Chloe, warm in his embrace, as her lips responded to his.

Chloe wound her arms around Bret's neck, trusting him to hold her up. Because she was pretty sure her knees didn't work anymore.

She'd kissed a few men in her day, although granted, not in quite a while. But she would have remembered if it had ever been anywhere near this intense. At first his kiss was urgent, almost fierce. Then it grew softer, and that was even more devastating. The longer he held her, the slower their kisses got. And the faster her heart beat.

This entire day, and the weeks before it, had all been leading up to this. It felt so wonderfully inevitable.

Gradually, something intruded at the edge of her mind, like the distant sound of her clock radio's persistent beeping when she surfaced from a deep sleep and realized it had been going off for several minutes.

Bret was her boss. And she was a fool to forget it. If she wanted people to take her seriously, this wasn't the way to do it. She had to have a little self-control.

Or, in this case, a *lot* of self-control.

If Dr. Macias could see her *now*—

That woke her up. With sheer force of will, she slid her hands back down where they'd started when they were pinned between her and Bret. She pushed back, and Bret broke the kiss. She steadied herself, forcing her eyes to focus.

"Bret." It was hard to speak. "We can't do this." She paused, trying to find words to formulate the reasons. She looked up at him. That didn't help. Under the apartment's dim porch lamp, his eyes were fathomlessly dark. She closed her eyes, drew a deep breath, and tried to draw in some common sense along with it. "You're my boss," she said. Could he possibly understand? "Neither of us would look good. But I'd look worse."

His arms had loosened around her, but he hadn't let

go. He gazed down at her in the weak illumination from the porch light.

"You're right." He didn't pull back. Instead, with the outer edge of one finger, he traced a line from the tip of her chin to her jawline, never taking his eyes from hers. If he kept doing that—just looking at her that way, just touching her with one finger—she was a goner. Pushing him away the first time had taken all the willpower she had.

Then Bret took a step back, and the cold air seemed to rush in between them, like an unwelcome third party. He straightened almost imperceptibly, squaring his shoulders and taking on the taut posture she saw every day at work. In seconds, he changed back into the Bret she knew from the office.

"It never happened." His tone was so neutral, so convincing, she almost believed him.

While Chloe steadied herself with a hand on the doorknob, Bret stepped back again. "Have a good night."

He turned and walked away, his steps brisk but not rushed, while Chloe stared after him, her lips still warm, her heart still hammering.

Chapter 13

Chloe stepped into the apartment and shut the door firmly behind her, taking care not to show how hard it was to walk a straight line.

What had *happened* out there?

Bret was gone and the apartment was dark, so she was putting on her show of steadiness for no one. Still wobbly, Chloe reached for the light switch. In that fraction of a moment, she wondered why the scent of pine should hit her so strongly after just a few hours of being in Barstow, and why the smell seemed stronger inside. Then the lights came on, and she had her answer.

A humble Christmas tree stood in front of the drawn curtains, decked out in the oddball conglomeration of ornaments she and her roommates had pooled from their families' old tree decorations.

Kate and Tiffany had gotten the tree without her. She batted away a childish disappointment at missing out on the ritual. When did they all have time to get the tree together, anyway? December was already nearly halfway over, and it was darned rare for all three of them to be together these days.

Chloe crossed over to the tree and bent to plug in the lights. The multicolored bulbs winked on, and she went back to the entryway to turn off the living room light again. The tree glowed brighter in the darkened room, and the cast-off ornaments looked a little better, too.

She sat on the couch and hugged a well-worn throw pillow to her chest as she stared at the tree.

Spend the day with Bret, you said. It will be fun, you said.

And it had been, up to and including those last few wonderful minutes, before she did what she had to do and put a stop to it.

Now her job would be a bigger train wreck than it had ever been, and she'd probably lost a budding friendship in the bargain.

Chloe scrunched the pillow harder. This day had had a warning label written all over it. She'd known it and she'd ignored it. Obviously, she and Bret weren't meant to be just friends, at least not if they were going to spend hours and hours alone together.

Or maybe he'd just grabbed her in an impulsive moment and was already wondering what in the world had gotten into him. Despite the blow to her pride, in a way, that would be better. That way, they could shrug it off and get back to business as usual.

Yeah, right.

Even if Bret could shrug it off—could she?

She watched the colored lights go blurry in front of her eyes. It didn't count as crying as long as she blinked before—

"Hey! Is that—"

Startled, Chloe squealed, jumped up, and spun around. Kate, startled by Chloe's shriek, shrieked back.

Her roommate stood in the doorway to the hall in purple sweats, hair rumpled. Down the hall behind her, a dim light showed from the now-open bedroom door.

"What are you doing here in the dark?" Chloe panted.

"I took a nap. It wasn't dark when I went to lie down. What are *you* doing in the dark?"

Chloe nodded toward the faint glow of their little tree. "It's not dark. I turned the tree on."

"Close enough." Kate walked over and snapped on the living room light. "You're squeezing the stuffing out of that pillow."

Chloe looked down and saw white fluff oozing from one of the pillow's tired seams. She poked it back in. "It's been doing that for a while."

She wondered if her mascara was running. Probably not, because Kate didn't appear to notice.

"How do you like the tree?" Kate asked. "We had a couple hours between the time I got home and Tiff went to work, so we decided to grab it."

Chloe contemplated the tree again. It was a little shorter than her own five-two, and with their second-hand ornaments, it definitely looked better in the dark, but . . .

She found a smile. "It looks great."

"Tiff saved some of your decorations for you to hang up." Kate nodded toward the coffee table, where a few of Chloe's favorites from home lay scattered.

Tiffany would think of that. Of course neither of them had meant to leave Chloe out. They probably even thought they were doing her a favor by surprising her with a decorated tree.

"Thanks." Chloe was tempted to hug her, but Kate wasn't the type to hug unless someone was crying or bleeding, and she had no intention of crying in front of Kate. Or admitting how badly she needed a hug. She dropped the world-weary pillow back on the couch before she squeezed any more life out of it.

"How was your thing?" Kate asked.

"Oh . . ." Chloe rejoined the pillow on the couch, feeling equally limp and worn out. "It was okay. Kind of a long day."

Liar, liar . . .

"That guy's working you like a dog." Kate passed into the kitchen, and Chloe heard the refrigerator door open. After a brief moment of assessment, the door closed again. Kate called, "Want to go out somewhere and get a bite?"

Chloe felt a weak smile pull at her lips, but at least she didn't have to force it this time. Going out to eat was one reason they never got around to springing for new throw pillows or Christmas ornaments. That, and the fact that this apartment was a way station.

"Well?" Kate returned to the kitchen doorway. "We could go hassle Tiffany. Make her run back and forth with special orders."

Chloe's smile widened in spite of herself. "You're mean."

"I was kidding. We can be nice."

"You go ahead. I'm wiped out."

"You sure?" Kate cocked a hand on her hip. She was nowhere near as intuitive as Tiffany, but Chloe squirmed a little under her examination, hoping again that her mascara hadn't smudged while she sat on the couch feeling sorry for herself.

Spending some time with her friends would be nice. She missed them, and it might get her mind off . . . things. But it would also mean keeping her smile in place, unless the mask cracked and she ended up spilling way more about Bret than she intended to tell. She didn't want to do that. She felt foolish enough as it was. Truthfully, she wasn't sure exactly *what* she felt. She needed some time alone to process.

Or maybe wallow.

"Not tonight." Chloe nodded toward the coffee table. "I'll stay here and hang my ornaments."

"That'll take about sixty seconds." Not one to over-examine, Kate started toward the bedroom to change. "I could bring you something back. What kind of pie do you want?"

All right, Kate had some intuition after all.

"Banana, if they've got it. No, wait." Chloe reconsidered. "Pecan."

After all, it was Christmastime.

Bret hit the ball sharply to the left, and Jake Wyndham raced across the racquetball court to hit it. Too late. The ball hit the floor a second time as Jake crashed into the wall.

Jake let out a sigh of defeat and slouched against the wall to catch his breath. The ball bounced near his feet, unheeded. That had been game point.

Bret saw fit not to gloat. Instead, he asked, "One more?"

"No, thanks. I don't think Mandy wants to be a young widow." Racquet still in hand, Jake brushed damp brown hair off his forehead with the back of his wrist. He gave a wry grin. "Have you got any pent-up anger issues?"

Bret kept his expression carefully neutral. "Not that I know of."

Bret bent and scooped up the ball with his racquet, bounced it on the mesh, and caught it in his hand. Like Jake, he was out of breath, but he felt better. A wonderful thing, adrenaline.

He'd been climbing the walls since last night. He couldn't get those last moments with Chloe out of his mind, and he needed to. He'd started something he couldn't finish, couldn't even pursue to page two, and he had to vent somehow. So this afternoon, he'd called Jake and challenged him to a round of racquetball at the community center. They'd only played a few times before, and Jake always trounced Bret soundly.

Not today.

Jake crossed the room to the opposite corner, where his towel and water bottle waited.

He slid down the wall, sat on the varnished floorboards, and took a long drink from his bottle. Bret joined Jake and picked up his own water, but didn't sit down as he drank.

"Thanks for getting away," Bret said. "I'll bet the hotel is crazy busy."

"Can't complain." Jake rested the back of his head against the wall, eyes closed, but his tone held a note of satisfaction. He'd started up the hotel less than two years ago on a wing and a prayer, and Bret knew garnering support from the town hadn't been easy. Jake cracked one eye open again. "What about you? Why the sudden urge to be athletic?"

Bret shrugged. "Just feeling competitive, I guess."

"I'm competitive. Today you're lethal," Jake said. Both eyes were open now. "Sure there's nothing up with you?"

That was the trouble with Jake. Too perceptive.

Bret bounced the ball with the racquet. "If there was I'd write to Dear Abby."

He heard the terseness in his own voice as Jake's expression shuttered faintly. It was one thing to discourage prying. Being flat-out rude was another.

He didn't apologize, but he shifted to a friendly topic. "How's Mandy?"

Right choice. Jake's distant look vanished. After all, Mandy was his favorite subject. "Great. This is her time of year. Other people get stressed out, but she thrives on it."

Oh, right. To talk about Mandy led right into Christmas. Bret wondered how much Jake bought into the whole Santa-sighting thing, but he didn't ask. Jake had always struck him as a rational sort. Still, it did seem that people in Tall Pine tended to be more . . . fanciful these days.

Bret said, "She's doing a great job with that little coffee bar."

Jake nodded. "That went way beyond what either of us expected. Turns out she's got a real knack for hospitality. And since we brought Liv in to help with the business end, it's filled a lot of the gaps for both of us. Mandy can focus on what she does best, and the customers love her."

Jake's smile said the rest. Between all the visions of Christmastime and wedded bliss, Bret's satisfaction at kicking Jake's butt started to wane.

"It was nice seeing you at the Inn a few weeks ago," Jake added. "How'd you like the hot chocolate?"

They really had a thing about the hot chocolate there. "Good, especially considering I'm not a chocolate fan. I'm more of a coffee guy."

"Sorry about that. Mandy can be a little . . . persistent with her sales pitch."

"Like Joan of Arc with the English."

Jake chuckled. So Bret hadn't overstepped it on the snark that time.

Bret bounced the ball on his racquet as he felt that restlessness set in again. The game had been an unusual outlet, because he'd never tended to be very athletic. Jake had invited him to go for a run once, and Bret had tried it. After all, cardiovascular exercise was an idea he agreed with in principle. In practice, he'd found it to be the height of masochism. He supposed he liked to do his huffing and puffing with purpose. Even if it was only a game.

He bent to pick up the vinyl cover for his racquet and zipped it shut. He'd caught his breath, but his body still felt heated up from the workout. Jake was right; he needed to quit while he was ahead. The two games had been pretty high-octane for someone whose usual exercise didn't extend far beyond his typing fingers.

He needed to change that, and he knew it. Avoiding most of the known carcinogens wasn't enough.

Jake stood. "Glad you called me up," he said. "We ought to do this more often."

"Okay. I promise not to put you in the hospital next time. Today was a fluke."

Bret hoped so, anyway. If it meant getting his mind on a more even keel, he'd cheerfully go back to losing.

When he arrived for work Monday morning, Chloe's white sedan was already in the parking lot. She'd beaten him to the office.

Of course, today he'd dawdled.

It never happened. Bret repeated the words in his mind like a mantra as he pushed open the door of the newsroom.

Chloe stood at her desk, phone held awkwardly against her shoulder while she leaned over to scribble on a notepad. She'd obviously just walked in and caught the phone ringing. Her purse dangled on her shoulder, and she still wore her coat; underneath, he glimpsed a soft-looking sweater the color of butter.

She looked up when Bret walked in, and he saw recollection fill her eyes. He felt it all the way to the marrow of his bones.

Everything froze as their gazes locked. Quickly, Chloe shifted her attention back to her notepad. Her purse slid off her shoulder.

Bret recovered his stride, passed her with a nod, and went straight to the editor's office, closing the ineffectual glass door behind him.

It never happened, he reminded himself. *Shut it off. Keep it in. Forget it.*

He could do this. He'd been doing it, in one form or another, for the past seven years.

He sat behind McCrea's desk and turned on his computer. A moment later an e-mail came in from Chloe.

Had a call that there's a mountain lion stuck on one of the old power lines across from the pizza place. Ned's not in yet. Want me to check it out?

Chloe didn't always use e-mail for quick questions, but this was a day when technology was a blessing. Smart girl.

He typed his reply: Go for it. Thanks.

A moment later she was gone, without ever having taken off her coat. Bret fully exhaled for the first time and went to start the coffee.

By Tuesday afternoon, Chloe was ready to scream.

She had absolutely no grounds for complaint. Bret rarely emerged from his office, but that wasn't unusual. He'd bypassed their weekly story conference due to the mountain lion sighting first thing Monday morning, asking her to e-mail him a rundown of proposed stories instead. Perfectly reasonable. And whenever he had reason to speak to her, he was unfailingly polite.

The politeness ate away at her. You were *polite* to people you barely knew. But what killed her was the way he didn't look at her. At all. Not since his expression of dismay when their eyes locked first thing Monday morning. Now, when they talked, he focused on some point just over her shoulder, as if she were some kind of mythical creature who could turn him to stone if he looked at her directly.

It was one of those quiet afternoons, all three of them settled in to file their stories for tomorrow's edition. Bret left his office and passed by without a word, on some unspecified errand through the door that led to the photo department. Chloe ignored the way he ignored her and tried to concentrate on the story on her screen. She sipped her coffee. Stale coffee, when what she really wanted was an energy drink. And maybe a bottle of Jack Daniel's for the other hand. If only to get *some* kind of reaction out of Bret.

Grow up and get over it. If he could do the Vulcan thing, so could she. After all, she'd pushed *him* away, and she'd been right to do it. Now, if only she could get the sensory flashbacks to stop. Being kissed by Bret had been like a drink of water after a long drought. Except that a drink of water, as far as she recalled, had never made fire shoot out of her fingers and toes.

Where *had* he learned to kiss like that?

Sherry, maybe. At that thought, Chloe picked up a pen and flung it down on her desktop. It knocked over her paper clip holder and sent the little silver clips scattering.

"Hey." Chuck paused his typing to glance over his shoulder. "You interrupted my nap."

"Sorry." Chloe placed her fingertips over her eyelids and rubbed, trying not to smudge her makeup. "I'm just really tired of looking at that screen."

Her fingers helped to cool the scratchy feeling from

her eyes, and anything else that might be making them burn.

"Are you okay?" Chuck's voice came more clearly this time, and when she lowered her hands, he'd turned around to face her.

Now Mr. Switzerland was looking at her askance, and that absolutely wouldn't do.

"Just a little stir-crazy." Chloe stood to stretch, arching one arm over her head, then the other. At least Bret had been out of the room when she chucked the pen. She righted the paper clip holder and looked again at the story on her screen. All two and a half lines of it.

Instead of sitting down again, she grabbed her coat off the back of her chair. "Know what? I'm going to try a change of scenery. I'll be back."

She picked up the pad with the notes from her interview, another notepad for writing a rough draft—she'd long since given up on the briefcase—and left.

Bret returned from Ned's office to find Chloe's desk vacant, her screen blank. The blinking light on her monitor told him it had gone into sleep mode, rather than being turned off. So, most likely, she'd be back. After all, why wouldn't she be?

He took advantage of the moment to get a cup of coffee. He hadn't been drinking coffee as often lately, because doing so involved walking past Chloe's desk. It was like a divorce, and she got custody of the coffee maker.

Even without Bret's usual consumption, he found the pot less than half full. She was sure going through the stuff. Maybe she was one of those people with a natural immunity to caffeine. He remembered the way she'd nodded off next to him in the car, a somehow-intimate memory he should be trying to forget.

Aware of Chuck's presence a few feet away, Bret stirred in the powdered creamer and refrained from asking where Chloe was. But as he raised his cup, he thought about the way she always closed her eyes when she took that first drink of coffee, as if to savor the moment.

Bret took a sip. Hideous. The stuff must have been sitting there since first thing this morning, and conscientious Chloe hadn't wanted to waste a third of a pot by pouring it out.

Bret shuddered and started a new pot. "What we need is one of those pod coffee makers."

"Some people try getting some sleep at night," Chuck said dryly.

"That would be inefficient." What had he been doing last night? Oh, yeah. Tossing and turning. Right.

Bret leaned against the wall next to the brewer as the coffee started to trickle into the pot. He eyed Chuck with borderline suspicion. "You never drink coffee. That's not natural."

"I got out of the habit. My wife used to be Mormon."

Bret frowned. "Used to be, meaning . . ."

"Before we met. But she never did acquire a taste for coffee. So I . . . got out of the habit." His broad, loose shoulders shrugged. On the surface Chuck seemed unaffected. But his overly nonchalant attitude gave Bret the feeling he probably missed her. A lot.

It was unusual for Chuck to talk about his wife. Bret

knew that she'd died about four years ago, and that Chuck had moved to Tall Pine because he had an aunt up here who helped him with his two girls. Bret never brought it up, maybe out of tact.

Tact, schmact. He hadn't asked because he knew the story wasn't a happy one, and he hadn't wanted to risk dealing with it. The same way he never talked to anyone about his mother's death. Newcomers didn't need to know, and he'd just as soon longtime locals forgot. Or, at least, didn't remind him.

The coffee maker was taking its sweet time, though Bret knew from experience that it took exactly eight minutes to brew a pot. He decided he'd been out here long enough to make the question seem offhand. Casually, he asked, "Where'd Chloe go?"

"Somewhere else to write. She said she needed a change of scenery."

"I'll get her some postcards," Bret said. "Maybe that'll keep her at her desk."

The coffee trickled into the pot like sand into the bottom of an hourglass. It had been going for about four minutes, he estimated.

He heard Chuck's chair creak a bit. "By any chance could there be an elephant in the room here?"

Bret turned his head sharply. Chuck was leaning back as if he were on a lounge chair in the middle of summer.

"If there is it's going to stay muzzled," Bret said. "Or corralled. Or whatever it is they do with elephants."

"Okay, okay." Chuck raised both hands. "But *hypothetically*, I don't see anything wrong with two attractive, red-blooded kids—"

"Hypothetically, I'm her boss," Bret said. "And you have a vivid imagination," he added, half a beat too late.

"Is there some kind of law against it? Or a company policy?"

Chuck didn't look like the devil. But his line of conversation was appealing and persuasive. In the face of those simple questions, Bret's personal code of conduct seemed a little less . . . imperative.

But Chloe had pushed him away, and Chloe had her reasons. Good ones.

"If there's not a rule against it, there should be. A boss and an employee—there's nothing ethical about that."

"You're not the one who hired her. And I sure haven't seen any favoritism. If anything, you make things about five times harder on her than you need to."

"Tell that to the chamber of commerce." At Chuck's blank look, Bret shook his head. "Never mind. It's a moot point."

"Sounds like you've given it some thought."

First Jake, and now Chuck. What was this, get-in-touch-with-your-feelings week?

"Sounds like *you've* got too much time on your hands," Bret said.

Probably still about two minutes to go on the coffee. But he'd stood here long enough. He slid the pot out from under the stream of coffee, slipped his mug in its place, and poured in some coffee from the pot without letting any of it spill. The result would probably be just about as bitter and nasty as the pot he'd poured out, but he had work to do. And having Chuck play amateur Oprah Winfrey wasn't helping.

* * *

When Chloe left the Pine 'n' Dine at four, the afternoon had gone gray. She'd spent over an hour writing there and finally had a decent first draft to show for it. Not bad, considering that her pen had barely moved for the first twenty minutes. She'd been too busy composing mental discussions with Bret. Because she knew she had to go back to the office, and she was already dreading it.

The silent treatment had never been big in her family, and this was getting darned close to it. With all of Bret's distant civility, the office felt like a glacier, or a sensory deprivation tank. Almost as if she was being punished. She didn't think Bret meant it that way. But something had to change. She never thought she'd miss the days when he was just her professional nemesis. Looking back, it seemed so much easier.

Sherry hadn't been at the diner. Just as well. In her current frame of mind, Chloe was bound to ask too many of the wrong questions, and that could get embarrassing fast.

A light fog had settled over Evergreen Lane as Chloe started toward the public parking lot. It wasn't dark yet, but you couldn't call it daylight either. The Christmas lights had come on, and she wondered whether the grayness had triggered a sensor to turn them on, or a proactive human had hit a switch.

The colored lights against the gray-white mist had a strange beauty. Not quite gloomy, but—wistful? Melancholy? Unable to resist, Chloe backtracked half a block so she could turn around and capture more of the view with her phone's camera.

Pensive was the word, she decided. The foggy street matched her mood in an almost soothing way. She took a few more photos, longing to capture it, knowing that a flat rectangle could never quite re-create the feeling.

She lowered her phone to review the pictures. When she reached the end of the Evergreen Lane photos she kept going, thumbing back to the ones she'd taken at the Harvey House in Barstow. She reached the picture she'd taken of Bret on the stairs, and Chloe bit her lip.

It was a lucky shot, as most of her best pictures were— a moment of happenstance when things came together just right. He'd looked good in that gray blazer, the same one he wore every darned day. But there was something different in his demeanor, a little looser, more relaxed. She'd shifted the camera slightly and gotten it just in time—a quick click before he caught her aiming it at him, before the moment got away.

It was a good picture of Bret, but it was more than that. It was the way he was looking at Chloe. Not at Daddy's girl, not at a piece of arm candy—but at *her*. She could see a slight softening of his usual sharpness. He wasn't quite smiling, but almost. She enlarged the photo with her thumb and forefinger, like the glutton for punishment she was.

Her phone had been worth the extra money she'd paid for it. The image enlarged beautifully, and the expression on his face was there. The same look he'd gotten when he started to leave her at her door, right before he spun around and—

She hadn't imagined it.

It never happened, Bret had said after they kissed. This picture assured her it *did* happen. Not just the kiss, but that day. Like Camelot, one brief and shining moment. One glimpse of what things might have been like in some alternate universe.

With a few quick jabs of her finger, she deleted the picture.

And just as quickly, retrieved it again.

Back at the office, she plunked down in her seat and started typing up the rough draft from her notepad. A few minutes later, Bret walked out, stopping only long enough to pull his overcoat off the rack near the door. It was all she could do to keep from screaming under her breath. But she didn't want to draw Chuck's attention any more than she already had. It could be her paranoid imagination, but he seemed to be casting a few more curious glances today, breaking his pattern of laid-back observer. Not that she could blame him. Things *were* pretty weird around here today.

Typing the words from her notepad reminded her of her old process. Even in college, she'd done most of her first drafts longhand on legal pads. In the back of her mind, she imagined Bret's voice, admonishing her against doing the same work twice. But it wasn't quite true. She always revised as she typed.

A few minutes before five, Chuck stood and shook on his coat. "Chloe?"

She gulped and looked up, doing her best to keep her expression vacant. "What?"

"There's snow in the forecast for tonight. I checked

Facebook, and it's already coming down on some of those streets higher up the hill. Don't stay too late."

She glanced toward Bret's door. He'd left it open, so he'd definitely be coming back to the office tonight.

She nodded. "Okay."

Chuck left. She finished typing the story, fleshed it out, smoothed it over, and sent it to Bret's in-box. By that time it was after five-thirty. Usually she was here until about six. If she left now, she could avoid crossing paths with Bret.

Part of her *wanted* to cross paths with Bret. To tell him . . . what? To stop being so polite? It had almost made sense at the Pine 'n' Dine, when she was talking to him in her head. Now she wasn't so sure.

Chloe sighed, then e-mailed herself the notes she'd typed during a phone interview earlier today. She could work on it at home and get a head start on tomorrow's workload. If she left now, she could avoid Bret *and* the worst of the snow. Definitely the smart way to go, she decided.

As she walked down the hall, she could see the white flakes falling in the parking lot through the glass door of the employee entrance. The late afternoon chill hadn't been so bad, but it would be colder now. And wet. And if they'd gotten much snow, she'd need to scrape her windshield before she got into her car.

Chloe waited a moment, her hand on the door. In the security lights of the parking lot, the fine white particles glinted against the now-dark sky. She could barely make out the bumper of the car nearest the door.

She tucked her head down, pushed open the door,

and plunged outside. Cold and wet, but at least the wind wasn't blowing. Chloe pulled her coat around her and glimpsed the grille of the first car she passed. It had a Mustang pony logo in the center. Her heart twinged.

She raised her head to locate her car, a few spaces down the short row in front of the sidewalk. And saw him.

Actually, she could only see the back of Bret's black overcoat, collar upturned against the snow, and his dark hair above the collar, already dotted with white flakes of snow. Leaning over the hood of her car, he was using the edge of a credit card to scrape the crust of snow from her windshield.

Chloe slowed her steps. She heard the rasp of plastic against glass, probably the very sound that had kept Bret from hearing her approach.

She reached the front of her car, and he turned to look up with a start. Guiltily, as if she'd caught him slashing her tires instead of clearing her windshield. He stepped back with an awkward nod.

She'd been frustrated all day. She still was. But he'd just done her a kindness. In the snow. All her roughly composed speeches died away.

Not that it would have done her any good. The cold, wet night didn't exactly invite conversation. Even if she'd been prepared to clear the air with Bret, this wasn't the time.

And he was already circling the rear of the car next to hers, taking the long route away from Chloe to get back to the sidewalk.

"Be careful on the road," he said over his shoulder. "Good night."

She watched him stride briskly toward the employee door with the sure steps of someone who had years of experience walking over fresh snow.

"Thanks," she called belatedly after him.

He disappeared into the building, like one of Dickens's lesser-known Christmas ghosts.

Chapter 14

"Close the door." Tiffany's abrupt tone didn't sound like Tiffany.

Chloe hadn't even stepped all the way into the apartment, but with the icy air rushing in on her heels, she was happy to oblige. After she did, she saw the reason for Tiffany's urgency. A little brown and white cat trotted purposefully across the living room to meet her.

"What—" Chloe began.

"He was under the car in the parking lot when we left work," Tiffany said. "Trying to keep out of the snow. He's lucky we didn't squish him."

The cat wound rapidly around Chloe's ankles, apparently in a big hurry to rub off as much fur as possible onto the bottom half of her slacks. She could hear his purr from where she stood. Unable to resist, she dropped to the floor and knelt to pet him. The feeling of the soft, slightly bedraggled fur set off an ache in her throat.

The surprise guest raced back and forth under her hand as she stroked its back. Cats were usually aloof.

Not this one. He—She?—had the gangly, scrawny look of a cat that wasn't quite full-grown.

Kate emerged from the bathroom, dressed in the sweats she'd undoubtedly just pulled on after taking off her uniform. Tiffany still wore her dated pink dress from the Pine 'n' Dine.

Kate said, "We were thinking of calling him Rascal."

Her roommate's tone carried the hint of a challenge. Chloe looked up at Kate, who was clearly braced for an argument. Because, of course, their apartment rental agreement didn't allow pets.

The cat let out a raspy meow when Chloe stopped petting him. He reared up on two legs to rub the top of his head against her hand.

"Are you guys nuts?" Chloe scooped up the cat, rewarded by an even louder raspy purr as he bumped his head against her chin.

Kate and Tiffany stared at her as if trying to regroup.

"You've got no imagination," Chloe said into the silence. "'Rascal'? Haven't you ever heard of a thesaurus? Or a baby name book?"

"Yeah, pick up one of those around here and we'd have the town talking for days."

"Search the Internet, then."

The cat climbed toward her shoulder, looking for a place to hide in her hair. Chloe turned her ear toward his muzzle and listened to that wheezy buzz saw of a purr. She hadn't had a pet since her first cat, Nipsy, died during her freshman year of college. She closed her eyes and stroked him some more.

"The apartment manager is going to kill us." Kate,

caught off guard, was now playing a halfhearted devil's advocate.

"She'll have to find out about him first," Chloe said.

"We were afraid you'd say no," Tiffany said. "You're the one who's usually a stickler for the rules."

Was that who she was? If Chloe was the responsible one in this bunch, they were all in deep trouble.

"We don't have to call him Rascal," Tiffany said, her eyeliner faintly smeared. "How about Catsby?"

That was pretty good, actually. Tiffany knew the way to her heart was a literary reference, and Chloe did love F. Scott Fitzgerald. But . . .

An idea seized her. "Hemingway," she said. "His name is Hemingway."

Tiffany and Kate exchanged looks, as if to confirm that Chloe had just lost her mind.

Kate gave another shrug. "O-kay."

The talk turned to cat food and litter boxes. Chloe kept petting Hemingway and let his noisy purr drown out the sound of her common sense. It wasn't a great idea and she knew it.

But tonight, a lovelorn, raspy-voiced feline was just what she needed.

Bret was doing his best to immerse himself in the words on his screen when a familiar voice broke in on his thoughts.

"Bret, this is awful."

Chloe stood in the door of his office. Not too far in, but she didn't look like she was about to budge. Posture straight, feet planted firmly on the ground, she blocked his only exit. It was late morning and she'd waited until Chuck left for an interview, so they had all the privacy they needed, and he had absolutely no means of escape.

Cornering him in his own office—or McCrea's office—was dirty pool. But she looked armed and ready for battle. Determined to break through his wall, which, for his money, was every bit as sturdy as a Lego tower.

Bret's mouth went dry. He told himself that if he couldn't handle a twenty-four-year-old cub reporter, he didn't know what.

He leaned back from his keyboard, but not too far, as if to remind her that he had important things to do. He folded his arms. "What's awful?"

It was a patent bluff, but he had to start somewhere.

"Don't," she said. "Don't *even*."

Okay, for a woman who made her living with words, that was weak. If she couldn't say the words, maybe he could make it through this.

But before he could formulate his next obtuse question, she added, "That thing that never happened."

Silently, Bret pulled in a deep breath.

He couldn't meet her eyes without reliving some part of it. Not just the sock-melting kiss, but the sheer joy of being with her that day. The way she laughed. The way she grabbed for her camera phone when she saw something she liked. Her moral indignation when he suggested that the Beatles's *Sgt. Pepper* album was overrated, and *Abbey Road* was probably their best work. The way she smiled at him, which wasn't quite the same way she smiled at anybody else.

Meeting her eyes brought all of that back. But he

couldn't avoid her eyes now, or his defense wouldn't hold water.

"Chloe, you were right. We're professionals. We can't—" He shook his head, keenly aware that they were in his employer's office, as if the walls were witnesses that could testify against him. "We just need to move past it."

"But this isn't like it never happened. It's emphasizing the fact that it *did* happen."

"In what way? What, exactly, am I doing wrong?"

He'd made sure his behavior was above reproach. On some hypothetical level he was aware that this was a sexual harassment suit begging to happen, although he didn't think Chloe had that in her. Still, he'd written and read enough news to know that people often did things you would never expect. Especially when they were angry or hurt. But that wasn't what really worried him.

It was himself he couldn't trust.

"Stop being so polite to me," she said. "I hate it. We were just starting—"

"To be friends?" He couldn't keep the bitter edge out of his voice. Like it or not, *friends* was a word every guy hated hearing from the woman he was attracted to. Yes, he supposed that at some tottering midpoint, they'd been friends. But Bret had fallen over to the other side of that, and he couldn't see going back. Yes, he liked Chloe. It was what drew him to her so strongly, with a pull that went beyond physical attraction. But trying to separate that liking from the part of him that wanted to close the distance across the room between them and—

Well, that could take years.

She'd been a willing participant. He didn't think he'd imagined that. Her parted lips, her arms around his neck, that slightly confused look when he pulled back. He'd put that look there, and he couldn't help feeling some satisfaction from that.

It made it that much harder for him to ignore that there was something between them. Something that went beyond an impetuous moment of heat. He never did anything impetuous, rarely did anything on impulse, and couldn't remember the last time he'd done something because he so purely and simply *wanted* to.

Now she wanted to be friends?

And they said men were the ones who compartmentalized.

Focus, Radner. What had he been saying?

"This isn't about being friends." With difficulty, he picked up the conversational thread. "We're colleagues, first and foremost. Anything that jeopardizes that is bad for both of us."

"It's a little hard to be colleagues when we can't even stay in the same room together."

"You're the one who left yesterday."

"I needed air. It's hard for me to write when the air is thick. And you left right after I came back."

"I had an interview." Another patent lie.

"Bret." She closed her eyes briefly before meeting his again. "I'm not trying to make this worse than it is. I just want a comfortable working relationship. If we could get back to where we were, even last Friday . . ."

The rest dangled in the air. *Time travel isn't an option,* Bret thought, but he didn't feel up to the comeback.

Bret looked beyond the lift of her chin and the set of

her jaw. Her gray-green eyes were steady, and he had to give her credit. This wasn't an attack. She wasn't even being unreasonable. She was making an honest effort to cut through this mess, and however ill-advised, that took guts. More guts than he had.

She wasn't asking him to confess to anything. She just wanted a little détente, a truce in what wasn't even a war.

But he didn't know how to deal with it differently. When he was near her, everything wanted to spill out. He wanted to say he'd meant every bit of it, that there was no other human being he'd rather spend time with, which was saying a lot, because most of the time he enjoyed being alone.

Of course, he couldn't say that. Something akin to panic clutched at his throat. He was out of moves. He had to say something, maybe something to make her so angry she'd turn and leave. Because that might be the only way out of this.

"Bret?" Jen's voice came over the intercom on his phone. "You have a call on line two."

He raised a finger to Chloe. Saved by the bell.

Or so he thought, until he answered the phone.

"This is Bret," he said into the phone, his tone no different than the dozens of other times Chloe had heard him say it.

Then everything changed.

In her life, Chloe had seen plenty of people blush, even turn red. But although she'd read it in hundreds of books, she didn't think she'd actually seen anyone go pale before.

As Bret listened silently to the voice Chloe couldn't hear on the other end of the line, he rose from his chair as if lifted by marionette strings. He said only four words: "I'll be right there."

He hung up and rounded the desk. "Sorry," he murmured, brushing past Chloe as she stepped back. With a quick economy of movement, he made straight for the door of the newsroom, snatching his overcoat off the rack so quickly that the rack tottered.

Chloe stared after him, a cold knot forming in her stomach. Whatever had happened, their little melodrama suddenly seemed very secondary.

She went out to the front office and asked Jen, "Who was on the phone for Bret?"

The receptionist's light brown eyebrows furrowed. "Winston Frazier. Why?"

Chloe wrapped her arms around herself. "Bret just left"—his movements had been too purposeful for a bat out of hell—"in a big rush."

Jen's frown deepened. "Let me know when you hear anything. I'll do the same."

The older woman was obviously fond of Bret, and Chloe wondered how much Jen knew about him. But she resisted the urge to ask any prying questions.

Chloe did the only thing she could think of under the circumstances. She went back to her desk and did her best to write coherently.

* * *

Nonresponsive. It was one of Bret's least favorite

hospital words.

Bret sat beside Winston Frazier in one of the dated vinyl chairs in the waiting area of Tall Pine Hospital's emergency ward. If it turned out to be enough of an emergency, they'd send an air ambulance to transfer Bret's father to one of the larger hospitals down the hill. It had come to that once before, resulting in a heart bypass four years ago.

"I came over to pick him up for lunch, and he was slumped on the couch," Winston said. "I couldn't wake him up."

Bret nodded. He'd heard it before. Winston's needle was stuck, replaying the same story. That was atypical for him, the only indication that he was anything other than his old crusty self.

Winston had seen his dad through a lot, but this was the first time he'd had the dubious honor of being on hand for the initial medical emergency. It looked and sounded a lot like a stroke, but in Bret's experience, it would take quite a while before they heard any results on the tests the hospital was running right now.

What Bret wondered, but now wasn't the time to ask, was how Winston had gotten into his father's house. David let a lot of things slide, but even in Tall Pine, he wasn't one to leave doors unlocked. The sight of Winston, in his perpetual button-down shirt, clambering in through a window would have been something to witness.

Bret hoped one day he'd be able to laugh about it. It all depended on how things turned out today.

"You were meeting for lunch," he realized. "You haven't eaten."

"It's only been about an hour," Winston said. "It's not like I'm going to keel over."

Bret glanced at the time on his cell. One forty-five. Which made it closer to two hours, he estimated, since Winston found his dad "nonresponsive." Looking at the time reminded him of something else: the office.

He'd left a story up on his screen and Chloe basically standing in a cloud of dust. He ought to touch base. He doubted there was much danger of missing any major medical developments at the moment. His dad hadn't regained consciousness, but his vital signs were stable.

Bret stood. "I'll check the cafeteria and see what kind of health food they have in the vending machines."

"I told you, I don't need anything."

Bret aimed a meaningful look at Winston. "Maybe not, but I don't want to wind up looking after *two* of you."

He left the waiting area, but before he went to the cafeteria, he walked outside. The hospital's eighty-year-old concrete walls made cell reception hit or miss, even with Bret's service provider. And anyway, Winston probably would have chucked Bret's phone across the room if he tried to use it to text or e-mail the office. The older man didn't have a lot of patience with modern technology.

Outside, the recent snow glared brightly on either side of the carefully shoveled walkway in front of the hospital. *Fa-la-la-la-la.*

The incongruity of the sunshine hit him full force. For the first time since Winston's call, Bret had a moment alone to react. Maybe that wasn't a good thing.

Before he tried to contact anyone, he leaned against

the rough, irregular stones of the building's wall and closed his eyes. He sucked in several deep breaths.

Not again.

It was a desperate, two-word prayer, but God would know what he meant. Not another parent. Not at Christmastime, again. God wouldn't do that to him. Right?

As if God didn't have bigger things on His mind than how Bret's father's fate might affect Bret personally. This wasn't about Bret, it was about David Radner. His dad's disregard for his own health carried risks and consequences. But still. Surely God had a few more plans for David, instead of letting him passively run out the clock?

Please, he added. *Amen.*

A few deep breaths later, he turned his attention to something he had some control over. He sent a message to Chloe's e-mail: I'll be out for a few hours. Tell Chuck to write his head off and send the stories your way when he's done. Give them a good going-over. And I left a story up on my screen. It's mostly done. See if you can turn it into English.

He tapped the "send" button and waited.

Chloe's reply was quick. Will do. Where are you?

He'd known that was coming. He bit his lip. Tall Pine Hospital. Family emergency.

Chloe wrote back: Who?

Bret's jaw tightened. My father.

No more questions, please, he willed.

He had reasons for e-mailing rather than calling. Number one, he didn't need to worry about his voice giving anything away. Number two, it gave him an excuse to be brief.

227

Number three, it didn't seem as real if he didn't say it out loud.

Her response came back: I hope everything's okay.

A platitude, really. The kind of thing anyone would say. But from Chloe, it felt genuine. And thinking about the fingers that had typed it stirred emotions Bret had no right to feel, especially now.

Bret closed his eyes again and tried to focus on the jagged stones digging into his back. Somehow, during the past few weeks, he'd forgotten about *this*.

He'd been fighting to keep Chloe at a proper distance for professional reasons. It was the right thing to do, for him and for her, because it was the ethical thing to do. This way, he wasn't a boss involved with an employee, and she wasn't the pretty blonde too many people already took at face value. It was all true. But those reasons were just the beginning.

Anyone who got close to him became a part of this scenario. The medical crises, the ups, the downs. Especially the downs. Somehow that had never occurred to him before. The point had been moot, since he'd never gotten too involved with anyone since he came home from D.C. Or maybe that was another reason, subconsciously, that his relationships had a way of crashing before they really got started.

If he kept everyone at arm's length, no one had to see him like *this*.

He gulped in cold air, remembering that other December, seven years ago, when everything had been peeled away and he'd felt like he was walking around without his top layer of skin.

Tamp it down.

Keep her out of it.

Thinking about Chloe in those terms was ridiculous. He barely knew her, really, although something at the core of his being insisted otherwise.

He visualized the paper, in its orderly physical columns, and tried to piece together everything that needed to happen to get it on the stands tomorrow. One column at a time. It helped. When he had his thoughts sufficiently gathered, he worked up another e-mail of instructions, this time to the layout department.

Once he knew he wasn't going to fall apart, he went back inside to search for cafeteria food.

And to wait some more.

Chloe relayed Bret's instructions to Chuck, then made a quick trip to the reception area to give Jen the update.

She walked back into the office, temporarily at a loss. She'd come in this morning loaded for bear, wasted a lot of energy trying to pin Bret down, and had spent the last two hours trying to write an article since Bret shot out of here. Now that it was written, her circling thoughts had free rein, and she had trouble even reading her own words to check the story over. She had a feeling Bret's article would sound a lot more like English than hers did.

"Doing okay?" Chuck offered.

"I'm fine." Her father wasn't the one in the hospital. Thank God.

One more look at her article, she decided, to get the

thing polished up and done before she tackled Bret's. She sat down at her desk. "Do you have any idea what's wrong?"

Chuck shook his head. "He doesn't really talk about his family. I'm pretty sure his mother's gone."

Chloe took a sip of cold coffee and stared at her screen. The words looked like gibberish. She forced her eyes to the top of the article and started reading again, line by line.

In the next few hours, Chuck churned out five stories with mind-blowing efficiency, and Chloe cleaned them up, managing not to groan out loud over the misused punctuation. The execution was messy, but the words themselves were clean and direct.

"I don't know how you do it," she said.

"Necessity. I don't second-guess. I need to be out of here on time. Kids grow up fast."

Chloe nodded wordlessly. She'd picked up bits and pieces about Chuck's wife, and it sounded like the girls had lost a great mom. But he was determined not to let his aunt, a woman in her sixties, take over Annie's role completely.

A few minutes before five, she had a text from Bret. On my way back in. Chloe relayed the message to Chuck.

"Good." Chuck pushed back from his desk, but didn't reach for his coat. "Need anything from me?"

It seemed like everything in the office was code these days. Chloe had the feeling Chuck was really asking her whether she wanted him to stay. If it weren't for her, she was sure Chuck would have waited long enough to talk to Bret.

"I'm good," she said. "Thanks."

Chuck picked up his coat. "Give Bret my best," he said, and left.

He seemed to understand a lot more than he was saying.

Chloe eyed the congealing coffee in her mug and got up to make a fresh pot. It was a safe bet that it wouldn't go to waste tonight.

Bret walked in ten minutes later. With a characteristic nod, he hung his overcoat on the rack. His posture was intact, but his face looked weary and shadowed.

"How's your dad?" Chloe looked up from the screen she hadn't really been reading.

"Fine. Thanks for asking." The corners of his mouth tugged up faintly, but Chloe wouldn't have called it a smile. "False alarm. More or less."

He returned to his office. Chloe poured herself a fresh cup of coffee that, for once, she didn't really need. A few minutes later, an e-mail from Bret landed in her in-box.

Stories look fine. Have a good night. You've earned it.

It wasn't unusual for Bret to e-mail her from the next room, regardless of his mood. But after a day like this, she couldn't just leave. She went to his office and stood inside the doorway—not too far this time—and waited for him to acknowledge her.

He looked up from his screen. Blank, expectant, and tired.

"There's fresh coffee," she said. "Is there anything else I can do to help?"

"You already have. Thanks." His eyes went back to his screen, a pretty clear dismissal.

She shouldn't press. She'd already put her hand in the cage once today, and she still couldn't seem to leave it alone. "What happened?"

With a heavy sigh, Bret pulled back from his computer. "Extreme hypoglycemia. It looked like a stroke at first. But it just means maintaining a proper diet. We'll see how that goes." His lips twitched. "I got them to keep him overnight, so we don't chance going through the same thing tomorrow morning."

"How old is he?"

"Sixty-six. I have a sister in Cincinnati who's eight years older than me. I came along a little late in the game."

Old age wasn't something she'd pictured yet for her parents. "My folks are in their fifties."

"Enjoy it while you can." His voice was dull and flat.

Okay, that *did* sound like a dismissal. Reminding herself of her turtle shell, Chloe started to turn away.

"Chloe." Bret's voice was quieter.

She turned back. He rubbed the bridge of his nose under his glasses. "I'm sorry. That sounded terrible. All I meant was—"

"I know what you meant."

For a moment, his expression was unguarded, the pain in his eyes clearly visible. Pain, fatigue, and maybe something else.

Before she could put a name to it, the shutters went up again. "Okay." His eyes returned to the screen. "Like I said, false alarm. Now, if you'll excuse me, I can probably get out of here in about a couple of hours if I buckle down."

"Bret—"

"Chloe. I'm all right."

She glimpsed his eyes again. Hurting. Exhausted. "Okay," she said. "Good night."

She ached to do more, but clearly that was off the table.

That conversation, that ridiculous conversation that she'd started this morning, seemed like years ago. What had she hoped to accomplish? What Bret wanted, what he needed, was for her to be a reporter. No more, no less. She could do that.

Bret had more on his plate than she realized, and she wasn't helping. She needed to stop fussing over that-thing-that-never-happened.

In short, she needed to grow up. And do her job.

Chapter 15

A pretty silver locket for her mom. *Click.*

A sports watch, with lots of bells and whistles, for her dad. *Click.*

Gift cards for Todd and Joel, because they liked to pick out their own gifts. *Click. Click.*

Chloe sat on the couch with her laptop Sunday night, finishing her Christmas shopping. It seemed like she'd spent most of her December in front of a computer screen, one way or another.

She'd made the time to go shopping on Evergreen Lane yesterday, where she'd found nice presents for Tiffany, Kate, and Sherry. She'd even found a silly key chain for Chuck. But she'd been buying presents for her family ever since she'd been old enough to shop, and it was getting harder and harder to find special gifts she hadn't already thought of for them.

Hemingway tried to help. Purring loudly, he started to stroll across her laptop. Chloe scooped him up and planted him back on the couch beside her, only to have him try again from the other side. After being thwarted three times, he rubbed his nose insistently against

Chloe's elbow, which almost made her order ten gift baskets for Aunt Janice.

It had taken no effort for Tiffany and Kate to wheedle Hemingway into their home. Now Chloe had become his go-to person. Maybe because her hours were more predictable, or because she sat still on the couch longer. Maybe because she always had that thing opened up on her lap, taking her attention from him. Or maybe just because it made her lap warm.

Whatever the reason, she was grateful to have him around, pesky paw pads and all.

Chloe rubbed behind Hemingway's ears as she looked up from the screen. She took a few moments to focus on the flashing lights of their little tree, and to listen to the Train Christmas CD she'd put on.

Christmastime was passing her by faster than a sled with a slick coat of wax on the runners. Working full-time during the holidays always made it hard to celebrate. Working more than full-time for the *Tall Pine Gazette*, trying to pretend things were normal at the office with Bret—that was even harder.

Bret. Without even trying, she'd thought of a dozen gift ideas for him. She was sure he'd prefer she didn't give him anything at all. Unable to resist, she'd finally bought a coffee mug. Surely that was safe. But she probably wouldn't have the nerve to give it to him. Long after she moved on from the *Gazette*, wherever she ended up, she'd likely find herself sipping from a mug that read DEADLINES AMUSE ME.

Like it or not, in spite of all her efforts, she'd fallen for her boss. She didn't really know how Bret felt at this point, except that she obviously made him intensely uncomfortable. If she hadn't tried to talk about their kiss that day, maybe he would have forgotten about it already.

She knew she wouldn't have.

With a guttural moan that made Hemingway look at her askance, Chloe closed her laptop. Tiffany and Kate wouldn't be home from work for a couple of hours; she resolved to take that time to put her stress on hold.

She gathered Hemingway up in her arms. Now that he had her full attention, he squirmed as if he suspected some kind of trick. But she could be persistent, too. Chloe held him up to her shoulder and stroked him as his raspy purr filled her ears. He quickly forgot he'd been trying to escape.

She lay back on the couch, and Hemingway settled on top of her in the classic sphinx pose. She breathed in the scent of the tree and let the music flood her ears as Pat Monahan sang about tinsel and lights.

"Merry Christmas, buddy," she said. "You like music, too, don't you?"

He meowed through a purr, giving her a whiff of cat food. But hey, he seemed to know she'd asked him a question.

She rubbed the soft fur around Hemingway's ears until she fell asleep.

"Thanks, Mona," Bret said as he paid his lunch tab at the Pine 'n' Dine.

The brown-haired waitress smiled shyly from behind the register as she took his money and made change. So Ramona Billone had graduated high school and was now waiting tables at the Pine 'n' Dine. Another one of those Tall Pine rites of passage, like that apartment complex. You got out of school and either went on to college or worked at one of the local eateries. Bret remembered being waited on by Ramona's sister Kelly a few years back.

It occurred to Bret, as he went back to the table to leave the tip, that Mona had probably filled Chloe's spot at the diner.

He'd avoided the Pine 'n' Dine for the past week or so, trying not to run into one of Chloe's roommates, or Sherry, who'd ratted him out to Chloe about the fact that they'd dated. But it was impossible to avoid anyone in Tall Pine for too long, logistically speaking, so he'd chanced it today.

Bret stepped outside and turned the collar of his overcoat up against the chilly afternoon air. Truth be told, he was getting tired of avoiding people, period. It took a lot of energy.

As he walked toward the public parking lot, he approached a boy and a girl standing near the brick wall outside the row of shops. They were situated between Isabel's Antiques and The North Pole Christmas store, where they couldn't be accused of standing in front of either business. A TV tray stood on the walkway beside them.

They couldn't have been there long. Bret hadn't passed them on his way into the Pine 'n' Dine. Also, they hadn't frozen rock solid yet. This had to be the coldest day so far this season, allowing the town to hold on to its coating of snow. If the skies stayed clear, it would be great for the tourist trade this weekend.

But standing on the sidewalk on a Tuesday afternoon, the two kids weren't likely to do too well with their wares. It was way too early for Girl Scout cookies, and a little too late for Boy Scout popcorn. Bret squinted as he got closer to the improvised display table and its paltry display of—

The boy, about eleven years old, stepped forward. "Would you like to buy some mistletoe?"

Hoo boy, kid. Have you got the wrong customer.

For a moment Bret had a surreal vision of himself launching into a full-scale rant, telling the two hapless kids how much he did *not* need mistletoe, how very little use he had for mistletoe, and how he was probably destined to die alone. In a van down by the river.

The picture was so ludicrous that he almost laughed, for the first time in days.

He looked at the pair of them. The boy was tottering right at that edge between childhood and early adolescence. The little girl, silent and big-eyed, was several years younger than her brother—probably six or seven. She had pulled up the fur-trimmed hood of her coat so that just her face poked out, and Bret couldn't even see the color of her hair. Where were their parents? Probably working, Bret surmised, unaware of this little enterprise.

Bret eyed the display of droopy green sprigs, tied with red ribbon and packaged in sandwich bags. "Sure," he said. "I'll take one."

He handed the boy a dollar bill and waved away the change. "Get your sister home."

"Yes, sir." The boy nodded, the picture of politeness. And in that instant, Bret *knew* this kid. Probably not even in junior high yet, he already had a sense of public relations. The kind of kid who knew just what to say to a friend's parents. In a few years, those parents had better keep an eye on their daughters.

What the boy had overlooked was that not all thirty-year-old single men cared to be called *sir*.

The little girl, on the other hand, looked at him with solemn eyes. He didn't think anything about her was fake.

"He *is* your brother, right?" Bret wasn't sure the huckster standing beside her was above recruiting a waifish little friend to boost his sales pitch.

Her surprise was genuine. "Yes."

"Why?" the boy asked, suddenly defensive.

The girl looked at Bret with imploring eyes. "Have you seen a cat?"

"Sophie." Her brother nudged her impatiently.

Bret ignored him. "You mean, have I ever seen a cat? Or did you lose a cat?"

"He got out the other night," she said plaintively. "When it snowed."

Her brother nudged her again, a bit more gently. "Sophie."

"It's okay," Bret said. "No, I haven't seen a cat lately."

The girl's eyes shimmered. If that cat had been out overnight in the snowstorm, Bret didn't give long odds for its survival. His voice softened. "But I'll ask around. Okay?"

The girl nodded vigorously. Her soulful gray eyes had no trace of green or even blue. It didn't matter.

Bret's voice roughened again. "How much mistletoe do you have left?"

"Just those." The boy nodded at the tray. About five bundles.

"I'll take the rest," Bret said, and handed the girl a ten-dollar bill.

When he got back to the office, Bret found Chloe alone in the newsroom. They'd reached a tacit understanding since the day his father was hospitalized. Bret tried not to be excessively polite, and Chloe didn't press him to talk. About anything.

But today they were alone, and he had a pocketful of mistletoe in his overcoat. Somehow it felt like a loaded combination. She looked up from her screen, her eyes quietly assessing, lips slightly parted, reminding him of that night at her door. *Stupid mistletoe.*

He greeted her with a nod and made for his office without stopping to hang his overcoat on the rack.

"Bret?" Chloe's voice called him back, and that sounded like trouble. Sure enough, when he turned, she said, "I'd like to ask you a favor."

He approached her desk with caution. "What?"

Her shoulders squared. "Tomorrow night's the town council meeting. I know that's my beat. But my roommates and some other friends are going out Christmas caroling and—" She paused and pushed through with that determined jut of her chin. "I just haven't had much Christmas. I wondered if there was any way you or Chuck could cover it."

Bret wanted to be annoyed, but he couldn't. Chloe had put in a lot of hours, and with everything he'd added into the mix, this had to be a rough Christmas for her.

"Why not," he heard himself say. "I'll get more out of the council meeting, and you'll sure as heck get more out of the caroling."

Okay, that sounded glum even to his own ears. He couldn't walk away on that note. He thought of the kids who'd sold him the mistletoe and remembered his errant promise.

He asked, "By any chance have you seen a cat?"

Chloe gave a sharp intake of breath. "Why?"

It wasn't the response he'd expected. Chloe looked at him wide-eyed, and Bret wondered if that was the look she used on traffic cops when they pulled her over.

"I ran into some kids today," he answered. "The little girl told me they lost a cat. I said I'd ask around."

Chloe blinked. "Tiffany and Kate saw one the other night." She sounded hesitant. "In the parking lot at the Pine 'n' Dine."

Bret tried to interpret the dismay in her expression. "Was it dead?"

She blinked again, and color flooded her face. "No."

She didn't say any more, but Bret started to put two and two together. About a month ago, the night the photocopier jammed, Bret had thought she made a pretty good liar. He hadn't known her very well then.

"Did you get the kids' number?" she asked.

"No. I didn't think of it. I thought it was a long shot. Maybe you could make up a flyer. You could . . . mention where the cat was last seen."

Like last night, he thought. *In your apartment. Maybe on your lap.*

Chloe bit her lip, and Bret was sure he'd nailed it.

She shifted in her chair and changed the subject. "I had a call before you came in," she said. "They're having a living Nativity at Tall Pine Community Church two nights before Christmas. Live people, real animals, the whole bit." A smile touched her lips. "They even got hold of a camel somewhere."

That was less than a week away. They should have started promoting it sooner. Of course, Bret would have known about it, if he'd set foot anywhere near the church in the past few weeks.

Chloe waited for his answer. She probably expected him to say no, or relegate it to a news brief. Bret wondered how hard she'd fight for it. Perversely, he decided to find out.

"And?" He kept a straight face. "You'd like to, what, interview the camel?"

Ignoring the quip, she persisted. "They haven't tried something like this in quite a few years. Pastor Craig's really getting the youth involved on this one. I think it's worth a nice advance piece."

"So do I."

Chloe, who'd already opened her mouth to argue further, went silent. She looked at him as if he were an imposter, and he almost felt bad for messing with her.

In truth, his mood felt lighter than it had in days. They were having a normal conversation, and the floor hadn't opened up under their feet.

"Christmas may not be my favorite thing," he said. "But I never said I don't believe in what it stands for. Get with Ned, see if you can set up a good photo while you're at it. Maybe they're doing some kind of walk-through rehearsal. If the camel isn't already booked for *Good Morning America*."

"Thanks, Bret." She smiled, that dimple showing below the corner of her mouth, and suddenly Bret wished for a herd of camels. Dangerous, he reminded himself. Especially with that mistletoe still in his pocket.

He started to move on, and Chloe sat forward, hands returning to her keyboard. She wore one of her cardigan sweaters again. In the colder weather, she still wore them in the office, and pulled on her coat over them when she left. This one was dark blue.

Dark blue, with traces of fine white hair clinging to the sleeves.

Bret couldn't resist. He reached over the desk and carefully pinched a few of the hairs off the cuff of Chloe's sleeve. She looked up, startled, and Bret stood stock still.

All he'd really touched had been yarn and cat fur. Absolutely no reason for anything like a sizzle to race up his arm, unless it was the flash of surprise in Chloe's eyes.

Surprise . . . and maybe a little guilt. Bret felt a deep tug inside. He knew she hadn't meant any harm. She'd been rescuing a stray animal, not trying to deprive a little girl of her pet.

"Don't worry," he said.

"About what?" She blinked rapidly. She'd never make it as a felon.

"That cat your roommates saw," Bret said. "Once you get some flyers up, I'm sure it'll all work out."

Chapter 16

Chloe rang the doorbell as her fellow carolers shuffled on the porch with stapled lyric sheets and flashlights.

"What page is it on again?" Gwen asked in a loud whisper.

"Six!" Kate hissed as the door swung open.

Aaron McNamara's mother stood in the doorway with a look of slight confusion as she surveyed the baker's dozen of carolers clustered on her porch. Christmas caroling wasn't unheard of in Tall Pine, but people still didn't always know how to respond to it.

Chloe's brother Joel strummed a slightly off-key chord on his guitar, and they launched into a ragged version of "Jingle Bells."

She'd seen carolers on Evergreen Lane perform in beautiful a cappella harmony for the tourists. This was nothing like that. Chloe and her friends had been doing this since junior high, and musical proficiency wasn't a requirement. All you needed was a lot of heart. And a little nerve.

Mrs. McNamara's puzzled look lifted, and she smiled. A moment later, her smile grew when she spotted Chloe in the group. She nodded to them and turned from the door, as if to round up other members of the household. That was what happened at their most successful stops. That, and sometimes cookies.

This time, Mrs. McNamara didn't get far, because Aaron was already rolling up behind her in his wheelchair, pushed by a pretty dark-haired girl. A couple followed behind them, holding clear mugs of what looked like eggnog. Chloe didn't know if the brunette with Aaron was the errant girlfriend, but spirits looked pretty bright.

Then Aaron and his friends started singing along, which made it a *great* stop. Before the song was over, a man in his forties stood behind the rest, shaking his head with faint amusement at the ruckus on the porch. He hadn't been there the day Chloe interviewed Aaron, but she guessed he was Aaron's father.

Joel strummed the last chord of the song with a flourish and shook his hand as if to loosen it. Chloe knew his fingers stung from the cold.

"I'm amazed you're out here tonight," Mrs. McNamara said.

"We wouldn't miss it," Chloe said. Her eyes fell on Aaron and his friends. "Merry Christmas."

In point of fact, she didn't know how long their group of carolers would hold out. Temperatures had already plummeted to the freezing point and didn't show any sign of stopping. They'd come to Aaron's house first, the one place she'd insisted was mandatory for the evening.

"Do you know 'O Holy Night'?" the girl behind Aaron asked, and looked puzzled when they all laughed.

"You do *not* want to hear us do 'O Holy Night,'" Mitch said.

"It's a little out of our range," Tiffany explained. "We tried it at one house years ago without any practice. We didn't realize how high it went until—"

"Until it was too late." Chloe couldn't help laughing. "I think that was one house that was really glad to see us go."

"How about 'Silent Night'?" Aaron asked.

"*That,* we can handle." Joel strummed an opening chord.

They stood close together and shivered their way through "Silent Night," and "We Wish You a Merry Christmas" while their audience joined in.

Aaron's house alone was worth the trip.

Afterward, they left their four-car caravan at the curb and proceeded to two more houses up the street. But the thin layer of snow still on the ground was just enough to get their shoes wet, knees were shaking, and hands were so numb it was hard to turn the pages of their song lyrics. Then Mitch's girlfriend started to cough, and they left, taking two other members of their company in their carload.

"If I don't get something hot to drink I'm going to die," Gwen announced.

Ten minutes later, the remaining nine carolers were at the Pine 'n' Dine, pushing together a group of tables at the back. Chloe found herself at the far end, next to Tiffany, across from no one, as Sherry brought their cups of coffee or hot chocolate.

"This isn't your station." Chloe picked up her cup of cocoa. She'd decided to take a break from coffee for the night. Maybe she'd even go to bed early.

"I didn't think anyone else could put up with you guys." Sherry nodded toward the counter, where Darla waited on a group of tourists. Darla had worked at the diner for over twenty years, and she didn't always have the longest fuse.

"Good point."

Sherry bustled her way down the table with the remaining cups. Chloe sipped her drink. Good, but it didn't compare to Mandy's recipe. She really ought to get back over to The Snowed Inn sometime soon.

"Are you falling asleep?"

Chloe jerked up out of a brown haze she didn't know she'd slipped into. But Tiffany had left her seat and Sherry was leaning in front of her, so some time must have passed.

She grinned weakly. "Sorry. I guess this is just the longest I've sat down without a computer screen in front of me for quite a while."

"How's Bret treating you these days?"

The question caught her off guard, and she looked away. She hadn't prepared her turtle shell for the Pine 'n' Dine.

"Good," she said, a fraction late.

"I was wondering how he's doing," Sherry said. "I haven't seen him in a while. Which is kind of unusual for him."

Tiny needles of useless jealousy prickled at Chloe. She pulled on a smile. "I may or may not have mentioned you told me about you two."

"That's old news." Sherry didn't miss a beat. Bret hadn't reacted much, either. So Bret's assessment during their trip to Barstow was probably true; whatever romance he and Sherry had had in the past, it was long over. Not that it made a difference to Chloe's situation.

"He wouldn't be thrilled with me right now," she said. "I let him do the town council meeting tonight so I could go caroling. Now here I sit."

"Playing hooky? I wouldn't worry about it."

Chloe sighed. Tiffany still hadn't returned. Joel, catacorner from her seat, looked like he was trying to make some long-overdue time with Gwen. Maybe that was why Sherry was talking to her. To keep her from being the wallflower at the table.

Keep your nose out of it, Chloe told herself.

Maybe just one intellectual question.

"Why doesn't Bret like Christmas, anyway?" Chloe lifted her cup to take a casual sip. Part of it sloshed onto the table before it made it to her mouth. So much for casual.

"It's definitely not his favorite time of year," Sherry said slowly.

Chloe waited, head tipped. It was one thing she'd learned from her experience interviewing: sometimes you didn't ask the next question right away. You waited to see where your interviewee would go.

Sherry inclined her head, too, as if deciding. "He never told you about his mom, did he?"

"No."

Sherry eyed Joel, but he had his full attention on Gwen, and Kate was talking to Lucy. "She died at Christmastime. Right after Bret got out of college. Cancer. It took about four months . . . but it was a really long four months."

"That would be hard." Chloe's voice came out a whisper, because there wasn't a lot of air in her lungs.

"It was." Sherry's eyes were directed somewhere over Chloe's head, as if she were seeing the past. "They waited until the end of the summer to tell him. And then he shot straight for home. He left behind a job offer at the *Washington Post* to do it. I think—"

"Job offer?" Chloe interrupted. "He had an internship at the *Washington Post.*"

Sherry nodded. "And his mom and dad waited until he was finished before they told him. They didn't want him running home any sooner, and they were right, because that's exactly what he did. He dropped everything."

"But a job offer? Are you sure?"

Sherry nodded. "Oh, yeah. I know because he only told *me*. He made me swear not to tell *them*. Those four months—he was in here for breakfast most mornings. We talked a lot. I think it was pretty much the only break he let himself take. He was there, at home, helping to take care of her. He lost weight, if you can picture that. And then, when she died, it was right before Christmas. I didn't see him again until a few months after the funeral. And when he started coming back in, he was Bret again. More or less." Sherry shrugged. "I think he felt uncomfortable that he'd told me so much. We've been friends ever since, but it's sort of an arm's-length thing."

"How can you tell with Bret?" Chloe asked. "It's like

recognizing the moods of Darth Vader. You're probably the love of his life."

Sherry looked at Chloe for a long moment. "No, I don't think so."

Chloe didn't miss what Sherry was implying, but her mind whirled with other thoughts. Bret and Christmas. His reaction to her little tree. His wry comment about getting more out of the town council meeting than caroling. And something Sherry had said: *I think breakfast at the diner was about the only break he let himself take.*

With a sense of apprehension, Chloe asked, "Did his mother die at home?"

"Yes."

Chloe's mouth went dry. "She was on hospice, wasn't she?"

Sherry nodded. "That's right. Why?"

Chloe asked, rhetorically, "You don't read the paper, do you?"

Her heart pounded in her ears. She stood up just as Tiffany returned to the table.

"I had to call back a message on my voice mail," Tiffany said. "A boy saw one of our flyers about the cat. His family lives a couple streets behind the parking lot here."

Chloe hesitated as she shrugged her coat on. "Did he describe the cat?"

They'd decided against putting a picture on the flyers. In case, for some reason, the wrong person wanted to make off with the cat they'd . . . appropriated.

Tiffany nodded. "Brown and white. Raspy meow. He said his mom can pick him up here in the morning. I'm sorry, Chloe."

"It's okay. He belongs with his owners." Trying her best to ignore the twinge she felt inside, she pushed in her chair. "Joel, could you give Tiffany and Kate a lift home? I've got—somewhere I need to go."

Bret descended the three wide concrete steps that led from the town hall to the sidewalk, almost grateful for the fierce cold that greeted him outside. The small crowd from the council meeting rapidly went their separate ways, not lingering to converse the way they usually would. Instead, they made straight for the public parking lot just past the town hall building. Less than a week before Christmas, the council members had practically outnumbered the audience, and Bret couldn't help noticing Jake hadn't been there. Jake, who had been the one to suggest last year that Tall Pine really should have a town council that met more than once a month.

And then Mark Farren, the new kid on the town council, had picked tonight of all nights to bring up the bright idea of putting parking meters on Evergreen Lane. Someone new came up with that brainstorm every few years, and it usually took about three meetings of arguments to put the suggestion back in its rightful place.

Somehow the council had found enough fuel in the old debate to spend an extra forty-five minutes on it before tabling it for the next meeting. Otherwise, everyone could have been home and warm by now.

Bret fisted his hands inside his coat pockets and drank in several gulps of brittle air. Tonight there was no cloud cover, and it made the cold dry and ruthless. The stars overhead were everywhere, like fine shards of smashed glass in the dark sky.

For some reason, instead of turning left for the parking lot like everyone else, Bret was drawn straight ahead by an unlikely beacon: the town Christmas tree. Festooned with big, old-fashioned multicolored bulbs, this was the thing Chloe had been in such a hurry to see them light up a few weeks ago.

Bret drew toward the tree with caution, the way he might approach a growling mastiff, until he stood at its base. He craned his neck to see the top; it was a long way up. Reputedly, the town had been named for the tree, and Bret had to admit, it certainly was a tall pine.

He tried to strip away the last seven years and see the tree the way Chloe saw it. The way he might have once seen it. Maybe he'd simply never paused long enough to look, even back then.

Somehow, the bite of the cold air helped. It cleared his head, made the colored lights stand out in brilliant detail. He tried to remember what Christmas had been like before.

What came to mind, strangely, was a line from a Christmas carol, taken from a Longfellow poem. *And wild and sweet, the words repeat . . . of peace on earth, good will to men.*

Bret closed his eyes, as if he could will it. An answer wasn't long in coming.

He heard a quiet crunch of footsteps on the scrupulously shoveled pavement that surrounded the tree. The steps were slow and careful, taking pains not to slip on any surprise patches of ice that might be hiding on the cold ground. Slow, careful—and light.

He turned to see Chloe walking up from the direction of the city parking lot.

"Hey, stalker." He greeted her without surprise. Her presence here felt somehow inevitable. "What happened to caroling?"

"It got cold. We wimped out." With a few remaining steps, she joined him beneath the tree. She wore the same light brown coat she threw over the back of her chair every day at work. Like Bret, she had her hands shoved into her pockets, arms pressed close to her sides as if to hold in warmth. Standing in the darkness, she reminded him, not for the first time, of the little match girl.

"It was too cold," he said, "so you decided to take a nice stroll through Antarctica?"

"We stopped at the Pine 'n' Dine first." In the illumination given off by the Christmas tree lights, her eyes searched his face. "I talked to Sherry. She told me about your mom." She paused. "And about the job offer from the *Post*."

Hands clenched in his pockets, he let out a long sigh that sent up generous plumes of white vapor. "I thought Sherry was more discreet than that."

"I don't think she's ever told anyone else."

"And she told you." Bret looked away, and there was that tree again. Why Sherry, after all these years, would talk about his private life to Chloe—

Maybe it was more proof that his old friend knew him too well.

"Bret, why are you still in Tall Pine now?" Chloe asked.

Are we really doing this? When it's twenty degrees outside?
But Bret stayed where he was. Maybe he was literally
frozen to the spot. "You know the timeline on this,
right? I called home with my flight information, and
before I could tell them I'd be going back to Washington permanently, I found out my mother was dying.
They waited for me to finish out the internship before
they told me. My mom didn't want me to come running back before it was over." He drew up his shoulders. "It was the longest four months of my life, and she
was gone so quick. And I don't ever, ever want to talk
about it."

He turned away from the tree, away from Chloe,
directing his eyes toward the vacant town square. And
for some reason, he kept talking anyway.

"We decorated for Christmas that year," he said on a
ragged sigh. "She wanted to. She loved Christmas. And
I think—" Pulling a hand out of his pocket, he pinched
the bridge of his nose. When he was sure he could
speak again, he said, "I think, human nature being what it
is, you think that if you put a Christmas tree up, that
means you've got to be around long enough to take it
back down. It didn't happen. After that—"

Dear God, why was he still talking? Because she'd
asked? Surely she hadn't asked for all *this*. If he ever
wanted to talk about this, which he didn't, he'd be
better off spilling his guts to some anonymous hospice
case worker. Someone he never had to see again. This
was Chloe, who stood behind him in absolute silence.
And he'd have to face her in the office after this.

But she'd asked, and maybe she'd understand.
Maybe he wanted her to understand. Maybe then she'd

see why all of this, why any idea of the two of them to-gether, was such a bad idea.

So he went on.

"After that, I couldn't turn around and go back to D.C. Between my mother and the *Washington Post*, you've got to know which one I'd want back. So—it felt wrong to want the job. There was almost a fiancée back there, too, but that never happened. I didn't go back, and she didn't come here. She didn't offer, and I didn't ask her to. It seemed like too much to ask. The kind of shape I was in by the end—I think maybe I was grateful."

And even Sherry had never known about that part. Somehow, a near-engagement to his college girlfriend of two years had receded into fine print. Just one more part of everything that was stripped away.

"Anyway. By the time I started feeling better, it was a year or so later. When I started to think about trying to start things up again at the *Post*, my father had his first heart attack."

Chloe echoed, "His *first* heart attack?"

Bret nodded. "If I was a mess, my dad was worse. He pretty much stopped caring about anything after my mother died. My sister was already settled back East with a family and a law career, and I was here. So I accepted the inevitable, and I stayed. And bought the Mustang. Early midlife crisis. I was twenty-four."

He pivoted back around to see Chloe's reaction. It was about what he expected. Her eyes were wide, a little shell-shocked. He supposed that was the effect he'd been looking for.

He shrugged. "You asked."

She parted her lips to form some sympathetic response.

Bret didn't wait. He walked past her, striding toward the parking lot. He felt raw, laid open, and he didn't want her to see it.

"Bret."

His name was short. How could it sound so different when *she* said it?

He stopped. Just a few strides would take him back to her. One more thing he couldn't want. He didn't go back to Chloe, but he didn't quite have it in him to ignore her, either. So at last, he turned around.

Across the small distance he'd put between them, she looked smaller and colder, more like the little match girl than ever. But her stunned expression had faded, and he fancied he saw a trace of that resolute set of her chin again as she crossed the space between them. Her boots grated on the cold pavement. When she reached him, her eyes were shimmering.

"Hey," he said. "Don't *you* cry."

"I'm not," she lied.

He kept his hands stashed in his pockets, because now that he'd finished his talking jag, he had to fight the part of him that ached to reach for her.

"Bret, I'm sorry." Her voice broke a little. "The hospice story—I swear, I didn't know. I must have pushed every button you've got."

"Yeah, I've thought about that." He dredged up a wry smile. "Tell me something. Do you have any memories before you came to work at the paper?"

She frowned. "Of course. Why?"

"Because sometimes I think you were put here on earth just to mess with me."

It got a shaky laugh out of her, which was what he wanted.

Then she stepped forward, wrapped her arms around his neck, and fell against him in a hug, which was not what he expected at all. It was the hug of a friend, he decided, one who didn't know what else to say. And it set off a whole marching band of emotions inside him.

Hadn't he been blunt enough, abrupt enough, to chase her away? But she kept reaching past all the barbed wire he put up, as if she could sense what he really wanted.

Bret closed his eyes tight. He didn't want to respond. Wasn't sure how, after years of keeping people back, especially Chloe. He felt someone's heart hammering between them, his or hers, he couldn't tell, and felt something loosen inside him. Slowly he put his arms around her, tentatively at first, then more tightly.

He couldn't let this happen. She'd reached past the wall he'd built up, and he'd have to rebuild. But for now, he rested his cheek against her hair and pulled her closer. Because, yes, he was a guy. And she pushed *that* button, too. He felt her trembling. Or maybe she was just shivering.

He spoke with his lips against her hair. "You're cold."

He pulled back, just enough, and before he knew what was happening, his lips found hers again.

A voice in his head tried to intrude.

This is a bad idea, remember?

You can't do this.

You're kissing your reporter in the middle of the town square.

And then he didn't hear a thing.

She was still shivering, and he could only hope it was

from more than the cold. But it didn't feel like a pity kiss. It felt like she'd been waiting for this as much as he had. Her fingertips dug into his shoulders as she pressed closer. Then her lips parted to his, and there was no mistaking the passion in her response.

Wild and sweet . . .

His eyes were closed, but in his mind's eye he saw the lights of the giant tree, and he knew he'd found a Christmas memory worth keeping.

At last he broke the kiss and buried his face in the soft hair falling at the side of her neck.

I love you.

The words wanted to tumble right out of his mouth, and Bret bit his tongue to keep them from coming out. Saying it would be all kinds of wrong. Not because it wasn't true, but because it wasn't fair. There was more pain to come, and he knew it. Bringing her into his life would be selfish. And, more selfishly, he didn't want anyone else around to see him go through it.

He pressed her closer, stealing a few more moments of warmth. Because that was exactly what it felt like: stealing. It would only get harder to let go. And it certainly wasn't getting any warmer out here.

He'd feel better in a month or so. He knew that. December was the worst. But he couldn't kid himself that things would get much easier. How many times would his father be in and out of the hospital? It could be quick or it could be slow, but he had no business wishing it on anyone.

So, with all his resolve, he took her by the shoulders and gently pushed her back. Saw her eyes looking up at him, questioning.

"I'm sorry," he gritted out. "I can't drag you into my mess."

An attempted smile played at her lips. "Don't I get a vote?"

He matched her faint smile with a humorless one of his own. "I think it kind of has to be unanimous, don't you?"

He wanted to say something else, but he didn't dare. He'd already said too much tonight. Anything he could add would only amount to, *Talk me out of doing the right thing.* And keeping Chloe from getting entangled in his problems really was the right thing.

Unable to help himself, he squeezed her shoulders one more time, because she was already starting to shiver again.

"Go home and get warm," he said. Then he turned and left, this time without looking back.

And this time, she didn't call his name after him.

Chapter 17

Hemingway thought the cardboard box on the living room floor was just great when it was his idea to jump inside.

He wasn't so keen on it when Chloe closed the flaps over him and sealed the box shut with packing tape.

He yowled, the box rattled, and an urgent paw shot out through one of the many crude, quarter-sized air holes Chloe and her roommates had cut into the box last night. They didn't have a cat carrier, so they'd re-purposed the box from a package Tiffany had gotten from her grandmother last week. It wouldn't have to hold him long, if Hemingway's family was on time for their rendezvous in the Pine 'n' Dine parking lot this morning.

"Ready?" Kate asked. She stood by the door in her pink uniform, car keys in hand.

"Yep." Already in her coat, Chloe scooped up the box, trying to hold on to both the top and bottom for security's sake. The box pitched back and forth as Hemingway moved inside his new confines.

Tiffany looped Chloe's car keys over Chloe's little

finger and peered through an air hole. "'Bye, sweetie. We'll miss you."

A paw darted out again, and Tiffany jumped back.

In the car, Hemingway's raspy voice took on a whole new vocabulary. At first his meows were long and drawn out, almost like moans. Chloe expected that. Most cats hated cars. But as she followed Kate to the diner, his vocals soared into what sounded like multi-syllable words, like the notes of a tenor auditioning for the Metropolitan Opera.

"It's okay, buddy." Chloe rested a hand on the box as the car reached a stoplight. "Maybe we should have called you Pavarotti."

A long brown and white paw came through an air hole and flailed around as if groping for a hand to hold. Chloe choked back something between a laugh and a sob. Her emotions were too close to the surface, and the time waiting for the stoplight gave them a chance to set in.

A cat is not a metaphor, she told herself.

After seeing Bret last night, giving up Hemingway felt that much harder. He wasn't her cat, never had been. Letting him go was the only thing to do. It would be nice to see Hemingway reunited with his people, she reminded herself. But he'd found his way into her heart in a short time, and . . . she was turning the cat into some kind of an analogy again.

Somewhere along the line, she'd forgotten her own very good reasons for not getting involved with Bret. He'd obliged her by supplying new ones. She needed to get a clue and move on with her life.

When the car moved forward again, Chloe kept her

hand on top of the box, afraid he might ram his way out like some kind of hyperactive jack-in-the-box. And to think Kate and Tiffany had gotten him home the first time with no box at all.

Chloe pulled into the employee lot behind the Pine 'n' Dine for the first time in nearly two months. This was a sad errand, but she hadn't wanted to just send Hemingway out the door this morning. He'd become her friend, and she wanted to give him a proper good-bye.

A long, ululating meow from the box let her know just how much Hemingway appreciated her efforts.

It wasn't even full daylight when, at a little before seven, a minivan pulled into the lot. It felt like a ransom drop, or a drug deal.

A woman and a little girl—not a boy—got out of the minivan, met by Kate. It hadn't warmed up since last night; she had to be literally freezing in her Pine 'n' Dine uniform, since her coat didn't cover her legs. By contrast, the little girl was barely visible under her hooded coat, snow boots, and what looked like ski pants. Mom had bundled her up well.

Chloe got out as the three of them approached the passenger side of her car, where the box waited. The mother, a pretty blond woman with a slightly frazzled expression, had an actual wire mesh cat carrier in hand. Transferring the cat could be tricky. Maybe they should just hand over the box. Except . . .

Chloe said, "Maybe you'd better take a look and make sure it's the right cat?"

The girl's gray eyes got bigger. The thought apparently

hadn't occurred to her. Chloe felt ashamed of her fleeting hope that they might have the wrong animal.

Hemingway rasped out a meow, a little less theatrically now that the car wasn't moving, and the box shook.

"It's him!" the girl exclaimed.

"Sophie," her mother cautioned. "Let's just be sure."

Carefully, holding down the box flaps, Chloe used a key to slice through the packing tape. The flaps came up, and she seized Hemingway before he could make a break for it. His claws instantly planted themselves in the front of her coat as he dug in, trying to climb over her shoulder. Chloe crouched to the little girl's level, and Sophie came forward to pet the cat.

"Careful, honey," her mother said. "When kitties get scared sometimes they bite or scratch. Or try to run away."

"Easy, buddy." Chloe pried the cat's claws out of the shoulder of her coat and lowered him so they could see his face. His hugely dilated pupils had replaced the irises almost completely.

"It's Garfield." Sophie's voice was tremulous as she launched into a hug that included both Chloe and the cat. A lump swelled in Chloe's throat.

"Garfield?" Chloe's voice faltered. "Like the cartoon cat?"

"He was more of an orange color when he was a kitten," the mother explained. "Thank you for taking care of him. Sophie's been beside herself for days."

For over a week, Chloe thought guiltily, as Kate politely refused the mother's attempts to offer a reward. Meanwhile, Sophie's shining eyes remained fixed on her pet.

Sophie wanted to hold Garfield, but they convinced her that wasn't a good idea. With some difficulty, the little girl's mother helped Chloe stuff him into the cat carrier. Inside his new wire mesh prison, the cat resumed his raspy song.

"It's okay, buddy," Chloe said thickly to No-Longer-Hemingway. "You're going home."

She knew the cat was where he belonged, and Sophie's smile soothed her heart. But it still gave her a sharp pang to see him go.

After the cat's owners drove away, Kate gave her a hug, which told Chloe she must be in *really* bad shape.

"Look at it this way," Kate said over her shoulder. "He was shallow, disloyal. There are lots of other cats in the sea."

Chloe laughed and sniffled. "I hope not. That'd be pretty bad for the cats."

"Okay, how's this: there's a cat out there for you somewhere and you'll know it when the right one comes along."

"Good enough." Chloe blinked hard, sniffed once more, and pulled back.

She was pretty sure these analogies were happenstance, that Kate didn't know Chloe had a lot more on her mind and heart than just a cat. Then again . . .

"Thanks," Chloe said. "Now you need to get to work and so do I."

When she got to the office, the black Mustang wasn't in the parking lot yet. Chloe took another box out of the trunk of her car and, in short order, took down the

Christmas decorations on her desk. Yes, it was depressing. More than a little. And maybe she shouldn't give up her decorations on someone else's account. But everything she'd done after Bret kissed her the first time had only made things worse. Well, she was finished with making things worse.

She started the coffee. Heaven knew she needed it.

When Bret came in a few minutes later, she made sure she was hard at work at her computer. He hung his coat and walked by, pausing briefly at the sight of her stripped-down desk.

Chloe made the mistake of looking up. As Bret's glance flicked from her desk to her face, his eyes barely showed recognition. It scraped her insides raw. She kept her hands on the keys and returned her eyes to the screen. And Bret went to his office.

She knew there was more underneath that stony gaze. A lot more. She'd felt it when he kissed her. But he was good at hiding it, and it still hurt.

Half an hour later, Bret stared at the piece that had just landed in his in-box. It was easily the most sentimental thing Chloe had ever written.

This morning, I gave my first Christmas present of the season. Or, to be honest, I gave something back.

And on it went, about the lost cat Chloe and her roommates had returned to a little girl and her mother. It talked about loving and letting go and what a pet

265

could mean to a child. Unabashed schmaltz, and somehow it worked. It worked on Bret, at any rate.

Only Chloe would name a cat Hemingway.

Emphatically, it wasn't news. It was a first-person column, not the kind of thing they usually ran in the *Gazette,* and Bret found it impossible to read it with any kind of objectivity. The piece was a slice of emotion laced with quirky humor, especially the part about the loud drive in the car to deliver the cat. And the payoff with the little girl's reaction . . .

Okay, it got him. But it wasn't news.

Chloe had obviously dashed off the piece this morning, and Bret had never seen her produce anything so quickly. It was clearly written from the heart; he doubted she was capable of writing any other way. But what to do with it?

Bret looked through his closed glass door at Chloe's desk, bereft of its little tree. He'd done that. Which shouldn't factor into his decision.

What would McCrea do? He might give her some fatherly advice about keeping emotion out of journalism.

Or he might run it.

It was Christmastime, after all. A time when sentiment could be pretty forgivable.

Bret set it aside until that afternoon, when it was time to work out the layout of tomorrow's edition. At last he decided to run it in the editorial section, giving it a nice side column on page three.

Merry Christmas, Chloe Davenport.

He wished he had something more to give her.

Chapter 18

"Okay, guys." Bret stood in his customary stance, arms folded, half leaning against the desk that he never came out to write at anymore. "It's D-day. As in Day Before Christmas. Let's do our best to make it a short one. We've got two papers to fill—tomorrow and the day after—so let's take a look at what we've got."

Chloe bit her lip. She'd been way off her stride the past few days, unable to sandbag any interviews to work ahead on. The silent tension between her and Bret was taking its toll, and so was the fatigue of the past several weeks.

While Bret turned his attention to Chuck, Chloe slid her notepad in front of her and hurriedly started jotting ideas for generic filler articles. The tradition of Boxing Day. The town's program for curbside recycling of Christmas trees. Coptic Christmas, which was celebrated in January . . .

"Chloe." Bret turned from Chuck, speaking in the tone of someone greeting a barely remembered junior high acquaintance.

She met his eyes, or tried to, because he was looking at an invisible person standing just beside her left ear.

"I had an e-mail from a family in Mount Douglas," Bret said. "Their boy's constructed a pretty impressive village of snowmen in their front yard. Can you go up, get a photo and an interview?"

"Mount Douglas?" Chloe stared at him. "Why'd they contact us?"

"Apparently their local paper had bigger fish to fry. But it sounds pretty unique."

Mount Douglas was nearly an hour away, and definitely outside their usual coverage area. Which Bret knew full well. He had something in mind here.

She tried, "Wouldn't a phone interview—"

"The boy's eight. I have a feeling he'd be a lot easier to work with in person. Plus, they e-mailed a picture, but it's pretty lousy. And you get great results on your phone camera."

And you wouldn't want to tie up a real photographer for the whole morning. You might need him for something important.

"The day before Christmas," Chloe said. She became aware of Chuck shifting around at the desk in front of hers, making an effort to be very busy at . . . something.

"It'll make a good front-page centerpiece for Christmas," Bret said. "Plus, there's snow in the forecast for tonight, so that snowman village won't be around after today."

In the time it would take her to get to Mount Douglas, do the interview, and come back, she could knock out . . . well, three news briefs, anyway. This assignment wasn't a great use of manpower, but clearly, that wasn't what it was about today.

Bret's eyes actually met hers, and she saw a silent appeal there. "Once you get back here and write that one up, you can be done for the day."

That was what this was about.

He was sending her out to cover the puff piece of the year, in another town, just to get her out of the office so he didn't have to deal with their awkward situation.

There was nothing else to say. "Okay," she said. "Forward me the e-mail."

In front of her, she thought she heard Chuck exhale.

Chloe called the family and set up the interview. They couldn't see her before eleven o'clock, but she left early and made a detour to her apartment to pick up her laptop. Maybe she could find a place to stop and write up the story before she drove back. That would get her out of the office that much quicker.

He was a heel.

After Chloe left, Bret sat in his office to bang out stories to fill the paper for the next two days. But it was hard to focus beyond his circling thoughts.

Of course Chloe saw through the pretext of the Mount Douglas story. Tomorrow was Christmas and he'd sent her out the door like an idiot. As if that would help matters.

It didn't help. It made it worse. He hadn't been trying to hurt her. Just push her away. Even if that amounted to the same thing.

When this was over, he decided, he was changing his middle name to *I-shouldn't-have-done-that*.

When this was over.

What was *this,* and when was it over?

After his father died? A pretty bleak thing to put your life on hold for. After that, there'd be more guilt, more reasons to keep people at bay.

Sending Chloe out of the office the day before Christmas did nothing to alter the fact that he still had to deal with her on December twenty-sixth. And for the next month, until McCrea came back. The fact that being near her, and trying to act like nothing other than business had happened between them, felt like dining on a steady diet of ground glass.

His cell phone rang, and he answered without glancing at the caller ID. "This is Bret."

"Bret?" His sister's voice cut through the miles between here and Cincinnati. "Are you okay? What's wrong?"

He gave a weary chuckle. "You got all that from 'This is Bret'?"

"You don't sound like yourself."

Bret rested his head on the back of McCrea's chair and closed his eyes. "Busy day. How are you, Rosalyn?"

"Good. Except for the part where I'm helping Cindy with her college applications."

"College?" Bret did the math, as if Rosalyn wouldn't know how old her daughter was. Ten going on eleven when his mother died, fourteen when he and his father had visited that summer . . . okay, it added up.

"You should see the essays she's been doing. You'd be proud."

"I already am." Not that he could take any of the credit, but the girl was smart as a whip. Last time he saw her she'd been reading *The Picture of Dorian Gray*. During the summer. For fun. It had done his heart good.

"How's Dad?" Rosalyn asked. "Is he doing any better?"

"Not really." Bret pinched the bridge of his nose. "I kind of hoped this last hospital trip would be a wake-up call, but he keeps hitting the snooze button."

"I'm sorry, Bret." This was the unfortunate thing about Rosalyn's annual Christmas call. Sooner or later, she got to the guilt. "You've taken on so much."

"Rosalyn," he said gently, "I understand." Bret eyed the open door of his office, but Chuck was typing away at the far end of the room, out of earshot. "By the time Mom got sick, you were already settled on the other side of the country. You had your job, Dennis's job, you were bringing up Cindy . . . it's okay."

"It's not, though. It isn't fair. You're not responsible for the world turning on its axis. Dad . . . needs to take some personal responsibility."

He rubbed the bridge of his nose again. "Yeah, well, we're not going to solve the world's problems this morning. Do I still get a 'Merry Christmas' from you?"

"Sure, Bret. Merry Christmas."

"Love you."

After they hung up, Bret checked the forecast, called the art department, and asked them to work up a WHITE CHRISTMAS banner to have on standby for tomorrow's front page. They already had the MERRY CHRISTMAS banner they used every year ready to go; they could make a quick switch if the snow arrived on schedule tonight.

Bret tapped the mouse alongside his keyboard. Knocked out a piece on the town's annual New Year's

Eve square dance. And looked at the time. Ten after eleven.

Chloe would be in Mount Douglas by now, finding the right notes of personal interest in the piece of fluff he'd sent her off to write about. Granted, she'd make a great story out of it. They'd even gotten a few dozen e-mails in response to her piece about the cat. From a little column on page three of the editorial section.

Chloe had a way of making the most of things. She'd even tried to do that for him, despite his repeated efforts to brush her away. She'd probably given up for good by this time, and maybe that was the best thing for her.

Or maybe, just maybe, he could change that.

Chloe left the Marsden family's house shortly after noon. As she pulled out of the driveway, she took one more look at the snowman community, glittering like gems in the early afternoon sun. Big drifts of snow surrounded the little display; there was still plenty of raw material to spare. But at a population of fifteen, the snowman town included a policeman, with a navy cap and a toy sheriff's star; a doctor, complete with white coat and stethoscope; and a baker, with apron and rolling pin. Oh, and a cat. With adorable pine-needle whiskers.

Chloe had rightly deduced that one eight-year-old couldn't have built all this in less than a week, even on Christmas break. Under gentle questioning, he and his family had come clean with the details.

No, Joshua hadn't worked alone, but the village had

started out as his vision. When the neighbors saw him shoving snow around for hours, people of all ages had stepped in to help. To Chloe, the team effort made the story that much more magical. That, and the fact that so much work and ambition had gone into something that, by its very nature, couldn't last.

Bret might have assigned her the story just to get her out of the office, but she looked forward to writing it.

She started down Mount Douglas's main drag. Compared to Tall Pine, the place was a minor metropolis, but Main Street was still a two-lane road. And unlike Evergreen Lane, Main Street boasted chain restaurants with drive-through windows. Chloe kept an eye out for a quick lunch, and her eyes lit on a Starbucks at the next corner.

Starbucks had Wi-Fi. Because Mount Douglas actually had decent cell phone and Internet reception.

Maybe she didn't need to go back to the office at all.

She stopped in and wrote the story over a panini sandwich, then prepared to e-mail it to Bret. She bit her lip as she started to compose the note to accompany the story. She kept her tone as professional and neutral as possible.

Bret arrived at his father's house with a large bag of groceries and a smaller bag of chicken from the Pine 'n' Dine. Grilled, rather than their legendary, decadent fried chicken.

"Bret," his father said when he answered the door. "I wasn't expecting you."

"I know." Arms full, Bret moved past David to the

kitchen table, where he set down the bags. "I brought lunch."

But first, he started unloading groceries. He started by setting up a bowl of fruit in the middle of the kitchen table. Not that he hadn't tried this before.

His father joined him at the table. "Aren't you awfully busy at the paper?"

"Extremely. But my brain wasn't working too well, so I took a break. With a purpose." He unloaded a fresh batch of produce into the refrigerator and closed the door. With the added space between himself and his father, he took a deep breath. "We need to talk."

"You sound like your mother when you say that." With a faint smile, David Radner sat down at the kitchen table. If he was trying to look frail, he was doing a pretty good job.

"Maybe she and I have a lot in common." *Like looking after you.* Bret thought it, but he couldn't say it. Confrontation wasn't the idea here.

Plates. That was something to keep him busy moving. But knowing Sherry . . . "Are there plates in that bag?"

David peered inside. "Right here." He fished the plates and napkins out of the white bag, and the tantalizing scent of chicken wafted out. It might not be fried, but it still smelled darned good.

"Okay," Bret said. "So, what this is about . . ." A part of him wanted to remain standing, to retain the height advantage. And hold on to his nerve. But he sat, dishing chicken and rolls onto the sturdy paper plates. He sat back, brushed hair from his forehead. "Dad, I know you've heard this before. I love you and you mean a lot to me. And I don't mind helping you out. But—you need to help *me* out. I can't do it for you."

"I know."

Bret blinked. And searched his dad's eyes, a lighter brown than his own. Possibly he just wanted to say whatever it took to make Bret shut up. But there was something about his father's lack of surprise. "Did Rosalyn call you?"

"No, but Winston just left about twenty minutes ago. Said I needed to man up and take care of myself. Said I was turning you into a grumpy old man."

Dear Lord. By the time *Winston* called you grumpy . . . Bret asked, "And what'd you tell him?"

"That I noticed. You've been getting skinnier again. Not a good thing. But that's not all my fault, either. In fact, Winston sort of hinted that you might be using me as an excuse."

Bret felt a smile twitch at his lips. "Balderdash."

But it had a ring of truth. He couldn't pin everything on his dad.

He sat forward. Their food was getting cold. "I know it's been hard for you. But you're still here, and there's got to be a reason. I think it's time for you to find it." Bret shrugged. "Maybe try for the town council again. You wouldn't need to worry about conflict of interest anymore. We've got someone else at the paper covering that now." For a while, anyway.

"The cute blond reporter," David said.

"Yeah—" Bret couldn't gather up a denial. "She's more than cute, Dad."

"I knew it." His father reached for one of the containers of side dishes and pulled off the lid. "Cole slaw? Seriously?"

"Try it. It's hardly a health food."

They ate for a few minutes in silence.

"So," David said, "if Rosalyn calls, don't answer it?"

"No. Answer it. Just wish her a Merry Christmas."

Another pause.

Then his father said, "Does this mean I'll see you at church tonight?"

And that one *was* on Bret. Because while he'd avoided church during the Christmas season in the years since his mother's death, his dad remained a faithful attender throughout the year. Including the Christmas Eve service.

So David Radner still had the knack for negotiation from his town council days. Time for Bret to give a little, too. *Fair's fair.*

"You got it," he said. "I'll be there."

Chloe's e-mail to Bret took longer to write than the story. She read it over one more time before she finally clicked *Send*.

She looked up to find that Starbucks, quiet to begin with, was deserted. No surprise there. After all, it was Christmas Eve Day.

And she was going to have a good Christmas tomorrow with her family. Without thinking about Bret. Or his reaction to the e-mail she'd sent. She hadn't written it for the reaction. She'd written it to put all this behind her.

"Be careful out there," the lone barista behind the counter said as she left.

The significance of that remark hit her full force as she pushed through the door, out into a frigid world significantly different from the one she'd seen an hour and a half ago. She'd been so engrossed on her laptop she hadn't looked out the window.

The sky was gun metal gray, and it looked more like five p.m. than two o'clock in the afternoon. Nothing like the harsh, bright sunlight of a few hours ago. She didn't know if they'd get a white Christmas in Tall Pine, but up here in Mount Douglas, those clouds were unquestionably loaded with snow.

She should have driven back before she wrote the story. And the e-mail.

Chloe hurried to her car. Maybe she could still get home ahead of the storm.

Chapter 19

Where was Chloe?

Bret returned to the office to find both reporters' desks vacant. Chuck, presumably, had run out for lunch, hopefully a short one. Maybe Chloe had done the same.

He checked his e-mail and found a message from her, sent about half an hour ago.

Bret,

Attached is the snowman story, along with the photos. Hope you're happy with the results. I'm sending it from here so you'll have time to get a head start on the editing before I drive back down the hill. Unless you need anything else, I'll head straight home for Christmas Eve.

With the holiday crunch behind us, I think it would be better for me to go back to freelancing rather than working out of the office.

Let me know if this brings you up short. If not, I'll get to work generating some proposals from home to keep the paper stocked.

Thank you for a wonderful opportunity. I've learned a lot.

Hope you have a good Christmas,

Chloe

Very carefully worded, very professional. She'd written the e-mail in such a way that no one, say, from the corporate office, could read it and find anything amiss. Even Bret couldn't find any underlying bitterness or sarcasm, with the possible exception of four words.

I've learned a lot.

Okay. That stung a little.

He stared at the screen. He shouldn't be surprised. A few nights ago, she'd been in his arms. She'd given the indication that he might be worth the risk, the investment, and he'd turned away. He couldn't expect her to be endlessly patient while he made up his mind to turn into a human being.

If he'd been a little quicker to come around . . . if he hadn't sent her up to Mount Douglas today . . . if, if, and if.

Maybe he'd shut her out one too many times. Maybe he should leave it alone. But he'd be as defeatist as his father had been if he gave up without even trying.

He straightened in his chair and started to type.

Chloe had been on the road less than half an hour—long enough for the sky to go from ominous gray to premature darkness. Long enough for the snow to start, thick and heavy. Back home, at Tall Pine's lower elevation, they hadn't expected snow till around six o'clock. What a difference a few thousand feet made.

She hadn't seen another vehicle on the road in the past ten minutes. Because it was Christmas Eve, and because people who lived up here knew better than to go out in this.

She should have left sooner. And when she saw the

sky turning dark, she should have turned around while Mount Douglas was still close behind. How far had she driven? The snow and heavy, dusky light made everything unfamiliar. She only knew she was in some eerie no-man's-land between Mount Douglas and Tall Pine. And that if she turned around, she'd be driving uphill, straight into the thick of the storm.

As dicey as this was, pressing for home still made more sense.

She passed a yellow metal street sign. The name of the road wasn't encouraging: *Rabbit Trail.*

Chloe slowed—yet again—and leaned forward to squint through the windshield. It was like seeing the world from inside a snow globe. A really dark, scary snow globe. She negotiated the curves slowly and carefully, which gave the storm that much more time to catch up.

Biting her lip, she accelerated with care as she came out of the next curve.

The car skidded.

In slow motion, Chloe felt her rear wheels slide to the left. Toward the guardrail that stood between her and a steep drop.

It ran against her instincts, but she did what she'd been taught all her life: she steered the car in the direction of the skid. Toward the oncoming lane, and the guardrail. Her heart hammered as her car aimed for the edge, still skidding. It straightened its course in time, and she pulled the steering wheel to the right. A little too sharply. She skidded again.

Nothing was in slow motion anymore.

The car picked up downhill speed as it slid, this time toward the snow-covered mountain on her right.

Everything was a blur until the car hit something with a loud bang.

The next thing she knew, she was struggling for breath. She felt the safety belt biting into her shoulder. Chloe fought to pull in a short breath, then another, as she opened her eyes. A deflated white airbag drooped out of the steering wheel in front of her, and fine powder hung in the air. Chemicals from the airbag, she realized hazily.

She was still straining against the safety belt, but she didn't appear to be hanging upside down, thank God.

She took another breath.

Through the windshield, at first she saw only gray and white. As her eyes came into focus, Chloe saw that part of the gray was the thick trunk of a tree. The white, not surprisingly, was snow, which had probably softened the impact when she ran into the tree. The view through the passenger side was solid white. Apparently, the car was embedded in a snowbank.

Chloe twisted in her seat to look out the driver's side. She realized the car was tilted, not forward so much as to the right. Leaning to look out the driver's-side window felt a little like climbing uphill. To see out, she lowered the window a few inches. A nasty blast of cold air rushed in, bringing snow with it. She squinted through the gray and white. It looked as if her car had left the road altogether.

She pulled in another breath, this one deeper, then heaved a sigh. It could have been worse. A lot worse.

But it wasn't great.

* * *

Bret's reply to Chloe's e-mail was short, and he spent forty-five minutes trying to get it right.

Hi Chloe,

Thanks for the snowman piece, and for bailing me out during a stressful season. You made the Christmas crunch much more manageable.

Don't make any decisions until we've had a chance to talk.

Merry Christmas,

Bret

He hit *Send,* then checked the time again. Almost three-thirty. Weather permitting, she should be back in town by now.

Weather permitting. With a chilling sense of hindsight, Bret pulled up the weather on his computer as he dialed Chloe's cell number.

"The subscriber you are trying to reach is currently out of signal range. . . ." No surprise there.

Chuck popped his head in and echoed Bret's question of nearly an hour ago: "Where's Chloe?"

Bret stared at the forecast. The snowstorm still wasn't scheduled to hit Tall Pine until five p.m. Plenty of time for Chloe to get back safely. If she'd left in time.

But the database showed the storm had already descended full force on Mount Douglas, two thousand feet higher.

He texted Chloe: Are you all right?

No immediate reply. Of course, if she'd hit any weather, she could very well still be driving.

A moment later, he added: **Please let me know when you're back and safe.**

Remember your training, Chloe told herself. *What have you got?*

She'd have to make sure the tailpipe wasn't blocked by the snow before she tried to start the car again, or she ran the risk of sucking carbon monoxide fumes. Chloe switched on the car's flashing red hazard lights and looked behind her. She tried to make out the blinking of the lights through the falling snow, but it was hard to tell. There was a good chance the back end of the car was buried.

Only one way to know for sure.

She buttoned her coat up tight, pulled on her gloves, and pushed open the door. The first time, gravity made the door fall back. The second time, she held it open as she climbed out of the car and promptly sank knee-deep in snow. It soaked into her slacks and shoes, while more snow pelted her from the sky. She bent her head, trying to keep the snow out of her face, and stepped back to assess the situation.

The car was tilted, the driver's-side wheels off the ground, the passenger side shoved deep into the heaps of snow alongside the road. Chloe trudged to the back of the car and found what she feared: the tailpipe was buried. That meant no heater unless she could clear away the snow that buried the pipe. She tried digging at the hard-pack snow and only succeeded in soaking her gloves.

She fared a little better with the trunk, which was

higher up and only partly wedged into the hill. She got it open far enough to duck her head inside, which brought blessed relief from the snow blowing into her face.

Take a good look, 'cause you don't want to come out here again.

A flashlight with batteries that worked. Thank God. She used it to search for more resources.

A dirty beach towel from some forgotten trip to Prospect Lake. It might not keep her very warm, but it could help dry her feet. A tool kit? Maybe, if she got any MacGyver-type inspiration.

And two—count 'em, two—road flares. In her mind she heard her father's voice, admonishing her to be more prepared.

Chloe lit a flare and took it to the edge of the road to set on the rapidly disappearing pavement. She debated setting the other one as well and decided it was better to save it. Snow could cover the first one pretty fast.

As quickly as she could in the cold, she grabbed the rest of her treasures, left the trunk open for the extra bit of visibility, and scrambled back to the front door of the car. Before she got inside, she checked her phone for signal bars. Nothing. She held the phone high and moved it slowly overhead, watching for some change in the display. Not surprisingly, no bars appeared. It didn't take long for reception to disappear once you left Mount Douglas behind.

She tried to phone roadside assistance anyway and got the expected series of flat beeps. That left one more thing to try. Sometimes a text got through when a phone call wouldn't.

The first person she thought of to contact, ironically, was the person who sent her up here in the first place.

But she couldn't blame Bret for this. Yes, he'd sent her out of the office, for his own personal reasons. He'd also intended for her to go home early.

She didn't want to worry her parents prematurely. She could try Kate and Tiffany. But if she wanted a resourceful person with a cool head, she didn't think she could do better than Bret. This wasn't the time to indulge in pride, or hold a grudge. With numb fingers, she texted him.

The message bounced straight to her phone's out-box.

Maybe she'd decided to stay in Mount Douglas to wait out the storm, Bret thought.

Except that, knowing Chloe, she would have been intent on getting home for Christmas. And if she was still in Mount Douglas, she would have gotten his text. He didn't think she was petty or angry enough to ignore him.

Just in case, he texted her again: **Are you okay? Worried.**

He tried to skim the snowman story, but couldn't fight the sense that he was wasting valuable time. He sent Chloe's story and photo through for the front page and gave the green light to the WHITE CHRISTMAS banner. Then he turned to important matters.

He phoned emergency crews in both Tall Pine and Mount Douglas, but the harried dispatchers needed more to go on. With other, tangible emergency calls, they didn't have enough personnel to search the mountain highway for a motorist who *might* be in trouble.

By four o'clock, he was done waiting. Every fiber of his being insisted that something was very wrong.

He had snow tires on the Mustang, but he didn't think they'd cut it where he was going. He got on the phone in search of a vehicle with four-wheel-drive.

Did Chloe have chains in her trunk?

Imagining scenarios didn't do any good.

In minutes he'd arranged to pick up Scotty Leroux's truck. "I'll meet you at The Snowed Inn," Leroux said. "It's right off the main highway. That'll save you time."

Bret texted Chloe to let her know he was looking for her, although he had no idea whether she'd receive the message. Then he headed for the door.

"You're in charge," he told Chuck, who'd been pounding away at stories and trying to offer helpful suggestions.

"Seriously?"

Bret yanked his coat off the rack. "Sorry. I know it's Christmas Eve. Get together with the layout team, take what we've got, and have them put together two skinny papers."

"Right. I'll try not to burn it down."

Bret pulled on his coat and remembered one more difficult but necessary task. "I'll need the phone numbers for Chloe's roommates. And her parents."

"I'll call them."

"Just text me their numbers. I'll call while I'm picking up the truck." This was all his doing; he needed to deal with it. "Thanks."

Chuck nodded. "Go."

Bret started for the door. At the last minute, he reached back and snatched the scarf from Millie Bond off the coat rack.

* * *

Chloe huddled in the front seat, legs drawn up against her, as the temperature dropped. Surely a car would come by eventually. But so far, no one had.

Her foray into the snow had come at a heavy price. Her clothes were damp, and although the car provided shelter from the wind and snow, it was a long way from warm inside. She curled her bare toes under the towel she'd used to dry her feet. Her shoes had been soaked; her socks were worse. Why had she worn loafers today instead of boots?

Oh, right. Because she thought she'd be spending the day in a heated office. But she could have been home and warm by now if she'd left Mount Douglas right after she finished the interview. Or if she hadn't taken the extra time to e-mail Bret.

Twenty-twenty hindsight didn't help. She needed to cope with what had really happened, and she had to face the fact that she could be spending Christmas Eve in a freezing automobile. Chances of anyone seeing her white car in the snow were minimal, even with the hazard lights on. And with the airbag deployed, the horn didn't work. She'd tried.

She needed to stay alert, ready to flag someone down, if a car came by.

Staying alert was becoming a problem, too. A couple of times she'd caught herself nodding off, and she knew that wasn't a good thing. She forced herself to unwrap her folded arms and do mini-calisthenics. She needed to do whatever she could to stay warm . . . and awake.

* * *

At The Snowed Inn, Scotty Leroux was already waiting with his F-150. Impressive speed, especially from a guy Bret barely knew.

"Thanks," Bret said.

Leroux simply held out the keys. "Be careful up there."

Bret handed him the keys to the Mustang in return, so he wouldn't be leaving Scott short a vehicle.

Scott eyed the Mustang with a crooked grin. "Now, that's the trade of the century. If you ever want to swap straight across—"

"If I find Chloe I may just take you up on that." Bret climbed into the cab of the big truck. He heard what he'd said and corrected himself. "*When* I find her."

Before he could close the door, a small procession emerged from The Snowed Inn.

Scott's wife, Liv, came to the side of the truck and handed up two big plastic lidded cups of coffee. "One for you, one for Chloe, when you find her."

"With lots of cream. I told her. Here's some extra." Mandy handed him a thermos, along with two heavy blankets.

Jake was last. "I found two heat packs," he said. "She's going to be cold."

He wasn't kidding. The parking lot of The Snowed Inn had taken on a gray cast in the rapidly fading daylight, and a savage wind whipped at them from down the mountain. The storm was headed this way. And he was heading up into it.

Bret looked down at the four people who'd pulled all this together on fifteen minutes' notice. Three of them, he rarely even saw. There was no time to thank them adequately.

If I ever have a Christmas card list again . . .

He settled for, "You guys are amazing."

"Tell us about it." Leroux slammed the door of his truck and stepped back with a wave.

Bret waved back and gunned the motor. He had a lot of ground to cover.

Chloe tried to think about something besides the freezing air that seemed to close in around her and work its way past her skin. People used to survive in the elements with a lot less shelter than this car. In the pioneer days, mountain cabins probably weren't much warmer than this. Except that they'd undoubtedly keep a fire going.

A nice, roaring fire. She clung to the image, tried to take some warmth from it. She pictured herself building a roasty campfire on the floor of the passenger seat. No, she wasn't crazy enough to do it. Yet. But she was definitely getting loopy. She pictured laying twigs and needles for the kindling, building a tent of branches over it to let the air circulate, touching a match to it and watching the fire come to life—

Fire. That reminded Chloe of her lone flare in the road. She peered through her window and saw no light. It must have gone out some time ago.

She felt in her pocket for the remaining flare. It meant going back out there, and that sounded like the worst kind of masochism. But if she didn't, there was that much less chance of being seen.

Grimacing, she put on her wet socks and shoes and trudged back out. She ventured through the snow to the side of the road, legs growing number with every step, and walked past the rear of the car. She saw no sign of the first flare. It must be buried in the snow.

She stepped farther down the road and lit the second flare. The blast of heat inches from her fingers was enticing, but it wouldn't do her any good. Still, she briefly savored the heat as she held it.

It wouldn't be long before this flare, too, was extinguished or buried by the snow. Chloe said a silent prayer and set it down in the road. As she struggled her way back to the car, she felt a buzzing in her pocket.

Her cell phone. Holy crap, a text.

She dug the phone out of her pocket with frantic, numb fingers. It was from Bret. **Are you all right?**

Of course he hadn't gotten her first text, because she hadn't been able to send it. Chloe did her best not to move from the spot where her phone had buzzed. She retrieved the message from her out-box and re-sent it, holding her phone high over her head, hoping to catch whatever reception there was out here. After several seconds, she lowered the phone to check her screen.

The message had gone through.

She shut her eyes tight and prayed again. Her phone buzzed three more times. They were all texts from Bret, all more than an hour old. The first two relayed his growing concern. The third offered her some much-needed hope.

Looking for you. Stay warm.

As she read the last line, she nearly burst into maniacal laughter.

Bret worked his way up the mountain. The first part of the drive was torturous because he knew it wasn't likely he'd find Chloe this close to home. Still, he had to look, his eyes scouring both sides of the road for any sign of a white car in trouble.

Then he hit the snowstorm, and it got harder. It forced him to slow for safety's sake, and it made it that much harder to divide his attention between the road ahead and the search for any sign of Chloe alongside it. The snow grew heavier as he drove on through true darkness.

A while ago, he'd offered Scott Leroux his Mustang if he found Chloe. Soon, Bret was ready to promise him the Mustang, his firstborn child, and his immortal soul. A half-buried sign at the right told him he was ten miles from Mount Douglas.

Give me a break, Lord. A little help here?

Probably not the right tone for a prayer. Bret clutched the wheel a little harder, peered a little harder through the windshield.

And his cell phone, propped up in the console of the truck, notified him that he had a text.

Bret set his jaw. It could be important. Really, really important. White-knuckled, he waited for the next turnout and stopped, flashers on, while he checked his phone. If this was a notification from his carrier about some exciting new calling plan—

It was from Chloe.

Stuck in the snow coming home from Mt. Douglas. Please call Roadside Assistance. I'm somewhere south of Rabbit Trail.

Rabbit Trail?

The time displayed on the text was twenty minutes ago, but with the erratic mountain reception, that could mean anything. At least he had a location to watch for. Bret turned off his flashers and moved forward, eyes searching the other side of the road.

Five minutes later, he came to a half-buried sign for the Rabbit Trail turnoff. His heart lurched.

He'd missed her.

Bret swore softly and looked for the next place to turn around. Coming back down the hill, he traveled at a crawl, watching the side of the road for something. Anything. His eyes strained.

There.

Lying in the road, near the ever-growing bank of snow, was a guttering flare.

She was starting to doze again.

Chloe shook her head and rubbed her hands together vigorously, trying to force feeling back into them. Even the ache from the numbness was starting to fade. Within minutes, despite her efforts to fight it, she felt herself start to drift again. She bit her tongue, hard, until it bled. But soon she was sinking back against the upholstery of the car as the feeling of cold receded.

She jerked awake. The car was shaking, something rattling at the door. A rescuer, she decided, or a hungry bear.

The door opened with a crackle from the icy snow that coated it, bringing in a brutal blast of cold. At this point she would have been glad to see any human being short of a serial killer. She'd even take her chances with the bear, as long as it was warm.

But it was Bret who pulled her across the seat, into his arms. She curled up tight against him and buried her face in his coat to shut out the cold. His voice was the most welcome sound she'd ever heard.

"It's okay," he murmured. "I've got you."

Chapter 20

As Bret loaded her into the front seat of a truck she didn't recognize, Chloe felt as mobile as a sack of flour, and not nearly as useful. He heaped some heavy blankets on her and—not surprisingly for Bret—stopped to buckle her safety belt.

He started to step back when Chloe remembered something. She put a hand on his arm.

"My shoes." Her voice came out weak and rough.

"Your *shoes*?" Bret echoed incredulously.

"They got wet."

Bret studied her, his face in shadow under the dome light. She thought she saw something soft there as he nodded.

"Be right back." He closed her door. Chloe hunkered under the blankets and tried to absorb some warmth from them. She felt cold from the inside out. She clenched her hands between her legs.

A moment later Bret climbed into the driver's seat and closed the door. He deposited her shoes on the floor at her feet. "Two very wet shoes." He reached over and opened the glove box. "Two heat packs. You can thank Jake Wyndham." He pressed the buttons that activated them. "I'm putting these on top of your shoes. I think the socks are history."

He wrapped the blankets around her feet and rested them on top of two spots of heat that she could actually feel. Chloe let a sigh escape. Bret pulled off his coat and slid it under the blankets, the inside facing her, still warm from his body heat.

"You need your coat," she protested. Her voice cracked.

"Not like you do. And the heater's cranked."

Chloe couldn't tell.

Bret pulled off her gloves, finger by finger. "Okay. Basics." He took her hands and rubbed them together between his. His eyes stayed on hers, as if to make sure she was tracking on his words. "You have one job. Keep your circulation going. Move your fingers, toes, arms, legs, as much as you can."

He turned away, squinting at the thick snow that blew at the windshield. "And I have one job," he said. "Getting us back down the hill in one piece."

Before he put the truck in gear, he dialed a number, then maneuvered back onto the road. While Chloe diligently tried to feel her fingers and toes enough to move them, she listened as he spoke through the Bluetooth.

"Mrs. Davenport? I found her." Chloe heard the relief in his voice. God bless him for calling her mother first.

He listened, then glanced at her. "Really, really cold. But she's talking. I think she's going to be all right."

He paused again and nodded. "That's what I told her." He sent her a sidelong glance, and Chloe rubbed her hands together harder. "We've got a tricky drive ahead of us, but I'll get her home as soon as I can."

His next call was more succinct. "Chuck? Bret. She's

all right. Or she will be, once we get down the hill. Can you pass the word?"

There it was again. When it came to brevity, Hemingway had nothing on him.

He disconnected the call and looked her way again. "Fingers and toes," he reminded her, and focused his eyes ahead as they moved on through the darkness.

There was no way to get ahead of the storm. Bret could only keep going and hope that the worst of it didn't catch up to them. From time to time he spared a glance in Chloe's direction to make sure she was moving and alert. When some time had passed, she started to shiver, which he took as a good sign: the body's way of warming itself.

She'd felt so limp when he pulled her out of the car, barely moving. Except for the way she pressed her face against his chest, if only to escape from the cold.

"There's coffee in front of you, when you're ready," he said. "I'm not sure how warm it is anymore, but it should help a little."

He'd never touched his own coffee. He needed both hands on the wheel.

Now certainly wasn't the time for apologies, or repercussions, or any of the things that he wanted to say to her. He didn't even know how to start. Especially not when he had to keep watching the ever-more-obscure road and avoid the disorienting trap of staring into the white flakes that rushed at the windshield in an eerie, white-on-black 3-D effect.

Chloe had gone still beside him. A quick glimpse showed that her eyelids had fallen shut. He didn't know how dangerous dozing would be for her at this point, but he wasn't taking any chances. Fixing his eyes back on the road, Bret reached over and poked her arm sharply with one finger. He heard a quick breath as she straightened with a start.

"Hey," he said. "No sleeping. Let me hear . . . the alphabet. Backwards."

"Z, y, x . . ." She rattled it off in about twenty seconds.

That defeated the purpose. He felt half a laugh escape. "How'd you do that? It's supposed to force you to concentrate."

"I got really bored one day in second grade." She sounded more like herself.

"Okay." He needed for Chloe to concentrate on something else to stay awake, so he could concentrate on the drive. Bret made the next turn slowly and carefully. "How about . . . an animal for every letter of the alphabet. Backwards."

"Zebra . . . Yak . . ." Chloe paused. "Xylophone?"

"Good enough. Keep going."

"Walrus . . ." Another pause. "Vixen . . ."

Bret tightened his knuckles on the wheel, but something inside him relaxed. For someone who'd spent several hours in a freezing car, Chloe appeared to be doing remarkably well.

He didn't know how much longer he'd driven into the interminable night, or how far he'd gotten, when a call came through on his Bluetooth.

"Bret? It's Jake. I wanted to let you know, you only need to make it as far as the Inn tonight. We've got rooms for you both, and Chloe's parents are on their way here to help take care of her."

A handy thing, having a mother who was a retired

nurse. Bret already knew he'd have to face Chloe's family after what had happened, but this brought the reality that much closer.

"Thanks, Jake." Bret set his jaw as he rounded another precarious curve. "How hard is it snowing in Tall Pine?"

"It's . . . coming down." Jake sounded as close to being evasive as Bret had ever heard. "But don't worry. You'll make it."

Intellectually, he believed it, too. But he'd be glad when this drive was over.

Jake's offer did make Bret's mission easier. If he could just hold out until the road straightened, all he needed to do was watch for the turn off the highway for The Snowed Inn. He just hoped the snow hadn't covered it yet.

Chloe sat forward and reached for her coffee cup, another good sign.

He tightened his grip on the wheel, and this time it wasn't just the truck he was trying to control. *Focus. Get her home first.* If he let himself think about how he felt, how much danger he'd put her in—it would be the ultimate irony if he ended up driving her off the road when they were almost home.

They had to be close by now. Didn't they?

Bret made one more turn, and the road straightened. He released a long, slow exhale. Just a few more miles, in a straight line. The dizzying flakes still rushed at them, but as long as he spotted the turn for The Snowed Inn, they'd be all right.

"Almost there," Chloe said.

Bret leaned forward and squinted at what looked like lights up ahead. Two lines of lights.

Chloe leaned forward, too. "An accident?"

With that many lights, it would have to be an ugly one. But it looked too orderly for that. Almost like an airplane runway. "What the—"

As they got closer, Bret realized, with astonishment, what the lights were.

"Headlights," Chloe breathed.

It was unmistakable now. The lights came in pairs, on either side of the road, angled so that they illuminated the road leading to the turnoff.

"When Chloe Davenport gets lost in the snow, word gets around," Bret said.

Up to now, the grueling drive had made any real conversation impossible. Suddenly, it looked as if they were minutes away from being surrounded by people. Now, while they were still alone, he wanted to say something to Chloe. Something about what he'd put her through, what she meant to him, how desperate he'd been to get to her.

Words, idiot. He made his living by words. They were his stock in trade. But he'd spent over two hours white-knuckling the steering wheel, and now his tongue was thick.

All he could think of was, "If you think you can walk, you might want to get your shoes on."

"Right." Chloe bent forward, groping down at the floor in front of her.

They reached the double line of cars, snowflakes dancing erratically in the headlights. Bret recognized some of the cars, some of the faces behind the windshields, and realized they weren't just there for Chloe. He saw people he'd known all his life, people he'd interviewed, people he never would have guessed would give him a second thought. Ed Hollingsworth and Mel Kruger sat together in an old Thunderbird, their differences apparently patched up for the moment. Scott Leroux, behind the wheel of Bret's Mustang, flashed the high-beam lights on and off as they drove past.

At the turn, Jake Wyndham waved them into the driveway with an elaborate sweep of two flashlights. The cars ended there, but the Christmas lights that framed The Snowed Inn glowed ahead, and white-bagged luminaries lined the driveway. He would have had to be blind to miss it.

But for some reason the last few yards did look blurry as Bret pulled into the driveway, aware of the procession of cars following them. He brought the truck to a safe stop before he blinked hard, and the picture sharpened again.

Just in time, because the doors of each side of the truck were being pulled open.

When Bret's feet hit the ground from the unaccustomed height of the truck, his legs wobbled—whether from exhaustion, emotion, or just the length of time sitting tensed up in the vehicle, he wasn't sure. He covered by grasping the door of the truck with one hand and regarded the people approaching him.

Including his father, who'd opened the door.

Bret summoned a wry smile. "What, Rudolph wasn't available?" he said. He added, quietly, to the group clustered around him, "Thank you."

His dad grabbed him in a hug. He couldn't remember the last time they'd done that. "I should have known you'd find a way to worm out of church tonight," David said.

Over his father's shoulder, he glimpsed Winston Frazier and Millie Bond, and he found room to be grateful he'd grabbed the scarf Millie had made.

"Merry Christmas, Dad," Bret choked out. And turned to look for Chloe.

She'd been safely unloaded from the truck and was being engulfed in hugs from a woman almost as petite as she was, then a solidly built man. Chloe's parents, undoubtedly. And hanging in the background, two younger, blondish men who had to be her brothers. Bret thought he recognized Todd Davenport, who'd graduated a year or two after him.

As she stepped back from her parents' hugs, Chloe looked more wobbly on her feet than Bret. At least her legs appeared to be holding her up.

It didn't look like he'd have a chance to catch up to her tonight. Her mom would want to check her over.

But Chloe turned to look over her shoulder, past her brothers and her parents. He saw her mouth form the word more than he heard her. "Bret—"

"Excuse me," Bret said, even as his father gave him a shove in her direction.

This time it was Chloe's mother who stood in the way, putting her arms around Bret. "Thanks for getting my girl home."

Bret couldn't think of a thing to say. Surely Chloe's parents would be ready to shoot him by tomorrow, when it sank in that he was the one responsible for sending her up to Mount Douglas in the first place.

He'd have to take his medicine when the time came. For now, he caught Chloe's eyes over her mother's head and mouthed one word: "Tomorrow."

Chapter 21

Chloe opened her eyes to the sight of white, this time in a much more pleasant context.

A lacy canopy hung over her head, and a thick comforter covered her. Taking in the room around her, she was better able to appreciate the bridal suite at The Snowed Inn this morning. It was the only room they'd had vacant on Christmas Eve.

"We put a cot in The Man Cave for Bret," Mandy had told her last night. "We figured he'd be more comfortable there anyway."

Chloe sat up straight, and numerous muscles screamed in complaint, probably sore from all the shivering.

It was Christmas morning, and Bret was here in the hotel.

Her mom had put her in a hot tub after checking her over last night. She'd offered to take Chloe home, if that was what she wanted. Chloe had demurred, saying she'd rather just take advantage of Mandy and Jake's kind offer and go straight to bed.

And, though she'd rather her mother not guess at it,

she wanted to see if she'd read Bret's lips correctly last night. And find out what it meant.

Bret hadn't said much last night, understandably, and she had no idea where things stood between them now. One harrowing adventure in a blizzard didn't necessarily change everything else. First there hadn't been time to think. Then, on the drive home, there hadn't been time to talk.

She climbed gingerly out of bed, dressed in the long T-shirt Tiffany and Kate had brought her last night along with a few other supplies. Her feet sank into soft, thick carpet.

As she made her way to the bathroom, two objects on the floor caught her eye. Chloe bent to pick up her cell phone and a copy of the *Tall Pine Gazette*, both slim enough to be pushed under her door. No corporate-style hotel doors or key cards here at The Snowed Inn.

On top of the *Gazette* was a note on a slip of the hotel's note paper. Chloe recognized Bret's bold, slanted print:

I charged up your phone. Found it when I went back
for your shoes. Text me when you're ready to talk.
Want to make sure your fingers and toes still work.

The front page of the *Gazette* had a big WHITE CHRISTMAS banner, and news of the blizzard had knocked her snowman article and photo down to the bottom half of the front page. Running down the right-hand column was a brief story, written by Chuck, about last night's rescue effort. It was presented with a minimum of fuss and muss—and only a couple of punctuation errors—but Chloe doubted Bret was thrilled that Chuck had put their adventure in the news.

Bret's note didn't shed much light on what he wanted to say to her, and she wasn't entirely sure what to say to him. Only that she was anxious to find out.

She found the bag her roommates had thrown together and hurried to get ready.

Bret waited in the alcove at the end of the second-story hallway, looking out through a pair of glass-paned balcony doors. The view of last night's snowfall was spectacular under the morning sun, and the storm had left behind a fiercely clear blue sky. Bret had cracked one of the balcony doors open briefly as he contemplated talking to Chloe outside. Uh, no. Beautiful as it was, it was still freezing. She'd had more than enough of that last night.

He hadn't slept much. Everything he couldn't think of to say in the truck had been jostling around his brain all night. Even now, he struggled to put his thoughts into some kind of order.

Bret looked outside again. From here, he could see the chimney from one of the fireplaces in the lobby, and the rooftop of the first floor with its immaculate blanket of snow.

Almost immaculate.

Near the chimney, he saw what looked like—but couldn't be—footprints. As if they'd been left there by a pair of booted shoes.

That was just what it *looked* like.

Maybe Jake had done it for Mandy. Except that it

had still been snowing when Bret and Chloe got in last night. It would take one ambitious guy to create a set of footsteps on the rooftop after the snow finally stopped.

He reminded himself that Jake really loved Mandy. But that still didn't explain exactly how he would have accomplished it.

Bret turned and faced the Christmas tree that decorated the little alcove. Bret had asked Jake if there was a place around here, other than a hotel room, where a boy could be alone with a girl. As it happened, little nooks like this one were among the features Jake and Mandy had taken into account when they designed the inn. There was room to duck between the tree and the balcony for a little privacy, and an end table where two cups of coffee waited.

Before he could go insane from waiting, a text came through on his phone.

Chloe followed Bret's directions to the end of the hall, trying to keep her steps measured. He stood beside a Christmas tree that dripped with ornaments, tinsel, and tiny white lights. He wore a gray sweatshirt that didn't look like Bret; probably a loaner from Jake. With the light from the paned glass behind him, she couldn't read his face.

Her heart in her throat, her feet carried her down the hall toward him, picking up speed with a will of their own. Just as she reached him, he picked up a large mug and held it out to her. She stopped short before she crashed into him and accepted the cup.

"Thanks." She wafted the mug under her nose. Coffee

with cream. She sipped it. "I was kind of hoping for Mandy's hot chocolate."

"I asked about that. Jake said it was better if we were both clearheaded. Whatever that means."

"As long as it's hot. I never want to be that cold again."

"You won't be, if I have anything to say about it."

That sounded promising. Chloe lowered her cup and stared at him.

Don't get too excited. She reminded herself of all Bret's admonitions. Her heart might be gung-ho in big red capital letters, but that didn't mean everything had changed. Even though it was Christmas morning and Bret's gaze looked direct and purposeful as he set his coffee cup down on the little table and locked eyes with hers.

"Feel okay?" The bland words didn't match his intent expression.

She nodded. "Fine. Fingers and toes in working order." She flexed her fingers around her cup as if to illustrate. The truth was, she was fidgeting.

"I did have a cup of that hot chocolate with your parents last night, by the way. Mandy insisted. I don't know when she and Jake ever sleep. Anyway, your mom and dad are great people. And they were amazingly kind about your . . . adventure."

"You stayed up until my mom left my room?" She'd barely been able to keep her eyes open until her mother left.

"I needed to find out how you were doing. And since I was the one who sent you up to Mount Douglas, I wasn't just going to slink off to my room. I needed to

305

own up. I'm sure I took a few years off their lives. Maybe yours, too." Bret drew a deep breath. "It could have turned out so differently. I never should have sent you up there yesterday. I'd ask why you didn't come straight home, but I know why."

She bit her lip.

"Chloe . . ." He closed his eyes briefly—whether to avoid her gaze or to gather his thoughts, she wasn't sure—then opened them again. "I know I keep pushing you back with both hands. It's a bad habit. I've gotten pretty good at holding people at arm's length. It felt so much safer, keeping people at a distance. Playing the objective journalist. It was all just an excuse."

He reached up, brushing at a strand of hair on her forehead. Chloe held perfectly still, afraid to interrupt.

"It's funny," Bret said. "Before you showed up, I pretty much thought I was okay. Then you showed up and everything came spilling out in a few weeks."

"Bret, it's—"

"Shh." He cracked a wry smile. "I've been working through this stuff in my head for hours and I need to get it out while I still have the guts. Then you can let me know . . . whether it makes any sense."

His eyes, behind the glasses, had lost all their sharpness for the moment. Chloe was pretty sure she was reading them right.

"Last night I had to get to you," he said. "Nothing else mattered. I even left Chuck in charge of the paper, for heaven's sake."

"It looks like he did a pretty good job."

"Yeah . . . just don't look too closely at the commas." Bret shook his head. "Never mind. Back to you."

His eyes searched her face, and she held still under the weight of his gaze. "You're way too important to me, and I know I've been hard to deal with. But if you're not totally fed up, I think it's probably time to get over the fact that I'm your boss. Your *temporary* boss."

She nodded, set her cup down, and stepped toward him.

"But." Bret rested his hands on her shoulders, gently holding her back. "I want you to think about this first. You need to know what you're getting into with me."

His thumbs made soft, light circles against her shoulders. That was supposed to help her *think?* "I'm a fixer-upper, and that's not your job. I need to do the work myself. But if you have any patience left, I'm selfish enough to ask you to try to bear with me. Because you're smart, you're beautiful . . . and you know how to get at the heart of things better than anyone I've ever known. I know my life isn't perfect, and it never will be. But I think I'm ready to take a chance on going through the rough stuff with someone else." Bret rested a hand on her cheek. "People don't change all at once, and we need to go slow," he said. "But I know how I feel. I love you."

Chloe waited a beat. Bret was waiting, too.

She raised her eyebrows. "Do I get a say?"

"Of course."

"Okay." She tried to move forward, but Bret still held her back. "I don't think I need much time. Bret, I love you. You're funny, you're smart, you're loyal, and you care about people way more than you want to admit. You didn't fool me. Not all the time, anyway." A smile spread across her face. "I also happen to know you're pretty passionate."

"About that. I made myself a promise." Bret relaxed and moved closer. "I told myself if I ever got a chance to kiss you again, no one's pushing anyone away. Is it a deal?"

Her eyes misted. "Deal."

"Good." He pulled her to him at last. "Because we happen to be standing under mistletoe. I don't think you can walk five feet in this place without—"

Chloe didn't let him finish. She cut him off with a kiss.

Because sometimes, there were better things than words.

Epilogue

From the *Tall Pine Gazette*, January 31

by Bret Radner, Acting Editor

A month ago, I saw the most beautiful Christmas lights I'll ever see: the ones that lit my way home to Tall Pine after a long drive through a snowstorm. Some of you were there that night, and you helped me find my way back in more ways than one.

From that experience, I learned three things:

1) No one who lives in a mountain community should ever own a white car.

2) Tall Pine is long overdue for a cell phone tower.

3) No man is an island. I've tried to be, and in a community like Tall Pine, that just doesn't work.

You won't let it, and for that, I'm deeply grateful.

You won't catch me complaining again about a lack of real news in Tall Pine. Outside a town like this, stories like mine wouldn't draw much interest. But a certain young woman has helped me realize that those small, everyday stories are well worth telling, and I plan to keep telling them here for a long time to come.

About that young woman.

After Christmas Eve, if you haven't guessed how I feel about Chloe Davenport—well, you don't have much imagination.

But as of now, I'm no longer her boss. I'm happy to turn the reins of the *Gazette* back over to Frank McCrea and go back to full-time reporting. This is a great relief to me from a personal and professional standpoint.

Having your girlfriend work for you is questionable.

Having your wife work for you is *out* of the question.

Invitations are in the mail.

Dear Reader,

Thanks for joining me on my latest journey down Evergreen Lane. My characters would be walking around in a vacuum if not for you.

Because I'm not as prolific as many authors (I'm working on that), I realize there's a good-sized gap between books. While you wait for the next one, you're invited to check out my other Evergreen Lane novels— *Do You Believe in Santa?* and *We Need a Little Christmas*— as well as my Christmas standalone, *No Christmas Like the Present.*

And yes, I do realize that people don't *only* fall in love during the Christmas season. I'm working on that, too. For news on upcoming releases, be sure to sign up for my mailing list. Just e-mail me at sierra_donovan@yahoo.com with the subject line, "Newsletter." You can also sign up by clicking the tab on my Facebook page, www.facebook.com/sierra.donovan.romance.

When I'm not busy writing (no, seriously, I am) you're likely to catch me posting silly things about dogs, cats, and Christmas. And books. And coffee and chocolate.

There's a little piece of my heart in everything I write, and it's my joy to share it with you. See you next time!

Best,
Sierra Donovan
www.sierradonovan.com

Connect with